DATE DUE

AN INTRODUCTION TO GOLDEN AGE DRAMA IN SPAIN

STURGIS E. LEAVITT

KENAN PROFESSOR OF SPANISH EMERITUS
UNIVERSITY OF NORTH CAROLINA

AN INTRODUCTION TO
GOLDEN AGE DRAMA IN SPAIN

Estudios de Hispanófila

19

ESTUDIOS DE HISPANÓFILA

DEPARTMENT OF ROMANCE LANGUAGES
UNIVERSITY OF NORTH CAROLINA

Distribuido por:

EDITORIAL CASTALIA
Zurbano, 39
MADRID, 10 — España

Printed in Spain

depósito legal: v. 5.578 - 1971

Artes Gráficas Soler, S. A. — Jávea, 28 — Valencia (8) — 1971

CONTENTS

FOREWORD

This study of Golden Age drama in Spain is a reconstruction of lectures and commentary that comprised a course, presented over the years at the University of North Carolina. The students of that day found the course interesting, and it is hoped that present-day students will have the same reaction. For one thing, the course introduced suggestions by which plays of a later period might be judged, even plays of modern times, though to a lesser degree, perhaps.

Students (and readers) should first of all try to "see" the plays that appeared in the theaters in Spain in the seventeenth century. They should be aware of the limitations of the stage of that period, and observe that these limitations afforded opportunities for scenes and situations not possible on the stage today. They should realize that the plays were put on by professional actors and actresses, many of them of no mean ability. The audience was what we may call of average intelligence. These people had had little or no education, but they knew right well what they liked. They had paid good money to see the show, and they expected to get their money's worth. They had a perfect right to.

In considering the plays, the series of events that make up the plot should be carefully scrutinized, and some questions asked. For example: Are these events logical in sequence? Do the characters act in a believable manner? Are the characters and their actions "stacked" so as to bring about a predetermined conclusion that is not the logical result of what has gone before?

Another point of view is to consider the plays as saleable items. We can take it for granted that the author had in mind a sale to the manager of a dramatic company, who would read the play with an eye for its presentation on the stage. If accepted, what, he would ask, were its chances of success? In his company he had a high-strung actress. Was there a good part in the play for her? Would she be satisfied with it, and not make trouble? He might also ask: Were there features in the play, such as dramatic situations, humor, or other elements that would have special appeal to the audience? In short, did the play look like a good buy?

Before coming to a consideration of Siglo de Oro productions, it is important to review earlier plays and the type of audience that witnessed them. By so doing, we may better appreciate the development of the Spanish theater from plays for select, non-paying audiences, on to various "experimental" efforts for paying audiences, up to the extraordinary flowering of the Golden Age, our principal concern. Unfortunately, as we shall see in the last chapter, these Siglo de Oro plays eventually lose their identity.

The text of the Golden Age plays under consideration here has been taken from the series, Clásicos Castellanos, and the quotations given are from these volumes:

PEDRO CALDERÓN DE LA BARCA

Comedias de capa y espada. Edición, prólogo y notas de Ángel Valbuena Briones. Madrid, 1962.

Autos Sacramentales. I. Prólogo, edición y notas de Ángel Valbuena Prat. Madrid, 1962.

GUILLÉN DE CASTRO

La mocedades del Cid. Cuarta edición. Notas de Víctor Said Armesto. Madrid, [1945].

AGUSTÍN MORETO

Teatro. Cuarta edición. Edición, prólogo y notas de Narciso Alonso Cortés. Madrid, [1955].

FRANCISCO DE ROJAS ZORRILLA

Teatro. Edición y notas de F. Ruiz Morcuende. Madrid, 1917.

JUAN RUIZ DE ALARCÓN

Teatro. Cuarta edición. Prólogo y notas de Alfonso Reyes. Madrid, 1948.

TIRSO DE MOLINA

Comedias. I. El vergonzoso en palacio y El Burlador de Sevilla. Prólogo y notas de Américo Castro. Madrid, [1948].

LOPE DE VEGA

Comedias. I. Prólogo y notas de J. A. Ocerín y R. M. Tenreiro. Madrid, 1920.

Chapter I

EARLY SPANISH DRAMA

Drama in Spain goes back quite a ways, and the first example we have is a little play of a religious nature, the *Auto de los Reyes Magos*. It was probably given at the time of the Epiphany, and presumably presented on a raised stage, in the open air. The actors were amateurs, and no admission was charged.

The plot. Three wise men, one at a time, see the star, and decide to go and worship the Saviour. On their way they stop at the court of Herod and tell him of their mission. He cannot believe that there can be another king than he, and so he calls upon his advisers (priests, grammarians, astrologers, and rhetoricians). They are in disagreement, and Herod becomes exceedingly angry. Here the manuscript breaks off and we can only surmise how the *auto* came out.

It is generally agreed that the manuscript of this religious play is of the twelfth century. It was written in a variety of verse and has elements of humor, as when the Magi question what they have seen, and when Herod goes into a frenzy when his councellors cannot agree. It really has a lot to recommend it. It is quite easy to read, and well worth the effort. [1]

It seems strange that no other plays of this early period have been preserved, nor anything of the sort for about 300 years. There is evidence, however, that there were dramatic productions, and this is to be found in a codification of laws called the *Siete Partidas*, a project of Alfonso el Sabio (1220?-1284). In this interesting legal compilation, we find laws and commentary dealing with many aspects of life of the times. Among the topics discussed are plays, and it seems reasonable to infer that if there were laws about plays, there were plays. Here is one of the articles of this famous law code:

"Priests should not play backgammon, nor roll dice; ...nor should they devise indecent plays *(juegos de escarnio)* for people to come and see,

---

[1] It is included in J. D. M. Ford, *Old Spanish Readings*, New York, 1966.

as priests [sometimes] do; and if other people perform them, priests should not go to see them, because many ugly and improper things (*villanías y descomposturas*) are perpetrated there; nor should this sort of thing be given in churches... But there are plays that priests may put on, such as the birth of Our Savior Jesus Christ which shows how the angel came to the shepherds and told them how He was born... But this should be done in a seemly manner, with great devotion... They should not be performed in small towns, nor in vile places, nor in order to make money." [2]

This law shows that not only were religious plays given at the time, but secular plays as well. Exactly what was meant by "juegos por escarnio" is not crystal clear, but the words "villanías y descomposturas" seem to indicate that in some of them there were unseemly incidents. It is unfortunate that none of these "juegos de escarnio" have survived. One cannot but wonder whether their vulgarity would be considered very shocking.

William H. Shoemaker in *The Multiple Stage in the Fifteenth and Sixteenth Centuries* (Princeton, 1935) devotes attention to a considerable number of religious plays that were performed either in the churches or outside them. These plays continued through the sixteenth century and led up to the seventeenth century *autos sacramentales* which reached near perfection, as we shall see, in the work of Calderón de la Barca. There is no evidence that any admission was charged for these religious plays.

Some approaches to drama have been pointed out in histories of Spanish literature. There was, for example, the *Representación de Nuestro Señor*, written by Gómez Manrique between 1467 and 1481, but this was for nuns in a convent and not a public performance. There was the *Diálogo entre el Amor y un viejo*, printed in the *Cancionero general* of 1569. This is not really a play, but as the title indicates, a dialogue. And there is the *Celestina* (1501), which in the earliest versions is called the *Comedia de Calisto y Melibea*, and in later editions a *Tragicomedia*. In this unusual work there were at first sixteen acts (*cenas*), and later *twenty-one*. Obviously such a long composition could not be put upon the stage. It is a dramatized novel. [3]

---

[2] The Spanish version is: Los clerigos ... non deben jugar tablas nin dados ... nin deben ser facedores de juegos por escarnio porque los vengan a ver las gentes como los facen, et si otros homes los fecieren non deben los clerigos hi venir porque se facen hi muchas villanias et deaposturas, nin deben otrosi estas cosas facer en las eglesias... Pero representaciones hi ha que pueden los clerigos facer, asi como de la nascencia de nuestro señor Jesu Cristo en que demuestra como ... era nacido ... mas esto deben facer apuestamente et con grant devocion ... et non lo deben facer en las aldeas, nin en lugares viles, nin por ganar dineros con ello. *Siete Partidas, Primera Parte*, Título VI, Ley XXXIV.

[3] The Department of Spanish and Portuguese at the University of Wisconsin presented in 1954 *La Celestina*, "a dramatic reading of one of the masterpieces of

At the end of the fifteenth century and in the early sixteenth century three dramatists of note were writing at about the same time in three different places, in Spain, Italy and Portugal. These men are important in the history of Spanish drama, but, as we shall see, their productions were for select audiences who did not pay admission. Rather, their plays were performed for patrons who had them staged for the enjoyment of their friends, who no doubt had had a good dinner (it did not cost anything) and something good to drink. The audience was in good humor even before the play started and naturally it was favorably disposed toward anything that was provided by way of entertainment. All of it was splendid. [4]

JUAN DEL ENCINA (1468?-1529?)

It is generally conceded that Juan del Encina was the founder of Spanish drama. He studied at the University of Salamanca, where he received minor orders. Probably through the influence of the chancellor of the university, he entered the service of the Duque de Alba. He evidently held an important position in the household of the Duke as an entertainer (musician, poet, playwright and actor). J. P. W. Crawford calls him "the outstanding musical composer of his generation."

The Duque de Alba could not have been at home much of the time, for he was constantly fighting wars. His name was Fadrique Álvarez de Toledo, and he was the son of the first Duque de Alba, García Álvarez de Toledo. In his youth he fought for the Reyes Católicos. In 1482, for example, at the head of a large force he devastated the territory of the Moorish King of Granada. In 1487, still fighting the Moors, the Reyes Católicos gave him the city of Huéscar. Appointed Captain General, he went on to Catalonia, where he forced the French King to return Rousillon to Ferdinand. In 1512 the conquest of Navarra was entrusted to him, and he carried out this assignment with great dispatch. Later, he rendered

---

Spanish literature." A version of the *Celestina* by Huberto Pérez de la Ossa, a "Tragicomedia en dos partes divididas en catorce cuadros," was put on in Madrid in 1956-1957. There have been others.

[4] In this connection we may imagine a situation like the following: The time is the present. Susie has been away at the Conservatory, taking piano lessons. She has come home all steamed up with her progress and gives a concert to which she invites her friends. The performance is mediocre, but the public applauds generously. Susie is no stupendous artist, but she has done the best she could. It has been a pleasant evening, even though there were no refreshments. There wasn't anywhere else to go to that night, anyway. *But,* if there had been an admission charge, every one present would have said that Susie's playing was "lousy."

service to Charles V in Flanders and in Italy, and was rewarded with the Golden Fleece.

Even if the Duke was away most of the time, his family and retainers stayed at home, and there was all the more reason for them to look for entertainment. A very special event in the career of Juan del Encina must have been the performance of his play *Representación de amor* in 1497 in the castle of Alba de Tormes or at Salamanca. In the audience were the Duque de Alba, Prince John of Castile, and his bride, Margarita de Austria. The *representación* is a sort of burlesque on the power of love.

Juan del Encina did quite a lot of travelling. He made two visits to Rome, where he enjoyed the favor of Cardinal Arborea and Pope Julian II. Some of his plays were presented in the palace of the Spanish ambassador. In 1519 he made a pilgrimage to Jerusalem and published an account of it. In 1516 he was appointed to a church office (Prior) of the cathedral in Leon. He probably died in Leon around 1530.

Encina's first two plays *(églogas)* were presented at Christmas time in the palace of his patron the Duque de Alba. In the first, two shepherds appear, and one, Juan (probably Juan del Encina) salutes the Duke and says he has a present (i. e., his play) for his mistress, the wife of the Duke. His companion mocks him ("no vales un pato"), and asks what his patron has ever given him. To this Juan cagily replies that he hasn't given him anything yet, but that he will. Most of the play deals with praise of the Duke and Duchess. They could hardly fail to respond with some remuneration.

The second play, which is much longer, has the same two shepherds in it, and also Matthew, Mark, Luke and John. They speak of the birth of the Savior and its significance. They sing and dance and set off to worship the Christ Child. The play ends in a carol *(villancico)*, probably composed by Juan del Encina. The audience probably found the music agreeable, if nothing more.

After a number of plays of this general type, the author becomes more ambitious and we have an *Égloga en requesta de unos amores*. First, there is a summary of the plot, if we can call it a plot. Then a sheperdess, Pascuala, appears, going along with her flock. A shepherd, Mingo, makes love to her. While he is thus engaged, a squire *(escudero)* comes along. He is also in love with Pascuala. In the contest, the squire wins her hand, and for her sake becomes a shepherd. A sequel to this play has the same characters. The squire is tired of country life, and invites the two shepherds to a life at court. The two accept, and there is some comic effect as the two try to adopt the airs of courtly life.

One of Encina's most ambitious plays is the *Égloga de Plácida y Vitoriano*. In this rather strange play we have what seems at first sight to be an unhappy love affair between Plácida and Vitoriano, in the course of which she commits suicide. Vitoriano is about to do likewise, but is restrained by no less a person than Venus. Plácida is brought back to life through the intervention of Mercury. As one might expect, after such a miraculous event, happy songs are sung. In this loosely constructed play the characters scrupulously avoid each other and indulge in a long series of laments.

Encina also has a farcical play, the *Auto del repelón,* in which students from the University of Salamanca play tricks upon some shepherds, who ultimately take their revenge.

Most of Encina's works were published in his *Cancionero,* Salamanca, 1496. There were seven editions between 1496 and 1516. The *Cancionero* begins with an "Arte de la poesía castellana," an adaptation of the eclogues of Virgil. The *Plácida y Vitoriano* is not included in the *Cancionero.*

Lucas Fernández (1474-1542)

Juan del Encina had a rival both in his musical and dramatic career. This was Lucas Fernández, who was a musician of considerable note, as well as a dramatist. In 1498 the position of *cantor* in the cathedral of Salamanca became vacant and both Encina and Fernández were candidates for the vacancy. Fernández received the appointment and Encina decided to seek his fortune in Italy. According to some accounts, Fernández continued in his post at the cathedral until shortly before his death.

Unlike Encina, Fernández did not enjoy the favors of a patron. His three *églogas* were presented at church festivals, such as Christmas and Easter. He also wrote five *comedias salvajes,* which we can perhaps translate as non-religious plays. These deal with the love affairs of shepherds and shepherdesses, more or less in the same manner as those of Encina. They were probably performed at betrothal festivities.

Bartolomé de Torres Naharro (1524?-...?)

Bartolomé de Torres Naharro was a Spanish dramatist who did all his writing in Italy. [5] He was born in Extremadura, near Badajoz. On a voyage to Italy he was shipwrecked, captured by pirates, and taken to Africa. He was ransomed and finally reached Rome, probably about 1507.

---

[5] About one sixth of the population of Rome was Spanish. See E. P. Rodocanachi, *La première renaissance. Rome en temps de Jules II et de Leon X.* Paris, 1912.

Such experiences could well fill a book, but Torres Naharro did not write one. In fact, he makes no reference anywhere to his enforced stay in Africa. In Rome he enjoyed the favor of a number of patrons, among them Bernardino Carvajal, Cardinal de Santa Cruz. [6] Torres was fortunate enough to have his plays presented at gatherings of distinguished personages, sometimes including the Pope. The period of his greatest activity as a playwright was between 1514 and 1516. He returned to Spain soon after the publication of his *Propalladia*; and he died in León. The date of his death is uncertain.

The *Propalladia* is dedicated to Fabrizio Colonna, the "General of the Pope." Through the good offices of Colonna, Torres entered the services of Hernando d'Ávalos, Marqués de Pescara, and husband of Fabrizio's talented daughter, the "divine Vittoria Colonna." Torres moved in the very best circles.

Torres explains *Propalladia* (Naples, 1517; another edition, 1524) as "the first things of Pallas." He first pays his respects to the ancients and then discusses comedy and tragedy at considerable length. Comedy, he says, is an ingenious arrangement of notable events, ending happily, and in dialogue. He classifies plays into two types: *comedia a noticia,* by which he seems to mean comedy of manners; and *comedia a fantasía,* a play that is wholly imaginary. *Comedias,* he explains, should have five acts *(jornadas),* with not too many, nor too few characters, a reasonable number being six to twelve. These personages should act and talk as befits their station in life. Each of his plays is preceded by an *introyto,* which gives a fairly detailed summary of the plot. If we study the language and imagine the gestures which probably accompanied these *introytos,* we may infer that Torres' audiences could not have been at all squeamish.

Torres has two plays of the *noticia* type: the *Comedia tinelaria,* which presents the rough side of a servants's dining hall; and the *Comedia soldadesca,* which gives a picture of an army recruiting office. His most ambitious play of the *fantasía* type is the *Comedia Himenea,* which is a prototype of the *capa y espada* plays of the seventeenth century. M. Romera Navarro calls it "una de las piezas más acabadas y primorosas del primitivo teatro español." It certainly deserves special mention.

In brief, the plot of *Himenea* is as follows: Himeneo is in love with Febea, but her brother, the Marquis, is opposed. Eventually, Febea lets her lover into her house at night and the brother unexpectedly enters. Himeneo runs away, leaving the girl to face the consequences. Eventually,

---

[6] Bernardino Carvajal was held in high esteem by several popes. However, he was excommunicated in 1511 for attempting to unseat Pope Julius, and his property was confiscated. He was later restored to favor and his property returned.

and fortunately, let it be said, he returns and explains that his intentions are honorable. This, of course, makes everything all right. There is a parallel love affair between two servants, set on a lower plane.

GIL VICENTE (1453?-1536?)

At the Portuguese court in Lisbon we find interest in the drama, and this took form in both Spanish and Portuguese. The Queen was Catherine of Castile, sister of the Emperor, Charles V, and her retinue included many influential men and women from Spain. The Kings of Portugal, Manuel I and later, John III, were greatly interested in the arts, and were generous patrons. The setting was favorable for court entertainment.

The man in charge of this sort of activity was Gil Vicente, and he was well fitted for the responsibility. He is considered to have been one of the greatest playwrights of Portugal. He was also a musician and an actor. Most of his plays are in Portuguese, but with a Spanish queen upon the throne, it was good policy to compose some plays in her language. Of his forty-four plays, some are in both Spanish and Portuguese, and eleven are wholly in Spanish.

The first play of Gil Vicente, the *Auto de la Visitación* (1502) is in Spanish and reminds one of the first play of Juan del Encina. It is a monologue spoken by a herdman (probably Gil Vicente himself), congratulating the royal family on the birth of a prince. The piece gave such satisfaction that the author was asked to repeat it on another occasion.

On this other occasion Gil Vicente decided to extend himself and presented a long and elaborate *Auto pastoril,* in which a number of shepherds appear. Of them, Gil (the author of the *auto,* no doubt) has the most to say. He is in love and very sad. His friend Lucas is also disturbed because he has lost his goats. Another friend, Silvestre, is bethrothed and Gil gives us an extended account of the girl's lineage. There is considerable "horsing around" until an angel announces the birth of the Christ Child. The shepherds find him in the manger, and here we have some very realistic details, such as the Christ Child being cold and in need of diapers *(pañizuelos)*. Praise of the Virgin follows. This *auto* is quite a show, as compared with the first effort of Gil Vicente.

After the success of these two plays Gil Vicente was really in business. His plays include a considerable number of *autos* (one of which is an *Auto de los Reyes Magos*), *comedias, tragicomedias* and farces. Of those in Spanish the most interesting is the *Comedia del viudo*. It begins with a lament of the widower over the loss of his wife. She was really somebody, and he gives a long account of her many good qualities. A priest makes a half-hearted attempt to comfort him by telling him that everybody must die some time, and this seems to change the widower's attitude to a certain extent. Thereupon, a neighbor *(compadre)* relates that his wife is still alive, and he wishes that she were dead. She is the bane of his life. This part of the play is pretty amusing.

The rest of the play has to do principally with the two daughters of the widower. A nobleman in disguise, Don Rosvel, is in love with the two girls. We do not learn how this came about, but, anyway, he can't make up his mind as to which one he loves best. Here the author introduces a neat little touch that must have won applause from the audience. Prince John is called from the audience to make the decision. Fortunately for all corcerned, Don Rosvel has a brother who shows up at this opportune moment. He takes the other girl.

It is evident that Gil Vicente imitated Juan del Encina in his earlier plays, but later he struck out for himself and displayed greater imagination in subject matter and in delineation of character. He was a greater poet than either Encina or Torres Naharro. [7] Menéndez y Pelayo says of him: "Su labor dramática... es la historia entera del teatro de su país."

Critics have pointed out that Juan del Encina and Torres Naharro were indebted to the early Italian theater. Gil Vicente seems to have had few, or no such contacts. What is important for us is that the plays of all three dramatists were given for select audiences, composed of people of high degree who paid no admission for the performances. When the audience changes to people from a lower station in life, and when admission is charged, the nature of the plays changes completely. It could not be otherwise.

---

[7] Testimony that the works of Gil Vicente are still of interest is a production in Madrid celebrating the 500th anniversary of his birth. This was at the Festivales de España in the summer of 1965. On this occasion a Portuguese company, which had been putting on the plays of Gil Vicente all over the Iberian Peninsula, presented selections from his works, beginning with the *Auto de la Visitación,* and including Portuguese as well as Spanish examples. The *Comedia de Rubena,* in Portuguese, was given in full. These plays were performed by first class actors, with elaborate staging. The performance in Madrid was a great success, as must have been the performances elsewhere.

SELECTED BIBLIOGRAPHY

General.

J. P. W. Crawford, *Spanish Drama before Lope de Vega.* Revised edition with bibliographical supplement by Warren T. M. McCready. Philadelphia, 1968.
N. D. Shergold, *A History of the Spanish Stage from Medieval Times Until the End of the Seventeenth Century.* Oxford, 1967.

Juan del Encina.

James R. Andrews, *Juan del Encina. Prometheus in Search of Prestige.* Berkeley, 1959.
Georges Cirot, "Le théâtre religieux d'Encina." *Bulletin Hispanique,* XLIII (1941), 5-35.
Emilio Cotarelo y Mori, "Juan del Encina y los orígenes del teatro español." *Estudios de historia literaria de España.* Madrid, 1901. Pp. 103-81.

Bartolomé de Torres Naharro.

J. E. Gillet, "Torres Naharro and the Spanish Drama of the Sixteenth Century." Homenaje... Adolfo Bonilla. Madrid, 1927-30. II, 437-68.
   Continuation, *Hispanic Review,* V (1937), 193-207.
A. Rodríguez Moñino, "El teatro de Torres Naharro," *Revista de Filología Española,* XXIV (1937), 37-82.
M. Romera Navarro, "Estudio sobre la comedia *Himenea* de Torres Naharro," *Romanic Review,* XII (1921), 50-72.

Gil Vicente.

Aubrey F. G. Bell, *Gil Vicente.* Oxford, 1921.
Jack Horace Parker, *Gil Vicente.* New York, 1967.

Chapter II

THE PROFESSIONAL THEATER—TRIAL PERIOD

With the advent of Lope de Rueda Spanish plays take on a new dimension. This "New Deal" may be considered as a trial period during which there is a much experimentation, as dramatists search for a type of play that will please a non-aristocratic audience. This audience is now made up of spectators who pay admission, and who are therefore more demanding than those who witnessed the plays of Juan del Encina, Torres Naharro and Gil Vicente. The first, and in some ways the most interesting, of the innovators was Lope de Rueda, a talented musician, actor and manager of a dramatic company.

Lope de Rueda (1510?-1565)

There were some Italian companies that travelled through Spain in the early part of the sixteenth century, putting on plays in the large towns and cities, but we have little information about them. What we do know for sure is that around the middle of the century, Lope de Rueda, with a strolling company of players brought plays to the common people of Spain and made them popular. These people paid admission, and this fact marks a new epoch in the history of Spanish drama. If an audience pays money to see a show, it wants to get its money's worth, and the dramatist has to aim to please and not be faced with a hostile mob.

Lope de Rueda was born in Sevilla. The date of his birth is uncertain. He was a gold beater by trade, an occupation that was remunerative and called for considerable skill. He abandoned this calling to become an actor, playwright and manager (autor de comedias) of a dramatic company. He died in Sevilla in 1565.

Lope de Rueda's wife was evidently a person of considerable talent. Before her marriage to Lope de Rueda her singing and dancing attracted the attention of the Duke of Medinaceli, Gastón de la Cerda, who hired her to sing and dance in his retinue. She must have had the appearance of some of the young girls of today, for the Duke made her cut her hair and dress as a page, so she could accompany him everywhere and dispel his melancholy (He was sick and lame). This was all to the good for the Duke, but not so good for her, because he neglected to pay her salary. It was only after his death and after she married Lope de Rueda, that she got what was due her. A suit was brought against the Duke's heirs and was settled in her favor.

Since Lope de Rueda was good actor, and his wife famous for her singing and dancing, the two must have formed the nucleus of an unusually attractive and popular company. It is too bad that Cervantes says nothing about Lope de Rueda's wife. He does call Lope de Rueda a "célebre español," and "varón insigne en la representación y en el entendimiento" (Prologue to *Ocho Comedias y Ocho Entremeses*).

Lope de Rueda was not adverse to putting on performances for special occasions, as when he participated in celebrating the return of Prince Philip from Flanders in 1551, or again in honor of Philip II when he was on his way to England to marry Mary Tudor. Lope de Rueda also put on two *autos sacramentales* for a Corpus Christi celebration in Sevilla in 1658. In the first instances he was undoubtedly rewarded in a substantial way by the sponsor of the celebrations; and in the case of the *autos sacramentales*, the author of such plays, as we shall see when we come to Calderón, was paid handsomely by the city fathers from public money. Writing an *auto* and having it accepted was "velvet."

The plays that Cervantes writes about were probably one-act comic plays *(pasos)* in prose. The best of these, out of ten that he wrote, is *Las aceitunas*. Here a man and his wife are arguing violently over the price they want to receive for their olives. Someone comes along and tries to settle the argument, only to find to his astonishment that the olive trees have not yet been planted!

Lope de Rueda has a number of other plays that are more ambitious than *Las aceitunas*, the best of which is *Eufemia*. This is a play in prose, divided not into acts, but into scenes. It begins with an "introyto," which gives a brief summary of the plot: Leonardo says farewell to his sister, Eufemia, and goes off to a far away place. There he enters the service of a rich man named Valiano. Out of envy another servant puts Leonardo in grave danger, but everything ends happily.

The brief sketch is only a taste of what actually happens. In the service of Valiano Leonardo waxes so eloquent over the charms of his sister that Valiano wants to marry her. But Paulo, another servant, tells Valiano that she is unworthy of him, because he (Paulo) has slept with the girl. In proof of this dastardly assertion he produces a hair that he says he took from a mole on her shoulder. This is pretty bad for Leonardo, and Valiano orders that he be put to death.

Not long after this, Eufemia receives a letter from her brother, calling her a "malvada hembra, abominable persona," and worse. Greatly puzzled by such words, Eufemia learns from her servant Christina that at one time a stranger asked her for a lock of Eufemia's hair, and she got it for him. Eufemia also learns about the danger her brother is in. Thereupon, she journeys to the land of Valiano and demands justice against Paulo, not for having slept with her, but for having stolen a jewel from under her pillow. Paulo swears by all that is holy that he never saw her before. Thereupon, Eufemia explains that she is none other than Leonardo's sister. Now it is Paulo that will be put to death, Leonardo freed, and Eufemia and Valiano married. Nice going!

The story is dramatic in itself and it is written in language that lends itself extremely well to spoken dialogue, but there is more, much more, whole sections that would appeal to a low-browed audience anywhere. There is, for example, a long dirty-word-calling battle between two servants. This reaches a climax when one of them learns the name of his opponent's father. At this, he tells his adversary to take his sword and cut him wide open. "Why?" asks the other. The answer is "Because your father saved me from the gallows many times, and if you do as I say, you will find his name written on my heart." This answer deserves a drink to celebrate friendship, and the two go off to get it.

There are other delightful interludes, such as a love dialogue between a negress and a servant, a complicated report to Eufemia on the imminent execution of her brother, and the cunning of a gypsy woman who fortells the future. Let the reader be warned, however, that the language of some of these passages is in dialect and hard to read. This dialect is only one feature that must have contributed to the enjoyment of Lope de Rueda's plays on the part of the audience. [1]

We should observe that in the plot summaries with which Lope de Rueda begins his plays, probably so the audience could be sure to follow the drift of the play, he tries to ingratiate himself with the spectators by calling them "Muy magníficos señores," "Nobles auditores," "Ilustres y agradecidos señores," etc. Lope de Rueda had an eye for the main chance.

It is interesting to note that Juan de Timoneda, something of a playwright himself, and who published Lope de Rueda's plays in 1567, makes a significant statement in an "Epístola satisfactoria al prudente lector: "...me dispuse...ponerlas (las comedias) en orden y someterlas bajo

---

[1] M. Romero Navarro, "Estudio de la *Comedia Himenea* de Torres Naharro," *Romanic Review*, XII (1921), 50-72.

la corrección de la santa madre iglesia. De las cuales por este respecto se han quitado algunas cosas no lícitas y mal sonantes, que algunos en vida de Lope habrán oído. Por tanto miren que no soy de culpar, que mi buena intención es la que me salva. *Et vale.*

It is clear, then, that in the original uncensored versions, Lope de Rueda had some lines and expressions that were somewhat risqué. These must have endeared him with the *hoi polloi* in his audiences. It is a great pity that these lines are lost forever and beyond recall. It would be enlightening, at least, to compare them with some of the expressions in the literature of today.

Juan de la Cueva (1550?-1620?)

Little is known about the life of Juan de la Cueva. He was born in Sevilla. With his brother, Claudio, who later became an *inquisidor* in the Santo Oficio, he went to Mexico in 1574 and stayed there for about two years. However, there is nothing in his plays that has any connection with his stay in Mexico. It was after his return to Sevilla that he began to write for the stage. His plays were put on in Sevilla, then a thriving and wealthy city, due to its connections with the New World.

Juan de la Cueva is the outstanding figure in the period of transition before Lope de Vega. He wrote some 14 plays, of which three are especially important to us, because they deal with events from Spanish chronicles and history. These three are *El reto de Zamora, Los siete infantes de Lara,* and *Bernardo del Carpio.* Other plays have to do with classic subjects, as for example, *Tragedia de Ayax Telamón,* and *La libertad de Roma por Mucio Scévola.* One of his non-historical plays is *El infamador,* sometimes looked upon as a precursor to Tirso de Molina's *El Burlador de Sevilla.* There is no basis for such a supposition.

El Infamador.—Leucino tells how rich he is and how with his money he can get anything he wants. His servant contradicts him, saying that he has never been able to seduce Eliodora. To this, Leucino replies that if he cannot, he will take revenge. Next in appearance is Teodora, a procuress, who relates in picturesque detail how badly she was treated when she tried to intercede for Leucino. She got what is commonly called a "bum's rush." With his servants to help him, Leucino offers violence to Eliodora. Just in the nick of time, no less a person than Nemesis, right out of Greek mythology, saves her from what is sometimes called a fate worse than death. This might well be the end of the play, but there is more to come.

In the second act another mythological character, Venus, takes a hand. Parenthetically, this part must have been real nice, if Venus looked anything like her statues and pictures. A second attempt upon Eliodora, this time with low-life characters, is planned, in the course of which a conjuring act gives hope of success.

The third act presents Venus again, and she once more tries her hand with Eliodora, but to no avail. Toward the end of the act Leucino and his servants accost Eliodora and in an attempted rape Eliodora stabs one of the servants to death. An officer of the law shows up and Leucino tells him that Eliodora killed the servant. The officer decides to lock up all three of them.

In the last act the girl's father sends his daughter, now in prison, a dose of poison to save her from disgrace. Lo and behold, the bottle of arsenic, or whatever it is, is changed into a bouquet of flowers. This is not all that is marvellous in the play. As a notary is about to enter the jail to notify Eliodora of her death sentence, two savages stop him. Thereafter, Diana, the Greek goddess, not just any human Diana, explains the slander commited by Leucino. The servant concerned with the violence in the preceding act is sentenced to be burned, and Leucino to be cast into the river. But here the river makes her appearance and protests. She doesn't want the guilty man thrown her way, and Diana sentences him to be buried alive. What a play!

El reto de Zamora.—King Sancho, angry because he has not been able to capture the city of Zamora, orders the Cid to deliver an ultimatum to his Sister, Doña Urraca — surrender, or all the inhabitants will be put to death. The Cid warns Sancho that in trying to take the city he is disobeying his father. Doña Urraca will not acceed to Sancho's demand, trusting in Heaven to protect her. Vellido, the villain, says this refusal means that they will all be a massacred. To prevent this he announces that he will kill the *monstruo,* and calls on Heaven to help him. He makes his way into Sancho's camp and offers to show him a way to take the city. A guard, evidently from the city walls, warns Sancho, but in spite of all this Sancho trusts Vellido and ventures with him out into no man's land. Vellido, asking aid from Heaven, kills Sancho. The Cid hears Sancho cry out, chases Vellido, but Vellido gets inside the city. Sancho lives long enough to say that Vellido was the murderer, and prays for time to make his peace with Heaven. The Cid and soldiers carry Sancho off.

In the second act the Cid wants vengeance on Zamora, and others declare that since the city gave refuge to Vellido, all the inhabitants are guilty. Diego Ordóñez is the challenger for the city, and Arias informs him that according to the rules of combat, he must fight with five opponents. Diego has never heard of this rule and nine days are agreed upon to decide the point. A committee is to be appointed, six from each side.

Diego Ordóñez wants to know if this "five man business" is *usada* or *inventada*. The Cid reports for the committee — five is the decision and the battle must be fought. Doña Urraca dissuades Arias from being the first to fight, she wants younger men to do it. Two of the sons are killed. In the third encounter Diego is carried out of the ring by his horse. This is a technical foul and gives rise to considerable discussion. The Cid separates the quarellers and says the judges will decide the outcome of the contest.

After a long discussion of the rules, the committee reaches a decision. Zamora shall be free, and Diego declared the winner. The Cid makes both parties swear that they will abide by the decision of the judges, and he announces it.

Los siete infantes de Lara.—Almanzor, King of the Moors, has his general, Viara, tell him about the battle between the Moors and the forces headed by the Siete Infantes. It was quite a battle — 10,000 Moors against 200 Christians. At last the six Christians who were still alive killed 2,000 Moors, but were finally overcome. Almazor calls in Gonzalo Bustos, who wants to know why he, only a messenger, has been imprisoned. Almanzor shows him a letter from Ruy Velázquez in which Almanzor is asked to kill Gonzalo, ambush the Infantes, and kill them, too. In a scene between Gonzalo and Zayda, the sister of Almanzor, she informs him that he (Gonzalo) is to be released, and tells him how much she loves him. Gonzalo assures her that he will never forget her.

After a while a tablo is set, there is a song, and after the meal Gonzalo asks to see his sons. Almanzor gives an account of the battle and shows him eight heads, those of the tutor and the seven Infantes. Gonzalo laments their death, and sets upon Almanzor's men to do vengeance, but he is restrained. Almanzor says he will now give Gonzalo his liberty.

Zayda tries witchcraft in order to keep Gonzalo with her. A little later she tells him, evidently for the first time, that she is nine months pregnant. Strangely enough, he hasn't noticed! She asks Gonzalo what she shall do with the son (Evidently, there is no chance of a girl). Gonzalo says to bring him up like other boys and when he is of age, to send him to him (his father). He gives her half of a ring to serve as identification. Zayda feels the pangs coming on, and soon after, a servant tells Almanzor that his sister has given birth to a son. This comes as a surprise to Almanzor ("¿Es posible lo que dices?"), but he takes the news in good spirit.

Zayda sends Mudarra, Gonzalo's son, to his father. This is a touching meeting. Gonzalo wants his son to become a Christian, and after some hesitation, he does so. He challenges Ruy Velázquez, who tries to run away, but Mudarra overtakes him and kills him. He then sets fire to Doña Lambra's house and she is burned up in it.

Comedia de la libertad de España por Bernardo del Carpio.—King Alfonso is very angry with his sister, Ximena. He feels that he has been dishonored by a love affair between her and the Conde de Saldaña. In consequence, she must retire to a convent. She does not offer much objection, but asks that her son be cared for by the King. The King orders the Count to be brought to court, without being given any idea why he is being summoned.

Count Tibaldo, torn between loyalty to the King and his friendship for Saldaña, delivers the message. The Count does not hesitate to comply, although he suspects that it bodes no good. At court he is berated by the King and his eyes are torn out (evidently, on stage!). The King swears everyone to secrecy, and says to have the son, Bernardo (2 years old), brought up in Asturias as his own son.

Time passes. The King decides to surrender Castilla to Charlemagne, for two reasons, so that a bastard (Bernardo) will never be king and so that the country will be saved from the Moors. Bernardo learns who he is and that his father is in prison. The King informs Bernardo that he has given his royal word to surrender Castilla, and then changes his mind and sends Bernardo off to fight Charlemagne.

Bernardo asks the King to free his father and this request is granted. We learn that Rolando is to lead the forces of Charlemagne. Charlemagne cannot understand why Alonso is changing his mind so (neither can we). He encourages his troops, especially Rolando. Bernardo looks for Rolando and finally kills him (not on the stage). Charlemagne withdraws, and takes the body of Rolando with him. The god of war, Mars, puts a laurel crown on Bernardo and praises him.

This play is not easy to read. The spelling has not been modernized in the edition of *Bibliófilos Españoles*,[2] and there are no indications of changes of scene. The language is declamatory, but even so, there are high dramatic moments and some of the incidents are deeply moving. It is really quite a play. The synopsis given here does not do it justice.

The plays of Juan de la Cueva are in four acts. In general, they are "talky," that is, the characters take a long time to express themselves. They sometimes act in an illogical manner. There is a good deal of violence in his plays, though usually in those dealing with Spanish history, the author is only following his sources. In his non-historical plays the

---

[2] *Comedias y tragedias de Juan de la Cueva.* Publicadas por la Sociedad de Bibliófilos Españoles. Madrid, 1917. 2 vols.

author resorts to the intervention of mythological characters, whose appearance, to say the least, is somewhat disconcerting. There are elements of humor in some of his plays, but it is not easy to find.

Some twenty-five years after his own plays were put upon the stage, Juan de la Cueva published an *Ejemplar poético* (1606). In this work he praises the ancients of classical literature, but says "...la invención, la gracia y traça es propia a la ingeniosa fábula de España," and finally "los sabios y prudentes dan a nuestras comedias la excelencia en artificio y pasos diferentes." Cueva was writing, not about his own plays (printed in 1583 and 1588), but about the plays of the time of Lope de Vega.

This pronouncement ranks with the one in Torres Naharro's *Propalladia* and with Lope's *Arte nuevo de hacer comedias* which, as we shall see, came out three years later.

Miguel de Cervantes Saavedra (1547-1616)

We know little about the early life of Cervantes. In 1569 we find him in Rome, where he enlisted in military service. As a simple soldier he took an active part in the naval Battle of Lepanto (1571), in which the Christian forces won a decisive victory over the Turks. In this battle Cervantes was wounded several times and lost the use of his left hand. All his life he was immensely proud of having taken part in this battle.

After further military service, in which he evidently distinguished himself, he set sail for Spain. He had with him letters of recommendation from men high in authority, among them Juan de Austria, commander of the armed forces in Italy. Instead of being a help to him, these letters almost proved to be his undoing. Captured by pirates and taken to Africa, his letters led his captors to believe that he was a man of consequence and a high ransom was set on him. The ransom arrived just as he was about to be sent to Constantinople, from which he probably would never have returned.

On his return to Spain without those important letters Cervantes was only one of many ex-service men looking for a job. The best he could get was collector of taxes, and at that he had plenty of troubles. He tried his hand at writing plays, without any great success.

Writing plays was not Cervantes' best line. His best work is prose fiction. The *Novelas Ejemplares* (1613) shows him to be a master in this field, and his *Don Quijote* (1605 and 1615) has no equal anywhere. In the *Quijote*, Part I, Chapter XLVIII, Cervantes severely criticizes the plays of his time for not conforming to the unities. They are full of "disparates," he says, and the authors claim that they have to be, because the "vulgo" wants them that way. A "felicísimo ingenio de estos reinos" [Lope de Vega] has written extremely good plays but, "por querer acomodarse a los representes, no han llegado todas, como han llegado algunas, al punto de la perfección que requieren."

In the prologue to his *Ocho comedias y ocho entremeses nunca representados* (1615) Cervantes writes about his own plays, but is not very precise about what they were, or how many he had written. He mentions by title *Los tratos de Argel, La destrucción de Numancia,* and *La batalla naval.* He says that he reduced *comedias* from five to three acts. (Two of his plays are in four acts.) He continues in the following manner:

"Fuí el primero que representase las imaginaciones y los pensamientos escondidos del alma, sacando figuras morales al teatro ... todas ellas [las comedias] se recitaron sin que se les ofreciese ofrenda de pepinos ni otra cosa arrojadiza; corrieron su carrera sin silbos, gritos ni baraúndas. Tuve otras cosas en que ocuparme, dejé la pluma y las comedias, y luego entró el monstruo de la naturaleza, el gran Lope de Vega, y alzóse con la monarquía cómica. Avasalló y puso debajo de su jurisdicción a todos los farsantes; llenó el mundo de comedias propias, felices y bien razonadas..."

He then mentions other playwrights who "no dejen de tenerse en precio." None of these, except Guillén de Castro, whom we shall mention later, are thought to be of much merit today.

Cervantes then tells about writing other plays, but found no one to take them. Finally, a bookseller told him that "me las comprara, si un autor de título (Lope de Vega?) no le hubiera dicho que de mi prosa se podía esperar mucho, pero del verso, nada." Cervantes says he looked over the *comedias* and *entremeses* that he had put away in a corner and thought they were not so bad after all. "Aburríme y vendíselas al tal librero ... él me las pagó razonablemente; yo cogí mi dinero con suavidad, sin tener cuenta con dimes y diretes de recitantes."

El trato de Argel.—In this play there are many characters, many long speeches, and little plot. We are expected to believe an incredible situation in which Aurelio, a Christian in love with Silvia, is loved by a married Moorish woman, who tries in vain to seduce him. The Moorish woman's husband is in love with Silvia and tries unsuccessfully to make her love him.

Also in the play are other Christians, including one named Saavedra, who has no special characteristics; two allegorical figures (Ocasión and Necesidad), who do not amount to very much; a sorceress; a devil; and a lion who appears briefly to rescue a Christian who is trying to escape. There is little that is believable about Moorish customs, or the fate and treatment of Christian captives.

El Cerco de Numancia.—Numancia is, or was, a city in Spain, the site of which was not known for a long time, but which was eventually located some three miles north of Soria. It is now a national monument. The city held out against the forces of Rome for twenty years. Its capture was finally entrusted to Scipio Aemilianus (the Younger), the Scipio who had overthrown Carthage. He, with about 60,000 soldiers against some 5,000 inhabitants of the city, captured it in 134 B.C. after a siege of fifteen months. There were no prisoners to be taken in triumph through the streets of Rome, the inhabitans of the city all died fighting or committed suicide.

There seems to be little point in giving the plot of this play, for there isn't any, except that Scipio resolves to capture the city by siege, rather than by direct assault, and the Numantians resist to the death.

The play is conceived on a grandiose scale, presenting the whole Roman army, and the city of Numancia. To do this on a narrow indoor stage would be difficult in the extreme. What it needs is an outdoor performance with a whole slew of supernumeraries in order to bring out the grand spectacle that it is.

In the framework of the epic struggle Cervantes centers our attention on a tragic love affair. Marandro's marriage to Lira has been prevented by the war. They are very much in love, but there is no hope of happiness, ever. She is on the point of starvation and Marandro, with a friend, make a rash foray into the Roman camp in an attempt to secure food. The friend is killed by the Roman soldiers, but Marandro succeeds in bringing back a little bread. Mortally wounded, he offers it to Lira, too late to do any good. The whole city is doomed.

Not only are the Roman army and the inhabitants of the city presented in this play, but a host of symbolic characters, among them Spain, War, Sickness, Hunger and Fame. And this is not all. We also have the River Duero, a demon, and a dead man.

The first of the scenes in which the Numantians have the soothsayer Marquino pry into the future is very elaborate. Unless it were presented with great skill it would come perilously close to the ridiculous. Another, in which a dead man is brought up from the grave is truly impressive. All the scenes in which the lovers appear are moving in the extreme, especially where Marandro offers Lira the bread which has cost him his life.

The characters in the play have a great deal of individuality: Scipio, with his merciless attitude; the desperation of the men in the city; the fear of the Roman soldiers on the part of the women; and the affection of Marandro and Lira for each other.

The language of the play is generally free from meaningless flights of style, or highly figurative language. There is a sincerity about the speeches of the individuals that gives them reality. [3]

SELECTED BIBLIOGRAPHY

JUAN DE LA CUEVA.

Francisco A de Icaza, "Juan de la Cueva," *Boletín de la Real Academia,* IV (1917), 469-83, 612-26.

S. G. Morby, "Notes on Juan de la Cueva: Versification and Dramatic Theory," *Hispanic Review,* VIII (1940), 213-18.

MIGUEL DE CERVANTES SAAVEDRA.

Armando Cotarelo y Valledor. *El teatro de Cervantes.* Madrid, 1915.

E. Juliá Martínez, "Estudio y técnica de las comedias de Cervantes," *Revista de Filología Española,* XXXII (1948), 339-65.

LOPE DE RUEDA.

Emilio Cotarelo y Mori, "Lope de Rueda, y el teatro español de su tiempo," in *Estudios de historia literaria de España,* pp. 150-75, 446-502.

---

[3] When Zaragoza was besieged in 1809 by French troops, General Palafox had this play performed in order to inspire the Spanish army.

CHAPTER III

THE PRESENTATION OF PLAYS IN THE GOLDEN AGE

Before we come to the dramatic productions of the Golden Age in Spain, it will be well to give some thought to plays in general. First of all, what is a play? A play is a composition in prose or in verse, and is intended to be presented before an audience that will pay to see it. If the play is successful, that is, if it pleases the public and has a good run, the author makes some money — and incidentally, a reputation that may help him sell another play.

A play is necessarily artificial. If it is in prose, the parts spoken by the actors cannot be exactly true to life, though they should seem so. If the play is in verse, it cannot possibly be true to life, but the lines should be easily intelligible.

The length of the play is limited by its playing time. It should not be so short that the audience will feel disappointed, and it must not be too long. The audience has to go home. The play is limited in the number of acts, and these acts are usually of more or less the same length. The *comedias* of the Golden Age in Spain were in verse and in three acts.

In more detail, a play consists of a series of scenes put together in an interesting story (plot). This story may be intended simply to amuse, and this is perfectly legitimate. The audience does not go to the theater to listen to a sermon, though some plays, and successful plays, may have a moral purpose. They may ridicule customs, condemn vices, or edify by presenting a great story, or a character from history. Some may combine several of these elements.

The students, as we have said before, should try to visualize the play, and think of it as presented by highly competent professional actors. He should ask some questions, some of which we have mentioned earlier in other terms. Is the author playing fair? Do the situations grow naturally out of what has gone before? Is the author distorting facts and characters in order that the play may arrive at its conclusion? Do we have to grant too much in order to believe in the outcome? Are the characters more or less consistent in their motives and actions?

In general, a play falls into a definite pattern. First, there is the exposition, in which the characters are introduced and the necessary antecedents explained. Almost invaribly, this takes place during the first act. [1]

The first scene of Act One is difficult for the author, for it is hard to be original here. A stock situation in some modern plays is to have the servants dusting off the furniture and talking about the excentricities of their masters. In cases like this, the audience would do well to go home. The rest of the play is not likely to be any good.

At the end of Act One something happens that initiates a conflict. From then on until very near the end of the next to the last act, there is a rising action which reaches a very important moment. This we may call the climax. Right after this, something usually happens that changes the entire course of the play, and leads directly to the conclusion. There may be an incident in the last act that temporarily suggests a different ending from what we expect, but this distraction is brief. The outcome, happy or tragic, should not be evident until the very end of the play. The play should stop there. Once the audience knows for sure how the play is coming out, it loses interest.

In judging the plays of the Golden Age, we should keep in mind what the theater of the time looked like. They were called *corrales* (yards) and there were two, the Corral del Príncipe and the Corral de la Cruz. The theaters were decidedly primitive as compared with the entertainment palaces of today. They were located in an open space between buildings, and had a canopy *(toldo)* over the auditorium, if we can call it that. The stage itself had a roof over it, though not at first.

There was a main entrance for the hoi polloi (standees) who paid only for standing room. Along the sides of the theater there were what we may call "bleacher seats," and these cost extra, as did a few moveable benches in front of the standees. The people of high degree viewed the performance from windows in the houses overlooking the corral, and entered through these private homes. The owners of the houses got a percentage for allowing spectators to tramp through their quarters. In the back of the theater there was a balcony, quite appropriately called the *cazuela* (stew pan) for women only, and the occupants of these seats were not of a very high degree, either morally or socially.

The stage had no front curtain *(telón)*. At the sides and back there were curtains which could be pulled aside to permit the exit and entrance

---

[1] A notable exception is Molière's *Tartuffe,* in which the principal character, Tartuffe, does not appear until the third act. Even so, he is there in spirit, because he is the subject of everyone's conversation.

of the actors. In the back of the stage there was a raised place called the *alto,* which could represent the wall of a city or the second story of a house. Also at the back of the stage there was a curtained-off recess behind which a tableau effect could be set up, to be revealed at an appropriate moment by drawing aside the curtain. [2] Sometimes this tableau represented a beautiful scene such as an altar with candles, or more often, a scene of horror, showing, for example, a man with his throat cut. This sort of revelation must have been pretty gruesome. Other than this there was practically no scenery. There was no back drop. This simplicity was in some ways a distinct advantage. No time would be lost in dropping the front curtain, putting on another set of scenery, and raising the curtain again. If a change of scenery was called for, the characters simply left the stage, the stage was empty for a moment, and the new characters came on. When they enter, the stage direction is "Salen," and when they go off, the stage direction is "Entran."

A new location might be identified by the dialogue: "A lot of new houses have been built in Madrid since I was here last," or by the costumes, suitable, let us say, for indoors or outdoors. A considerable number of scenes could be presented in a single act. The plays were given in the daytime. There were no lighting effects. Darkness could be presented by blowing out a candle and having the characters grope around as if in the dark. Two sets of characters, supposedly in a garden, could actually be quite near one another and yet one group could not "see" the other. The characters might walk back and forth across the stage and thus be going down a street. In the printing of plays today, the changes of scene are spelled out, but they were not so indicated in the early printings.

The actors furnished their own costumes, and evidently those of the women were quite elaborate. Those of the men varied in the extreme. There was little effort, apparently, to have them authentic. Women were on the stage from very early times, and sometimes the play called for them to dress as men.

The play began with a sort of spoken overture *(loa)* in which some idea of the play might be given. Then followed the three-act play in verse, with singing and dancing, or a one-act funny play, between the acts. The play closed with a "fin de fiesta."

The plays of the Golden Age would not be objectionable today, but there were some good souls in those times who termed them scandalous and immoral. In fact, some people were inclined to attribute national

---

[2] L. L. Barret, "The Inner Recess on the Public Stage in Renaissance Spain." *Report of the Modern Language Association Conference.* Evanston, Northwestern University Press, 1967.

disasters to the immorality of the theater. It may well have been true
that some of the dances were a little extreme for the time, but it is
doubtful that they would seem so today.

Whenever there was cause for national mourning, such as the death
of a member of the royal family, the theaters would be closed. At these
times the enemies of the theater might try to have them closed permanently.
But here is where the theaters had an ace in the hole. Certain hospitals
had a franchise on the theaters and received a monetary return from the
performance. Naturally, the hospitals did not want this easy money cut
off, and they soon brought pressure to bear to have the theaters opened
up again.

The hospitals had another concession, that of the sale of nuts, oranges
and a soft drink *(aloja)* for the spectators. These good people would save
up the shells and peelings to throw at the actors in case they were not
satisfied with the play or with the acting. The audience, though, usually
got its money's worth. They were pretty sure of enjoying the funny
character *(gracioso)*, or the songs and dances between the acts. It is
interesting to note that many of the plays close with lines addressed
directly to the audience, in which one of the actors says he hopes the
spectators liked the play. He sometimes even asks for applause.

We cannot be sure that the plays as we have them today are identical
with those presented on the stage. The manager of the company *(autor de
comedias)* may have made some changes in the lines in order to "improve"
the play. It was his play. He had paid good money for it. He could do
with it as he pleased.

Writing successful plays in those times was a good source of income.
For example, we know that Lope de Vega sometimes received as much as
500 reales for a play. This sum does not mean much until we translate it
into commodities. And this we can do. We have evidence that around 1605
a loaf of bread cost twelve maravidís. There were 34 maravidís in a real,
and with a little arithmetic we can arrive at the equivalent of 1400 loaves
of bread for a play. Not a bad return. [3]

It is a curious thing that the playwrights of that time seem to have
been reluctant to accept responsibility for having their plays printed. For
example, eight *partes* of the plays of Lope de Vega were printed with no
indication of his being responsible for the printing. Only in the *Novena
Parte* did he come out in the open, and then he offers excuses, saying that
his reason for publishing was that many of his plays were being printed
without his authorization. He, therefore, so he says, had these twelve

---

[3] Sturgis E. Leavitt, "Spanish *comedias* as Pot Boilers," *PMLA*, LXXXII (1967),
178-84.

printed, although "no las escribí con este ánimo, ni para que de los oídos del teatro se trasladaran a la censura de los aposentos." Such false modesty finds a possible explanation in the supposition that writing plays was considered at the time as a minor achievement. How the author got his plays back from the manager, if he wanted to print them, and how much he had to pay for them, is not known.

And if a dramatist wanted his plays back, what condition would they be in? They had probably been carried around from place to place, and none too carefully at that. In cases where a play was a flop, would the manager of the company not throw it away as unnecessary baggage? And if the play were a popular success, could it be that much handling had required making another copy? In such a case, can we suppose that the copy would be accurate?

In short, so many questions could be raised that we cannot touch upon them all. Any new light upon this whole subject would be an important contribution to scholarship.

SELECTED BIBLIOGRAPHY

Otis H. Green, "On the Attitude of the *vulgo* in the Spanish Siglo de Oro," *Studies in the Renaissance*, IV (1957), 190-200.

A. A. Parker, *The Approach to the Spanish Drama of the Golden Age*. London, 1957.

Arnold G. Reichenburger, "The Uniqueness of the *comedia*," *Hispanic Review*, XXVII (1959), 303-316.

Hugo Albert Rennert, *The Spanish Stage in the Time of Lope de Vega*. New York, 1908. New Edition, New York, Dover Publications, [1963]. Omits the "List of Spanish Actors and Actresses, 1560-1680," which appeared in the early edition.

Chapter IV

LOPE DE VEGA, *EL MONSTRUO DE LA NATURALEZA*

Lope de Vega Carpio (1562-1635)

If ever there was a man who kept busy during his lifetime, Lope de Vega would qualify for the record by any count. He had both licit and illicit love affairs and a number of children, some of them legitimate. He took part in the ill-starred naval expedition, mistakenly called the Invincible Armada; he was secretary to a number of noblemen, notably the great Duque de Sessa; he wrote novels and short stories, narrative poems and lyric poetry no end; and, what concerns us here, *comedias* too many to be added up. His biographer Juan Pérez de Montalván says he wrote 1800 plays, but this undoubtedly is a "bum count". We have titles to 726 plays, and taking out doubtful titles we have 470. Morley and Bruerton estimate that he wrote not more than 700, and more likely, around 600. [1] This is enough to keep scholars occupied for quite a while.

When we consider that in his extra-marital love affairs Lope fell madly in love (He never did anything by halves); when we consider that his duties as secretary must have been very time consuming; that some of his poems run to thousands of lines, not to speak of the number of plays that he wrote, one can only wonder how any man could do so much with only twenty-four hours in a day, as was the case then, just as it is now.

Lope's attitude toward his plays was not one of pride. In his *Arte nuevo de hacer comedias en este tiempo,* he is more than apologetic. [2] This composition in verse was addressed to the Academia de Madrid (whatever that was). In the first lines he attempts to ingratiate himself with his hearers by calling them "ingenios nobles, flor de España," and more along this line.

---

[1] Morley, S. Griswold, and Courtney Bruerton, "How Many *comedias* did Lope Write," *Hispania,* XIX (1936), 217-34.

[2] *Arte nuevo...,* ed. A. Morel-Fatio, *Bulletin Hispanique,* III (1901), 364-405.

He says that he knows the "reglas," but he notes that "...quien con arte ahora las [comedias] escribe muere sin fama y galadón..." As for himself, he says:

> y cuando he de escribir una comedia,
> encierro los preceptos con seis llaves
>
> ... ...
>
> y escribo por el arte que inventaron
> los que el vulgo aplauso pretendieron,
> porque como las paga el vulgo, es justo
> hablarle en necio para darles gusto.

Lope de Vega had as possible models the prose plays of Lope de Rueda, heavily laden with comic elements; the somewhat bombastic and stilted poetic works of Juan de la Cueva; and the spectacle show, *Numancia,* of Cervantes. What Lope did was make his own formula. With his immense production he, more or less — and rather more than less — set the standard for the seventeenth and a good part of the eighteenth centuries. His formula was a three-act play in a variety of verse, usually with some comic elements. He drew his subjects from many sources: mythology, history, literature, and his own fertile imagination. And here we should take Lope at his word and admit that he wrote to please the public.

El remedio en la desdicha.—Menéndez y Pelayo says of this play... "... es la mejor comedia de moros y cristianos en el repertorio de Lope, y aun en todo el teatro español, teniendo entre las comedias de su género la misma primacia que su modelo *El Abencerraje* entre las novelas." (*Obras de Lope,* XI, xli)

Questions have been raised about the date of composition of this play and whether the version we have is the original one. It has seemed too good to be the product of Lope's early years. As we search for clues, we note that the 1620 edition *(Parte XIII)* is dedicated to Doña Marcela del Carpio, the illegitimate daughter of Lope. Marcela was born in 1605, but the dedication may not have been in an early edition, if there was one, as Lope's statement, "saqué yo esta comedia en mis tiernos años," might imply. In the edition of the *Clásicos Castellanos* the editors state that the play "...puede ser la misma que con el título *Abencerraje y Narváez* se designa en la primera lista de *El Peregrino* (1604), pero Lope debe retocarla mucho para incluirla en su *Parte XIII.*" There are, indeed, evidences that the play may have been retouched, but there are also passages which have all the appearance of having been written by an inexperienced playwright.

One piece of evidence of an earlier date is a notation at the beginning of the play "Representóla Ríos, único representante." Nicolás de los Ríos, as the editors of the version at hand explain, was a famous actor, who died in 1610. This would indicate that the play was written before his death.

One indication that the play has been "retocada" — and not very carefully — is the occurrence of contradictory statements about the place where Narváez met Alora. In one place, it was "a unas rejas doradas," in another, it is "cuatro rejas azules," in another, it is back to "rejas doradas," and in still another it is "rejas azules."

In the second act Lope has a series of verses in six lines in which he uses the same six end-words in six stanzas, ending with a three-line stanza in which he introduces all six words. This sort of a stunt may well have appealed to Lope in his "tiernos años," but not likely at the height of his career.

At the beginning of Act Three we have a series of *octavas* in *esdrújulas,* which Menéndez y Pelayo characterizes as "ridículas — un pueril ensayo de gimnástica métrica." (*Obras de Lope,* XI, xxxviii.) Truly, it would seem that Lope in his later years would not have tried out such a silly exercise. Fortunately for us, although he might have been tempted to have a series of eight stanzas here, he has only six.

We may conclude that questions regarding the date of composition of this play and the possibility of an earlier edition remain unanswered, though the probability seems to be that what we have is the original version, or pretty close to it.

After all, the date of the play and the question of an early edition are not as important as the play itself, which we shall now consider. The stage directions at the opening of the play say that Abindarráez and Jarifa come out by two different entrances. The very first line, "Verdes y hermosas plantas," indicates that they are in a garden. The audience was supposed to use some imagination here. And even more imagination was needed to believe that the two walk around, as the stage directions say, "Sin verse."

It is not long before the attention of the audience is aroused by a remark of Abindarráez:

> Aquí vengo a quejarme
> ... ...
> ...de un imposible mal de amores,
> Que ya quiere acabarme.   ll. 47-50.

The same idea is expressed soon after:

> Que por mi hermana muero
> Y en tan dulce imposible desespero.   ll. 68-69.

So that the audience will not miss this important detail, the author repeats it again, this time in the words of Jarifa:

> Mi hermano adoro y quiere,
> Por imposibles muero.   ll. 78-79.

The idea of introducing a case of incest on the Spanish stage must have been startling, to say the least, and the idea is further emphasized later, when the two finally "see" each other and call each other brother and sister again and again.

However, in the course of the dialogue the author warns the audience that such a supposition as incest may not be correct:

> ABINDARRÁEZ.   ¡Ah, si mi hermana no fueras!
>
> ... ...
>
> JARIFA.   Todos nos llaman ansi,
> Y nuestros padres también;
> Que, a no serlo, no era bien
> Dejarnos juntos aquí.   ll. 92-99.

It is evident from these remarks that there is more than a possibility that they are not brother and sister, as they have been brought up to believe.

The important thing now is to have them know for a fact that they are not related, and here Lope is not at his best. A Moor, Alborán, brings the news that there will be no more war that year, and after that Abindarráez is left alone with the messenger. Why so? The reason given is that Abindarráez may want to find out some news. The fact is that the messenger has already given all the news that is really significant. At about the same time the father says he wants to speak alone with Jarifa and he goes with her off-stage. Really, there is nothing special for him to say to her. From a dramatic point of view this way of bringing the messenger and Abindarráez alone together is rather crudely done.

In the course of his conversation with Abindarráez the messenger mentions by name many prominent Spanish families as participants in the war. This is not significant news for Abindarráez, but Lope probably thought that the mention of these influential families might make a good impression upon some of them. It would do no harm to try. The messenger also gives a list of Moorish families engaged in the war, "accidentally" mentioning the family of Abindarráez. So it is that Abindarráez learns that he is the sole survivor of a massacre of his family. It must be said that such a startling revelation would have been better handled by Lope in his later years, and that he would have brought about a more dramatic effect.

It is quite evident that there is not enough material in the love affair of Abindarráez and Jarifa to make a three-act play. A secondary plot must be added. This plot concerns the love of the Spanish captain Narváez for a Moorish girl that he has seen in Coín. He confides in Nuño, an old war horse and his companion in arms. In the course of the confession Lope is evidently expressing his own ideas, when he has Narváez say of women in general:

> Hacémoslas malas obras,
> Y querémonoslas muy firmes.   ll. 494-96.

In the discussion of Narváez' affair, Nuño, one of the most interesting characters in the play, reveals his attitude towards his superior's love for a Moorish girl, when he says:

> Dime, señor, ¿de qué días
> Es este dolor de muelas?   ll. 514-15.

He does not think that Narváez has much of a problem:

> No será dificultoso
> Gozarla como la escribas.   ll. 534-35.

While a letter to the Moorish girl is being written, Nuño gives us his ideas about love. His "dama" is his armor, his lance and his horse. Love is all right once in a while:

> La mujer, fácil estopa,
> Es mancha de aceite, fuego,
> Que, si no se ataja luego,
> Cunde por toda la ropa.   ll. 612-15.

This sort of a private philosophy in one of the characters is good in any drama. In this case, as we shall see later, Nuño is consistent, or nearly so. He never disappoints us.

It must be said that Narváez does not give Nuño, who says he will dress up as a Moor to deliver the letter, very clear directions as to where the Moorish girl, Alara, lives. The address consists only of the "cuatro rejas azules." Nuño, however, sets out to deliver the message written by the captive, Arráez. Soon after Nuño leaves, Narváez, learning that Arráez is married and jealous of his wife, sets him free, admonishing him not to let his wife become aware that he suspects her of any wrong doing. In the conversation between Narváez and Arráez our suspicion is aroused that the woman that Narváez is in love with may be none other than the wife of Arráez:

NARVÁEZ.   ¿Tienes hermosa mujer?
ARRÁEZ.   No la hay más bella en Coín.   ll. 689-90.

The scene changes to one where Abindarráez has told Jarifa that they are not brother and sister, and there again Lope expresses his own feelings:

ABINDARRÁEZ.   Mas no es posible aprender
El amor y la poesía:
El hacer versos y amar,
Naturalmente ha de ser.   ll. 746-749.

After a mutual show of affection Jarifa solemnly gives her hand to Abindarráez. They are now man and wife. [3]

Nuño delivers the letter and is amazed to learn that the captive that wrote the letter is the husband of Alora. He has no scruples about taking advantage of this fact and suggests that she should go to Narváez and ransom her husband. She decides to do so, taking her jewels and money with her. Nuño is happy over his success as an ambassador of love.

In the final scene of Act One the father of Jarifa informs Abindarráez that he has been ordered away to another place and that Abindarráez must stay behind. Abindarráez can scarcely believe what he hears and is despondent in the extreme. Jarifa, however, is the strong character here:

Cuanto pueda llamarte
Para poder secretamente hablarte,
No habrá ocasión tan presto
Cuando te llame a verne.   ll. 976-977.

Jarifa is a girl well worth knowing.

At the beginning of Act Two we have a scene in which Narváez and his soldiers appear. This scene does not further the plot in any way, but it compensates for what may have seemed a weakness in Narváez in Act One. Into this group bursts Nuño in Moorish costume. He identifies himself to the audience by his blustering manner, but the soldiers and Narváez

---

[3] "… quando dice el home: yo te rescibo por mi mujer, et ella dice: yo te rescibo por mi marido ó otras palabras semejantes destas." (*Siete Partidas*, Part. IV, Título III, Ley 1). Though secret marriages in literary works were generally witnessed by servants, no witnesses were necessary to make the ceremony binding. From here on in the *Remedio en la desdicha* Abindarráez and Jarifa call each other *esposa* and *esposo*.

do not recognize him. This is a good scene, even though it is unlikely. After the audience has had its fun, Nuño reveals himself, and tells what he thinks is a good joke:

> El moro que escribió
> Era el dueño de quien yo
> La misma carta he llevado.   ll. 1197-1199.

He is greatly surprised to learn that the husband of Alara has been set free.

Alara appears, probably in a very alluring costume. It seems rather strange that Narváez would allow Nuño to be present at the interview, but he stays. From the point of view of the drama it is all to the good to have him do so, for his comments add no little zest to the situation. Alara wastes no time in declaring that she is ready to accept the love of Narváez, but the latter is moved by his sense of honor and sends her back home. In this scene we find that Nuño, who has previously said that he was insensitive to women, has been greatly taken by Alara. He makes this abundantly clear, when he says:

> Gózala, ¡pesia de mi vida!
> O si no, dámela a mí.   ll. 1275-1276.

In the next scene Abindarráez is shown bemoaning his fate. He does not want to eat, and only thinks of dying in the absence of Jarifa. He soon changes his mind, though, when he receives a letter brought by a messenger. The letter from Jarifa reads:

> Esposo: Mi padre es ido
> A Granada desde ayer,
> Venme aquesta noche a ver.   ll. 1457-1459.

This is good news, and Abindarráez decides to dress up in his best and go to see Jarifa. He will take a lance with him for protection, and here the author warns the audience that he may meet with trouble. The reason for the lance is:

> Por si al camino me salen
> Algunos cristianos perros.   ll. 1499-1500.

In a rather improbable scene the husband of Alara appears before the walls of the city in which Narváez is staying. He insults Narváez and challenges him to a duel. Narváez, however, assures Arráez that he has done no wrong to Alara, and Arráez goes away satisfied. This scene is not necessary to the play. It seems more like a filler than anything else. The only point to it is that the action of Arráez moves Narváez to go out on a raid.

In due time Nuño returns to say that he has delivered Alara safely. There is a very funny situation where Nuño takes off his Moorish costume which he calls "galgamentos" and "hopalandas." No doubt the actor who plays the part would get all tangled up in the garments. Here, the author shows Nuño, the non-womanizer, to be a sort of Dorothy Dix, or Ann Landers, with advice to the lovelorn. He tells how Alara cried all the way home, at which Nuño reacted as follows:

> Díjele mi razón, pero fué en vano.   l. 1720.

As Narváez and his men are out on their "raid," they hear someone singing. It is Abindarráez. It must be admitted that it is rather rash for Abindarráez to call attention to himself like this, but even so, it has good dramatic effect. As one expects, Abindarráez is set upon by the soldiers of Narváez. They are no match for Abindarráez, who conquers all five. A signal is given for Narváez, who arrives just in time to fight single handed with Abindarráez, who puts up a good battle and more than makes up for his defeatist attitude earlier in the act. He is finally overcome, and surrenders to Narváez. To the latter's surprise, Abindarráez laments in piteous terms. He asks to talk alone with Narváez, and Narváez sends the soldiers away. Nuño asks to stay, but Narváez has him leave. This is quite appropriate from a dramatic point of view, because Nuño would surely make some remarks that would distract the attention of the audience from Abindarráez's story of his love affair with Jarifa. As we have a right to expect, Narváez, who all along has shown remarkable generosity, frees Abindarráez. But there is one condition that proves to be very important. Abindarráez must return and give himself up in three days. This Abindarráez promises to do, and rejoices that he has found "El Remedio en la Desdicha." This is an appropriate end to Act Two.

Act Three starts off with Abindarráez reciting the "ridículous octavas" mentioned early in this account. This is no place for artificial metrical gymnastics, but rather for a moving expression of love on the part of Abindarráez. It is really impossible to believe that Lope in his later years would make an error like this.

Jarifa greets Abindarráez joyously, so joyously in fact that she does not even listen to some of the things he says, such as:

> Si no me esfuerzas,
> Para espirar casi estaba.   ll. 2139-2140.
> ... ...

> Hálleme agora la muerte,
> Que esta noche me ha buscado.   ll. 2160-2162.

She asks how he is, why he is late, but Abindarráez does not tell her. This is good drama, because his story would be long, and Abindarráez would be indulging in self praise. The two leave for the bridal chamber.

The "raid" is still on. A messenger brings a present for Narváez; with it is a letter from Alara, saying that her husband is treating her cruelly:

> ...Me han dado los cielos
> Mal galán y peor marido.   ll. 2275-2276.

As we would expect, Nuño is properly indignant. He blames Narváez for everything, and wants to go alone and punish Alara's husband. Narváez, however, decides to go, but he does permit Nuño to accompany him.

Time passes, and we see Abindarráez and Jarifa the next morning. This is the capital scene in the play. Jarifa is the picture of happiness, but Abindarráez responds with laments. A song by one of the servants does not change him. He repeats a refrain:

> Triste del alma mía
> Que dió tan triste fin a su porfía.   ll. 2474-2475.

Jarifa sends the servants away, and bursts forth in a bitter accusation. Abindarráez is like all men, he is not trustworthy. He has found her wanting in love's embrace. She is ready to kill herself.

Abindarráez cannot get a word in edgewise, but he finally has a chance to speak. When he does, the autor gives him a most unfortunate line:

> ... si escucharte podía,
> Fué querer tu amor probar.   ll. 1544-1545.

This is not the case at all, and he finally gets around to explain that he has been wounded in his fight with the Spanish soldiers. Here we have a most incredible part in the play. Jarifa has slept with Abindarráez all night and is not aware that he has been wounded, not once, but three times!

Abindarráez tells Jarifa that the reason for his sadness is because he has to return and give himself up to Narváez in three days. Jarifa is equal to the occasion and tells him that even if he wanted to stay, she would not permit it. Rather, she says:

> Que si prometistes uno,
> Es fuerza que le deis dos,

> Yo, que soy vuestra cautiva,
> Tengo de ir con su cautivo
> Porque, si en vos, mi bien, vivo,
> No es justo que sin vos viva.
> Tracemos partir a Alora
> Antes que mi padre venga.   ll. 2692-2699.

Now we pass to Alara and the danger she is in from her jealous husband. Narváez has been apprised of Arráez' intentions and has come to the place where Arráez is taking his wife. He overhears Arráez berating him in boasting terms, and the audience is on edge waiting for Narváez' move. To the satisfaction of the audience Narváez makes the husband eat his words.

In the meantime Jarifa's father has been trying to overtake the enamored couple. Needless to say, the play ends happily, even for Arráez, who is glad to escape with his life from the wrath of Narváez. The last words to the audience are:

> Aquí acaba, gran senado,
> El remedio en la desdicha.

The three principal elements to be considered in a play are plot, dramatic situations, and characters, We have already touched upon certain weaknesses in the plot, and we may add that a good part of the action depends upon chance. There are dramatic situations in every act — Jarifa and Abindarráez in Act I, the fight in Act Two, and the scene between Jarifa and Abindarráez in Act Three. With regard to the characters, it must be admitted that Abindarráez would be a sort of "weak sister," were it not for his fight with the soldiers. Narváez is a model of the Spanish *caballero*, brave and generous to a fault. He would appeal to a Spanish audience. Jarifa is the most interesting character, and it is right and proper that she should stand out among the rest. Her's is a good part for the actress. She has a chance to show a good deal of emotion. Of all the characters, Jarifa and Nuño, the old war-horse, are the ones we like best.

El mejor alcalde el rey.—This play has a straightforward plot and it is easy to keep track of the incidents. The first line gives the location of the action, Galicia, one of the most beautiful parts of Spain, and this fact is noted occasionally in the play. Incidentally, it is unusual in the plays of this period to find appreciation of natural scenery. It is evident from the costumes of the actors and from what they say that they are country folk. One of them is Pelayo, who attracts our attention right away by his sense of his own importance. Although he seems to be simple minded, every once in a while he shows that he is nobody's fool.

We should note Lope's skill in warning the audience that it may not be a good idea for Sancho to seek the approval of his overlord Don Tello. This warning is emphasized by the reluctance of Sancho to do as Nuño suggests:

> Yo voy de mala gana, finalmente,
> Iré pues tú lo mandas.   ll. 221-22.

This thought is repeated so that audience will not miss it:

> Tu padre, Elvira, me ha dado
> Consejo, aunque no le pido.   ll. 273-74.

The reaction of the audience is that Don Tello may not give his consent.

In the first scene, in which Don Tello and his sister Feliciana appear the solicitude of Feliciana for her brother is emphasized. This, as we shall see, is extremely important later. When Sancho states his case to Don Tello, the audience is temporarily relieved to see that Don Tello does not withhold his consent, but rather rewards Sancho handsomely. He even says he will attend the wedding. In this scene Pelayo distinguishes himself with unexpected remarks.

The audience is given a tip-off that the presence of Don Tello at the wedding may result in no good, when his servant Celio says of Elvira:

> ...es la moza más gallarda
> Que hay en toda Galicia.   ll. 504-5.

In the same vein is the remark of Don Tello that country girls have no attraction for him. The audience is led to think that he may change his mind when he sees how beautiful Elvira is. Sancho is more than pleased that Don Tello will honor him by his presence:

> Y aunque es dádiva excesiva,
> Más estimo haberme honrado
> Con venir a ser padrino.   ll. 529-30.

Nuño has the same thought:

> ¡Qué buen consejo te dí!   l. 544.

The audience has been partially prepared for Don Tello to be overcome by Elvira's beauty. But before this, Pelayo entertains the audience with his comical remarks. The high moment comes when Don Tello says:

> Pues, decid que no entra el cura.   l. 660.

Elvira's love for Sancho is made manifest when she tells him:

> Tú eres, Sancho mi marido,
> Ven esta noche a mi puerta.   ll. 715-716.

This invitation, as it turns out, plays right into the hands of Don Tello.

At the beginning of Act Two the audience is relieved to know that Elvira has not fallen a victim to Don Tello, when Elvira says:

> ¿De qué sirve atormentarme,
> Tello, con tanto rigor?   ll. 879-80.

The attitude of Feliciana toward her brother's efforts to overcome the resistance of Elvira has been interpreted in some quarters as hateful, because it has seemed that she was siding with him. This is not the case at all. She knows full well that nothing can be gained by opposing him openly, that the best she can do is to gain time, hoping against hope that something will happen to deliver Elvira from his clutches. [4]

When Nuño and Sancho come to Don Tello to plead with him for the release of Elvira, it does not seem probable that Don Tello would only tell Elvira to hide. He would more likely have had her locked up. Had he done this, the actress who plays the part of Elvira would have been deprived of a dramatic entrance. In this scene Feliciana's aside reveals clearly her stand in the matter of Elvira's captivity:

> ¿Cómo es posible liballa
> De un hombre fuera de sí?   ll. 1133-34.

After Nuño and Sancho are driven out of the castle, Pelayo lets us know that he is still around. He is quite right in objecting to laying his case before the King, who probably will not listen, but we must remember that this is an unusual king. He is young, was brought up in Galicia, and according to history greatly concerned about his subjects. Very properly, Pelayo goes along with Sancho. But the journey takes time, and so does a second journey later. What will Don Tello do in the meantime? A scene

---

[4] Sturgis E. Leavitt, "A Maligned Character in Lope's *El mejor alcalde el rey,*" *Bulletin of the Comediantes,* VII (1954), No. 2, 1-3. Feliciana's efforts to gain time is an important part of the play. Without Feliciana to intercede, the play would not be creditable.

Albert E. Sloman agrees in general with the above statements, but he has some reservations which deserve serious consideration: "[Feliciana] is above all a foil to her brother Don Tello, with whom she is inevitably associated, and she enriches the play as a character in her own right." *Bulletin of the Comediantes,* VII (1955), No. 2, 17-19.

in which Feliciana continues to intercede with her brother gives the illusion of lapse of time. Not enough, hardly, for Sancho and Pelayo to get to the King. In the appeal to the King there is an excellent moment, while the King is writing to Tello, for Pelayo to look around in the castle and be impressed by the tapestries. In this scene the King evidently takes a liking for Pelayo.

In almost no time at all Sancho is back with the letter and, now that we know the character of Don Tello, we are not surprised to have him treat it scornfully. At the close of the act Pelayo shows real good sense. He is the only one (audience included) to see straight when he tells Sancho — and the audience — that Elvira is safe. He is sure because,

> ...nos la hubiera vuelto
> Cuando la hubiera gozado.   ll. 1617-18.

Here Lope manifests his talent with a single word, "nos." Pelayo is as much interested in the case as anyone.

In the third act we note that more time elapses, as Sancho and Pelayo return to report to the King, and still more when the Count persuades the King to delay his visit to Don Tello. This delay hardly seems necessary to the plot. Surely, there has been delay enough already!

The author is very ingenious when he has the King, fearing that Pelayo will say too much, tells him how he can talk without being understood. The King decides to go in person to Don Tello, and here quite properly the title of the play is brought out:

> CONDE.   Enviad, que es justa ley,
> Para que haga justica,
> Algún alcalde a Galicia.
> REY.   El mejor alcalde el rey.   ll. 1773-75.

A fine example of the use of the *alto* is to be seen when Nuño has a chance to talk to Elvira. Nuño says:

> Parece que allí veo un blanco bulto,
> Si bien ya con la edad lo dificulto.   ll. 1792-93.

The audience is expected to imagine that Elvira, really only a few feet away on the stage, is talking from the tower. We know now that Elvira is still safe.

Sancho and Pelayo have returned, and Pelayo is beside himself to tell who is coming. He starts to do so more than once, and he is really funny when he remembers the admonition of the King. He has some good lines when he describes the officer who is coming, and has a proper answer when Nuño is surprised at his resourcefulness.

> NuÑo.   ¿Quién le ha enseñado a la bestia
> Estas malicias?
> PELAYO.   ¿No vengo
> De la corte? ¿Qué se espanta?   ll. 2023-24.

It is interesting to see how the King, when he arrives, greets his "friend" Pelayo, who now assumes the role of a true master of ceremonies, as he introduces his pals to the King.

Any objection of the part of the audience to the brevity of the testimony to the King is answered by the Conde:

> Con menos información
> Pudieras tener por cierto
> Que no te ha engañado Sancho,
> Porque la inocencia destos
> Es la prueba más bastante.   ll. 2115-19.

The capital scene of the play is, of course, the confrontation of Don Tello by the King. A group of the country people are present, and they make the scene more impressive. When the King reveals his identity, Pelayo cannot restrain himself any longer. With the greatest satisfaction he exclaims:

> Santo Domingo de Silos.   l. 2262.

The scene where Elvira appears to tell the King that she has been raped could have been greatly shortened. In very truth she could have told her story in four lines, or less, but Lope must afford the actress who plays the part of Elvira a chance to show her acting ability, and he gives her seventy-three lines. In a way, this is all to the good, for Elvira has not had much to say in the first two acts.

Lope does all right by the King, any king, when he has him say:

> Es traidor
> Todo hombre que no respeta
> A su rey, y que habla mal
> De su persona en ausencia.   ll. 2391-94.

The final lines state that the play is historic. It is — to a certain extent.

The most important part of this play is the plot. Some of the significant details of construction have been pointed out, but a more extended examination would reveal many cases of expert technique on the part of Lope. In each act there are dramatic situations: in Act One, the interruption of the wedding; in Act Two, the scenes in which Sancho and the King appear; and in Act Three, the intervention of the King. The characters in the play are not especially notable. None of them have characteristics that make them unforgettable, except perhaps Pelayo. This is all right, as far as it goes, but it is not enough. Some of the characters in a higher station in life might well have been improved, if the play is to be rated as a number one production.

RECOMMENDED READING

El Castigo sin Venganza. The Duque de Ferrara punishes his wife and his son for indiscretions and makes it appear that he had nothing to do with the killing.

Fuenteovejuna. A whole town rises against a despotic overlord and does him in. The principal actress has a good moment when she accuses the townsmen of being arrant cowards.

La Estrella de Sevilla. The King falls in love with a beautiful girl, La Estrella de Sevilla, and manages to enter her room at night. There he is surprised by her brother, Bustos. The King persuades her fiancé to kill Bustos and this act results in the separation of the two lovers. [5]

SELECTED BIBLIOGRAPHY

Francis C. Hayes, *Lope de Vega.* New York, 1967.
Marcelino Menéndez y Pelayo, *Estudios sobre el teatro de Lope de Vega.* Madrid, 1919-1925. 5 vols.
José F. Montesinos, *Estudios sobre Lope de Vega.* Mexico, 1958.
Hugo A. Rennert, *The Life of Lope de Vega.* Philadelphia, 1904. Translation by Américo Castro, Madrid, 1919. Reprint. Notas adicionales de F. Lázaro Carreter. Salamanca, 1969.
Rudolph Shevill, *The Dramatic Art of Lope de Vega.* Berkeley, 1918.
Guillermo de Torre, "Lope de Vega y la condición económico-social del escritor en el siglo xvii," *Cuadernos Hispanoamericanos,* Nos. 161-62 (May, June, 1963), 249-61.
Karl Vossler, *Lope de Vega y su tiempo.* Traducción, Ramón Gómez de la Serna. Madrid, 1933.

---

[5] It is generally agreed that this play was not written by Lope, but its authorship is uncertain. We have tried to show that it was the work of Andrés de Claramonte, a dramatist and manager of a dramatic company, but this ascription has been disputed. Sturgis E. Leavitt, *The Estrella de Sevilla and Claramonte.* Cambridge, Mass., 1931.

Chapter V

TIRSO DE MOLINA, PRIEST AND PLAYWRIGHT

TIRSO DE MOLINA (1584-1648)

Tirso de Molina is the pseudonym of Gabriel Téllez, a Mercedarian priest. Born in Madrid, he made a brief visit to Santo Domingo, lived for a time in Toledo, and wrote extensively for the stage. He claims to have written 400 plays, of which only about 80 have survived. Such a high mortality seems suspicious, in spite of the fact that this career was cut short in 1625 by a decree of a special committee called the Junta de Reformación. This body criticized his plays for being immoral,[1] banished him from Madrid and ordered him to cease writing plays. This was a harsh sentence, such as was dealt out to no other playwright of that period, or since. It seems as though there is more here than meets the eye. Could it have been that some personal grudge was the motive behind this decree? If any scholar could find out reason for such treatment, his fame would be made!

Tirso did write more plays, but not many. After his banishment from Madrid Tirso rose high in the order and became its historian. Few of us care much now about church history. Three of Tirso's plays were published in *Los Cigarrales de Toledo* (1624), a miscellany; four were published in *Doze comedias nuevas de Lope de Vega Carpio, y otros autores*, 1630. This last collection contained the *Burlador de Sevilla*.

El vergonzoso en palacio.—This play was one of those published in *Los Cigarrales de Toledo*. In it the date of its presentation is left uncertain. In his comment on the play Tirso praises his own work, saying that this *comedia* was "...celebrada con general aplauso (años ha) no solo entre todos los teatros de España, sino en los más célebres de Italia y entrambas

---

[1] "Trata del escándalo que causa un fraile mercenario que se llama Maestro Téllez, por otro nombre Tirso, con comedias que hace profanos y de malos incentivos y ejemplos."

Indias, con alabanzas de su autor...." It is interesting to note that he also says that "...uno de los mayores potentados de Castilla" once took the part of El vergonzoso. Who this was is not known.

In more ways than one *El vergonzoso* differs greatly from the plays of Lope. In the first place, the author takes his own good time about introducing the principal characters; too much time, we think. If we count the number of lines, we find that it takes 734 of them before we get to Avero, the scene of most of the action. All the early scenes have little to do with the main story, except the tip-off that Mireno, supposed to be of humble birth, is not really so. This idea is repeated again and again, so that no one in the audience could possibly fail to get it. Incidentally, the suspicion of noble origin that comes to Mireno is not very probable.

When we finally get to Avero, the action drags along until we come to where Mireno appears. Eventually, we see Madalena show her superiority over her sister, Serafina, when she tells her that she herself is the one who shall have Mireno. The real action has not started, though, and yet we are at the end of Act One.

At the beginning of Act Two Tirso shows us what he evidently thought was a characteristic of women, vacillation. Madalena changes her mind again and again. So many times, in fact, that her servant, Juana becomes quite impatient with her. In a scene with Mireno, Madalena takes the credit for freeing him from arrest (This is not true.), and completely dominates the conversation.

Madalena is evidently a person accustomed to having her own way. She makes it abundantly clear that she is in love with Mireno, who cannot believe it. In a monologue he reveals himself for what he is — a shy man at court. After "time out" for the secondary plot (Serafina's love affair), Madalena asks her father to employ Mireno to fill the vacant post of secretary. Here again she does not tell the truth (Again Tirso with women?), when she says that Mireno asked her to intercede for him, and that he writes an excellent hand. When she learns that the position has already been filled, she is quick-witted enough to ask that he be employed as *her* secretary. Madalena is quite a "gal." No man, much less Mireno, stands a chance in the world against a woman like her.

Another interesting situation is where Madalena decides to be more explicit with her bashful suitor, if we can call him a suitor. Madalena is the one who makes all the advances. She says:

> Diréle, no por razones,
> Sino por señas visibles,
> los tormentos invisibles
> que padezco por no hablar.   II, 641-44.

The rehearsal scene is heightened where Serafina teases her cousin Antonio, but even so, the main action of the play is interrupted for quite a while.

We finally see Madalena carry out her purpose of being more explicit when she hints broadly that she is in love with Mireno, and then declares herself openly as she pretends to stumble and gives him her hand to keep from falling:

> Sabed que al que es cortesano
> Le dan, al darle una mano,
> Para muchas cosas pie.   II, 1151-53.

Not entirely to our surprise, Mireno cannot believe what he hears. Here, very appropriately, is the ending of Act Two.

At the beginning of Act Three the father of Mireno gives an account of his misfortunes and reveals the noble birth of Mireno. It takes him a long time, too long, to tell his story. Such an extended narration comes at a bad time, because the audience now wants to see more of Madalena and Mireno. It finally does see Mireno when he relates his last experience to Tarso, who gives him plenty of good advice. In accepting Tarso's counsel to talk up, his determination is not very firm:

> Si la vergüenza
> Me da lugar, yo lo haré,
> Aunque pierda vida y fama.   III, 400-3.

In the next scene Madalena wonders what is the matter with Mireno and concludes that even if she told him outright, he wouldn't believe her. Still, she decides to make a try:

> ... abiertamente
> Le declararé mi amor,
> Contra el común orden y uso;
> Mas tiene que ser de modo
> Que diciéndoselo todo,
> Le he de dejar más confuso.   III, 447-52.

The author here dreams up a magnificent idea of having her pretend to talk in her sleep. The other scenes with Madalena and Mireno have been good, but this one is by far the best, properly so, at this stage of the action. Her declaration in her "sleep" entrances Mireno, but when she "wakes up," he does not dare to tell her just what she said. He changes the forthright statement:

>Días ha que os preferí
>Al conde de Vasconcelos.   III, 609-10.

to a future tense:

>Que he de ser preferido
>Al conde de Vasconcelos.   III, 663-4.

This is altogether too much for Madalena, and she quite properly admonishes him:

>Don Dionís, no creáis en sueños,
>Que los sueños, sueños son.

This final remark leaves Mireno more bewildered than ever. He says with deep regret:

>No he de hablar más en mi vida.   III, 651

Little does he know what kind of a woman he is dealing with!

He does not have to talk, for Madalena writes him a letter which cannot be misinterpreted:

>No da el tiempo más espacio
>Esta noche, en el jardín,
>Tendrán los temores fin
>Del Vergonzoso en Palacio.   III, 1186-89.

Mireno follows instructions, but when he does, another "Mireno" shows up unexpectedly and also enters the garden. Fortunately, in the dark the right man gets the right girl. Eventually, Mireno's true identity is revealed and the play ends with everybody, even Tarso, paired off.

El vergonzoso is unusual in having an extended criticism of the play by the author himself. As we have said, the play is included in a miscellany *Los Cigarrales de Toledo*. In this compilation, the play is supposed to have been given before a select audience assembled in the Cigarrales. At the close of the play some of the members of the audience criticize it unfavorably. One says that it is too long. Another, a pedant, criticizes it for not being authentic historically. He is especially displeased to have the author make the noble ladies, Madalena and Serafina, so "desenvueltas" as to admit strange men into their rooms at night. Another condemns it for not observing the classical rules of time and place. He thought that it was unlikely for Serafina to fall in love with her own picture, and that she could have lighted a candle and easily discovered who it was that came to her room in the dark.

"Poca razón tenéis tenido," rejoins another who, without answering all the details of the criticism previously expressed, some of which we must admit are quite valid, devotes himself principally to the questions of rules. He says that the play conforms to the rules of the time, that present day plays are superior to those of the ancients, and that Lope has set a standard that cannot be surpassed. He adds that, although Lope has said that he was only trying to please the public [Arte nuevo de hacer comedias], he is saying this out of his "natural modestia."

To this extended defense of the comedia there should be added the praise of plays in general that we find in the play itself (Act II, lines 745-82). In these two places Tirso is making one of the most brillant defenses of Lope and his school to be found anywhere. Tirso praises Lope highly, but he does not slavishly follow his technique. He evidently thought he had a "better idea."

As we have seen, the plot of the play is not complicated, except in the "mixture" of the two plots. The combination leaves us confused at times as to just where we are at. Upon reflection, it seems unlikely that Mireno, brought up in the country, should feel the stirrings of a nobleman. However, the author makes it appear more reasonable by having the others see something special in him. The selection of a secretary for the Duke is carried out in a very casual manner, and so is his consent to let Madalena have a man as her private secretary. The whole business of Serafina and her picture is indeed rather shaky, and so is the complication of two men getting into the garden, really the girls' rooms. And the play, with its almost four thousand lines, is too long, as the author himself admits. The part of Serafina could easily have been reduced and the play brought down to reasonable length.

With regard to scenes in the play, it is evident that the most important and the most interesting are the ones in which Madalena and Mireno appear. It would be hard to find in the abundance of Golden Age plays anything quite equal to what Tirso has done here.

The two characters, Madalena and Mireno, are of course, the most notable creations in the play. It may seem unlikely for a man to be so reticent as Mireno, but after all, we must remember that he believes himself to be of humble birth, that he has plenty of reason to doubt that a noble lady would ever fall in love with a man of his station in life. He has everything to lose, if he presumes too much. Madalena is evidently the kind of person that Tirso thinks women are. She is determined, resourceful, and unscrupulous. She is not the kind of person one would want to live with, but she is fascinating to watch. What more could anyone ask from a character in a play?

It is rather unusual in plays of this period to have two principal female roles in a *comedia*. Not only this, but the long recitation (rehearsal) of Serafina in Act Two is unnecessary in that it is only loosely connected with the main action. One cannot but wonder whether Tirso had some particular actresses in mind when he composed this play. There is one practical difficulty here. It might be hard to find a dramatic company with two first-rate actresses. And there might be some unpleasantness when it came to deciding which actress should have the better part, that of Madalena.

We should note Tirso's attitude toward women, as contrasted with that of Lope:

> Es posible que un hombre que se tiene
> Por hombre, como tú, hecho y derecho,
> Quisiese averiguar por tales medios
> Si fué forzada o no tu hermana? Dime:
>   Piensa de veras que en el mundo ha habido
> Mujer forzada?   II, 451-56.

Or again:

>   Yo aseguro
> Si como echa a galeras la justicia
> Los forzados, echara las forzadas,
> Que hubiera menos, y ésas más honradas.   II, 482-85.

Or still again:

>   Pero mujer y mudanza
> Tienen un principio mesma.   II, 957-958.

Strange as it may seem, the plays of Tirso de Molina have had a special appeal to critics belonging to what is erroneously called "the weaker sex."

Another thing. Tirso was not an easy versifier like Lope. It is doubtful for example, that Lope would have written verses like these:

>   Quítame la vida,
> De tantos, por honrada, perseguida.   I, 527-28.

>   ... y encubiertos
> Os libraréis mejor, hasta que el cielo
> O daros su favor, señor, comience. I, 537-38.

> Por la que debe guardar
> A la merced recibida
> De vuexcelencia mi vida,
> Bien los puede preguntar,
> Que mi fe su gusto es.   I, 177-181.

El burlador de Sevilla.—On the modern stage it is possible to do a lot of fancy things, but there is one thing it cannot do — represent darkness. The opening scene of this play, however, is in darkness and is an excellent example of what could be done in this respect on the stage of the Golden Age. Isabella is leading Don Juan by the hand (She knows the lay-out better than he) and he follows along under her guidance.

When Isabela cries out, the King appears — rather promptly, it must be said. Crafty man that he is, he does not want to know too much. He therefore entrusts the investigation to Pedro Tenorio, the Spanish ambassador. Here, we must admit that it seems strange that the ambassador would be lodged in the palace, and that the King would entrust a delicate matter like this to a foreigner. But Tirso is not fazed by unlikely details like this. He expects the audience to be so interested in the situation that they will not notice any unlikelihood.

The ambassador is "cagy." He, too, does not want to get unnecessarily involved. He has everybody retire from the scene, so he can have it out privately with the intruder. He learns who Don Juan is, and we find out that this is not his first offense:

> Tan gran traición en España
> Con otra noble mujer.   I, 79-80.

The ambassador's duty is to protect his nationals, and therefore he allows Don Juan to escape. When he reports to the King, he lies outrageously by telling him of the big fight Don Juan put up before getting away. If the King had not been so cautious, he would have proceeded with the investigation and found out what a liar the ambassador was. But, again with Tirso, that is not important. He must get along with the play. The most atrocious lie that follows is when the ambassador says of Isabela:

> Dice que es el Duque Octavio
> Que, con engaño y cautela,
> La gozó.   I, 149-51.

Evidently, the ambassador does not have much regard for the truth. Tirso, on his part, does not miss an opportunity like this to express his opinion of women, when he has the King remark:

> ¡Ah, pobre honor! Si eres alma
> Del [hombre] por qué te dejan
> En la mujer inconstante,
> Si es la misma ligereza.   I, 152-56.

When the King accuses Isabela of wrong doing, he is so indignant that he does not permit her to explain. And when she sees that it may be possible to pin the blame on Octavio, she acts in a way that is typical of Tirso:

> Mas no será el yerro tanto,
> Si el Duque Octavio lo enmienda.   I, 189-90.

And now the ambassador wants to get Octavio out of the way. He may talk too much. It takes quite a while for him to figure out a way to do it, and he stalls around with meaningless phrases, such as

> Cuando los negros gigantes,
> Plegando funestos toldos.   I, 278-80.

He finally frames up a plan with another lie, when he states that Isabela has said that Octavio was the guilty party. Octavio takes no chances with royal displeasure and he decides to leave town. The ambassador could not ask for anything better and tells him to get out right away. In this scene we have another comment from Tirso about women:

> Ya no hay cosa que me espante,
> Que la mujer más constante
> Es, en efecto, mujer.   I, 356-58.

One must admit that the characters we have seen so far are rather slippery, all of them.

Don Juan disobeys his uncle and decides to return to Spain, rather than go to Sicily or Milan. This disobedience nearly costs him his life, but Don Juan is unmoved by it. At this point the long speech by Tisbea makes us wonder whether it was written to give some particular actress some good lines.

When Don Juan and Catalinón escape from a watery grave, Tirso cannot refrain from bringing in a dirty joke by Catalinón. This sort of thing seems to be Tirso's trademark. One of the best lines in the play occurs when Don Juan recovers consciousness and asks where he is. The reply from Tisbea is:

> Ya puedes ver
> En brazos de una mujer.   I, 582-83.

Thereupon, Don Juan, who has just escaped death, starts to make love to a woman he has never seen before. To make this scene creditable and have its maximum effect, the actress who plays the part of Tisbea should be really good looking and be attractively dressed in peasant costume.

When Don Gonzalo reports on his mission to Portugal, we have some unintentional humor when the King wants to sit down. He needs to, because he would get pretty tired standing up all the time. Don Gonzalo's description of Lisbon makes one wonder whether the play was written to be performed there. [2]

The rustic scenes at the end of Act I are enlivened by country music, and this ought to please the city audience. At the end of the act the actress who plays the part of Tisbea has a chance to engage in highly emotional acting which is in violent contrast to her earlier disdainful attitude.

Early in Act Two we are apprised of the fact that Don Juan has escaped from the clutches of Tisbea's friends. He can still be counted on for more than escapades. Octavio is also in Seville. When Don Juan meets up with him, Don Juan shows his characteristic effrontery when he apologizes for not having said goodbye before he left Naples. Don Juan has not changed a bit.

In the scene with the father Don Juan is not disrespectful. Rather his attitude seems to be, "Well, father is getting old." Don Juan is not altogether bad.

In the scene between Don Juan and the Marquis, Don Juan makes it clear that he is well acquainted with the red light district of Seville. He inquires abut the denizens of this quarter and calls them by name. Don Juan is not "choosy" in his amours.

We get the usual tip-off when the Marquis tells how beautiful Doña Ana is, at which Don Juan shows great interest. In regard to the letter which is dropped down to him, we must remember that it could not have been in an envelope (When were envelopes invented, anyway?), but folded, with the edges tucked in. The actor who plays the part of Don Juan would twist the paper around in a seemingly careless manner and pretend to be surprised when it comes open.

In the part where Don Juan tells the Marquis about the promised interview with Doña Ana, it may seem that there is a mistake in the text. Don Juan tells the Marquis that he is invited to go to Doña Ana's house at twelve — and the door will be open at eleven! Having seen the boldness

---

[2] In a version of this play called *Tan largo me lo fiáis*, there is no description of Lisbon. Rather, when Don Juan talks with Octavio in Act Two, there is an elaborate account of Sevilla.

of Don Juan on previous occasions we have a right to suspect something of the same sort here. And we get it, if the lines referred to above are not changed.

What we have is a version of a con game. For example, A asks B how many coins he (A) has on a table. There are really only four, but A counts four, and then one more. He says: "I say there are five coins here, how many do you say there are?" The answer, of course if "Four." After insisting for a while, and getting B all steamed up, A says: "You say there are four, and I say there are five. Are you willing to make a bet?" B says "Yes" and A rejoins rather hurredly, "If I am wrong, will you set up the drinks?" B is anxious to collect and he says "Yes." Thereupon, A says: "I am wrong, there are only four." [3]

In the play Don Juan tells the Marquis to go to Doña Ana's house at twelve and seeing him all wrapped up in anticipation, openly adds that the door will be open at eleven. The Marquis hasn't been listening carefully, if at all, for he asks: "¿Qué decís?" To this Don Juan replies that the letter was given to him by an unknown person. This is not at all like what he really said, but the Marquis does notice the difference.

More music is introduced in another scene with the Marquis and again Tirso brings in what seems to be his favorite scatological joke. We really can get sort of tired of this type of humor. The attempt on Doña Ana fails and for the first time Don Juan is unsuccessful. But the affair has a tragic consequence, the death of Doña Ana's father. Here again the deed is ascribed to an innocent person, the Marquis. He had it coming to him, though, for having talked too much about his lady love.

We have folk music again in the scenes with Aminta, and the act ends with forebodings on the part of Batricio and the remark of Catalinón:

Canten, que ellos llorarán.   II,750.

This is a fitting end to the act.

The third act begins with the "Mal agüero" of Batricio. With him Don Juan employs a different technique. He tells him that he (Don Juan) has enjoyed the favors of Aminta for some time. Really, it is not likely that Batricio would believe this, for had Don Juan been in town before, everybody there would have known it and commented upon it. This is another case of Tirso's indifference to logic. In the words of Aminta, Tirso makes it clear what he thinks, not of women this time, but the court:

---

[3] Sturgis E. Leavitt, "A Note on the *Burlador de Sevilla*," *Romanic Review*, XX (1929), 157-59.

> La desvergüenza en España
> Se ha hecho cavallería.   III, 131-32.

With Aminta Don Juan shows utter recklessness when he tells her who he is, and swears that he will marry her, calling upon God to punish him, if he does not do so. His solemn promise has been interpreted by some commentators as phony, that he in reality is only swearing to her hand. This hardly seems to make sense. By this time Don Juan is so sure that he bears a charmed life that he is ready to swear to anything.

The net is closing in on Don Juan when Isabela meets Tisbea, and later, Octavio. And we come to the first of three spectacular scenes. The use of the back curtain is well illustrated when the statue of Don Gonzalo is revealed. Don Juan in an irreverent manner mocks him, but he accepts the invitation of the statue to dinner.

Very little time elapses, too little we feel, before we are transferred to Don Juan's home. The scene with the statue is well constructed. Catalinón is scared stiff when he goes to the door, and this gives the statue a dramatic entrance. There are moments of tragic humor when Catalinón is forced to talk with the statue, and there is appropriate music. At last Don Juan and the statue are left alone, quite properly so, alone for the solemn moment when Don Juan promises to accept the invitation of the statue. For once Don Juan experiences the sensation of fear, but he overcomes it and determines to go to the church as invited by Don Gonzalo. His reason for so deciding is something of a disappointment:

> Mañana iré a la capilla
> Donde convidado soy,
> Por que se admire y espante
> Sevilla de mi valor.   III, 684-87

Surely, if Tirso had really tried hard, he could have done better than this. But perhaps he did not want at this stage of the game to arouse any sympathy for Don Juan in the mind of the audience.

Soon after this, all the loose strings in the action are slowly but surely being drawn together. The victims of Don Juan are getting ready to make their complaints, yet it seems that there may be a happy solution. Don Juan, however, must be true to his word and go to the church to fulfill his promise to the statue. With him Juan for once admits failure:

> A tu hija no ofendí
> Que vió mis engaños antes.   III, 963-64.

And then comes the really important part of the play and the message it carries. Tirso, often so profuse in his dialogue, wastes no words here. The moral lesson is crystal clear. The rest of the play ties up the loose ends. Catalinón is spared from a fiery death and the technical reason for it is so that he can tell the story in detail. In this play the audience certainly got its money's worth.

The *Burlador* seems to have no plot in the strict sense of the word. It consists of a series of episodes in which one character is the principal figure. And yet, we may see a certain progressive action in these episodes. Each time, Don Juan becomes bolder and less fearful of retribution, and this constitutes a semblance of a plot. In the first episode he has the assistance of a third party, the ambassador; with Tisbea, he is unmoved by his narrow escape from death; in the case of Doña Ana, he kills a man and is undismayed; with Aminta, he dares to tell her who he is and solemnly swears to marry her. It is unnecessary to mention his attitude in the episodes with the statue. The audience would surely get the feeling that Don Juan is going too far and that eventually he will have to pay for his sins.

Each of these episodes has in them an interesting scene. There is the tricky action of the ambassador in the palace; Don Juan making love to Tisbea, as he lies with his head in her lap; the sly business of Don Juan with the Marquis; Don Juan at Aminta's party; and of course all the scenes with the statue. The surroundings in each case add color, as do the different stations in life of the persons involved. At times there is appropriate music.

With regard to the characters in the play, we are at a loss to find a single one that can possibly be considered admirable. Without exception each has a serious shortcoming: Isabela's rashness in letting a man into her room; the ambassador with his lying; Tisbea with her pride; and so on. It must be admitted that we would not care to be intimately associated with any of these people. And yet there is something fascinating about each one of them that makes them memorable. That is the acid test of creation of character.

One great difference from Lope is the "rough stuff" that occurs in the play. At times it becomes really vulgar. A typical example is the scene in which Tarso (now Brito) speaks of Daniel of the Bible being rescued from the lake(!), and beseeches Mireno to free him from the complicated breeches he has been forced to wear. The opportunity for the actor to make vulgar gestures here would endear him to the run-of-the-mine audience *(mosqueteros)*. We will say one thing — Tirso is not squeamish when it comes to situations like this.

The Don Juan theme has had a peculiar attraction for many authors: Molière with his *Festin de Pierre;* the Mozart opera, *Don Giovanni;* Byron's *Don Juan;* Bernard Shaw's *Man and Superman;* and, coming back to Spain, José Zorrilla's *Don Juan Tenorio.* Zorrilla's play is vastly different from Tirso's, for one thing, because Zorrilla was an adept versifier, and Tirso was not. The ending of Zorrilla's play carries with it no moral lesson. On the contrary, Don Juan is saved from damnation at the intercession of one of his lady loves. This highly lyrical play has been immensely popular in Spain and is given every year around all Souls Day, usually in more than one theater at a time. We have mentioned another version of *El burlador* called *Tan largo me lo fiáis,* the date of which is uncertain. Some critics have put it as late as the eighteenth century, but recently arguments have been advanced to set it even before the *Burlador.* [4]

RECOMMENDED READING

La prudencia en la mujer. The Queen Regent, María de Molina, defends herself and her son against the machinations of the nobles about her.

Ruth Lee Kennedy, "*La prudencia en la mujer* and the ambient that brought it forth," *PMLA,* LXIII (1948), 1131-90.

El condenado por desconfiado.

A hermit, Paulo, is deceived by the devil into thinking that his destiny will be the same as that of Enrico, who proves to be a bandit. In the end it is Enrico who is saved, and Paulo damned.

SELECTED BIBLIOGRAPHY

Alice M. Bushee, *Three Centuries of Tirso de Molina.* Philadelphia, 1939.

J. L. McCelland, *Tirso de Molina. Studies in Dramatic Realism.* Liverpool, 1948.

Tirso de Molina. *Obras dramáticas completas.* Edición crítica por Blanca de los Ríos. Madrid, 1946-1958. 3 vols. (Elaborate introduction and notes).

Tirso de Molina, *El burlador de Sevilla y Convidado de piedra.* An edition with Introduction, Notes and Glossary by Gerald E. Wade, [c. 1969].

Bruce Wardropper, "*El burlador de Sevilla.* A Tragedy of Errors," *Philological Quarterly,* XXXVI (1957), 61-71.

---

[4] Gerald E. Wade, and Robert J. Mayberry, "*Tan largo me lo fiáis* and *El burlador de Sevilla y El Convidado de piedra,*" *Bulletin of the Comediantes,* XIV (1962), No. 1, 1-14.

CHAPTER VI

JUAN RUIZ DE ALARCÓN, THE MORALIST

JUAN RUIZ DE ALARCÓN Y MENDOZA (1581?-1639)

Juan Ruiz de Alarcón, or Alarcón, as he is generally called, had more than two strikes against him before he ever came to bat. For one thing, he was a rank outsider (Mexican), and for another, he was woefully deformed (Someone wrote that you couldn't tell whether he was coming or going). He differed from his rivals in that he had an excellent academic education (advanced degrees from the University of Salamanca and the University of Mexico). He came from a high-class family and was proud of it; and he had more friends among the distinguished families of Madrid than any other playwright of his time. This last fact did not endear him to less fortunate writers.

Unlike playwrights of the time whose plays run into astronomical proportions, Alarcón wrote only some twenty plays. After abandoning the stage he took a dirty crack at the audience, calling it a "bestia fiera." No one else did anything like this. He evidently had no thought then of continuing to write for the stage. He did not need to, because through the influence of powerful friends, he got on the government payroll and was fixed for life.

His plays generally have a homey touch, but one, *El tejedor de Segovia*, would rank high in the romantic period. It seems as though Alarcón said to imself, "If what the audience wants is action, here is plenty of it."

La verdad sospechosa.—This play has good parts for two actresses, and the characters they represent are direct participants in the action, not partially super-imposed, as was the case with Tirso's *El vergonzoso.* An original touch is where the girls do not trust each other. Another feature of note is the relationship between father and son. The play is also unusual in that the characters are not too busy, or too preoccupied, to be polite to each other. It would be impossible to find another play of this period that has as many social amenities as this one.

The action of the play is not altogether easy to follow, because of its key factor — mistaken identity. But if the reader can keep clear in his mind which of the two girls is which, and which one Don García is in love with, the plot ought not to be too confusing.

The play opens with the return of Don García from the university. He has been away from home for a long time. With him is his tutor, El Letrado. Father and son greet each other affectionately, though one would perhaps expect the demonstration of affection to last longer. In the conversation that follows, note that Beltrán addresses El Letrado frequently as "Licenciado." It should be understood here that the degree of *Licenciado* is an advanced academic degree, and is highly prized. Beltrán evidently knows something about university degrees and their significance. He addresses the Letrado with his title the way students take pains to call their instructor "Doctor." It makes a good impression.

Beltrán very solicitously endeavors to make it easy for the Letrado to tell him about the bad habits of his son, and the Letrado does his best to soften the blow. This sort of consideration for others occurs again and again in the play. The revelation of El Letrado is a sad blow for Beltrán, but even so, it must be confessed that the father is not very considerate of the girl when he wants to palm off a "lemon" on her.

Alarcón's low opinion of the Court may well be back of Beltrán's rather extended comment toward the end of the scene with the Letrado. And it is significant to note the reference to the prevailing fashion of the time, the ruff collar. To tell the complete history of this kind of collar would take a long time. Suffice it to say that the collar was prohibited by a decree in 1624, and a less pretentious one not unlike what is worn today took its place. Since there was much discussion of this article of clothing at the time, Alarcón is bringing in a timely reference to a current style of dress. It may be a clue to the date of the first performance of the play.

The author gives Tristán individual touches by endowing him with an education and by his readiness with home-spun advice. In the scene with García and the girls, it is good drama to have Tristán unaware of his master's propensity for falsehood and to have him properly astounded by his lies to the girls. He acts here as a sort of mouthpiece for the audience. In due time the audience is further intrigued by his report:

> Doña Lucrecia de Luna
> Se llama la más hermosa.   ll. 551-552.

García is sure that the one he talked with is the prettiest, but Beltrán gives a tip-off to the audience that he may be misaken:

> Pues a mí la que calló
> Me pareció más hermosa.   ll. 565-66.

García's story of the banquet is a masterpiece of prose fiction. Tristán is quite right in saying that García ought to give him advance notice of his lies, so he can back him up in case of necessity. Here, and later on, we have to confess to considerable admiration for García's ingenuity. He is quite an operator, but he is not doing any harm to others, only to himself. Incidentally, the actor who plays this part has an opportunity to really "go to town" with pantomime.

When Beltrán consults Jacinta about marriage with his son, one could not wish for a more sensible remark than hers:

> Que el breve determinarse
> En cosas de tanto peso,
> O es tener muy poco seso,
> O gran gana de casarse.   ll. 921-24.

And she is just as practical in saying that she does not propose to wait forever for Juan to get his "hábito." In the meantime it will do no harm for her to look around.

The act ends rather abruptly, perhaps too abruptly, but rather effectively, with Juan accusing Jacinta of double-crossing him, and her replies. The attitude of both of them is natural and would be appreciated by the audience.

We go now to the Second Act. The girls in the play are not only good looking, but resourceful, as is shown by Lucrecia writing to García to pass by her balcony. The reason for this is to keep Juan from finding out about García, as he would certainly do, if García hung around Jacinta's balcony. The father finds out from Tristán what a liar his son is and rightly decides that scolding will do no good. By this solemn decision of his, the audience is invited to say to itself "Will he act this way, when he is faced with a really good big lie?"

The scene passes to Lucrecia's house and we have a homey touch when Jacinta tells of having taken a nap and dreaming of Juan. When she sees García from the balcony (*alto*) she suspects that something is wrong about his story. Her servant very solicitously tried to explain the apparent contradiction.

Right after this, Beltrán quite naturally forgets his resolve not to admonish his son, and gives him a real good lecture. He concludes by telling him that he is arranging for him to marry Jacinta. Here is a real challenge to García, and after a long wind-up to get his thoughts organized, he comes out with a perfectly gorgeous story explaining why he cannot marry. Beltrán's reaction to this amazing tale is quite understandable:

> Las circumstancias del caso
> Son tales, que se conoce
> Que la fuerça de la suerte
> Te destinó essa consorte,
> Y assí, no te culpo en más
> Que en callármelo.   III,1712-17.

After Beltrán hastens away to break off the marriage with Jacinta, García is left alone to reflect on his "victory" over his father. He admits that it was not very remarkable:

> Qué fácil de persuadir
> Quien tiene amor suele ser! II, 744-45.

When García meets Juan, he satisfactorily explains about the "fiesta by the river." He then insists upon a duel, but this is interrupted by Tristán, who tells Juan about the true facts. A very natural touch is when Tristán says he thought the story was phony all along. Like Hell he did!

Beneath the balcony (alto) Juan is accused of lying, and is chagrined to find that when he tells the truth by way of explanation, he is not believed. At this point we get the details of Lucrecia beginning to get interested in García. This has been partly promised in an earlier scene, when she says to Jacinta:

> Quo no te parece mal,
> Jacinta, que lo merece.   ll. 523-24.

On this note Act Two ends, and, it must be said, not in a very dramatic way.

When we come to Act Three we find Camino, Lucrecia's servant, delivering a letter to her. The most convincing proof — to him — that García is in love with her is that he gives him money. Lucrecia thinks it would be fine for García to be her suitor, but decides to proceed cautiously. She tells Camino to tell García that she tore up the letter (which she didn't) and, seeming to act on his own initiative, to tell García that he should go to the Church of the Magdalena that afternoon. Having seen Camino in action, the audience wonders just how well he will deliver this complicated message. We soon see how he balls it all up.

We now go back to García's house and his father wants to know if he has written to his wife. This scene is full of every day touches, including García's forgetting the name of his father-in-law. In another scene when Lucrecia and Jacinta are again together, the author introduces many feminine elements, such as insincere flattery. The "slight of hand" with the letter is cleverly managed, and García has a chance to make direct love to the one he is really in love with. The two girls are now heavily veiled, and it is impossible to tell them apart. It might seem that by this time one of the girls might begin to suspect something queer about the situation, but the play must go on. It would be incomplete without Tristán, who in spite of being fully informed of his master's propensity for falsehood, believes one of his biggest lies. We get a real good one and it is followed by a lot more, spun out by García, just for the fun of it.

Finally, García tells his father the truth and finds that he is not believed. This is quite a shock. After a series of homey touches the play ends in the discomfiture of García. He got what he deserved. All the same, we can't help but feel sort of sorry for him. He made a good try.

The plot of this play is decidedly ingenious and in places it is not easy to follow. It all depends on which one of the two girls is the prettiest, and from the start the audience is tipped off as to her identity. The plot is unusual in that the play does not come out happily for García. In the French version, *Le menteur*, by Corneille, the outcome is softened. Corneille thought so highly of Alarcón's play that he said that he would have given two of his best works to have been the originator of it.

All the lies of García are very elaborate and they are heightened by the reaction of the listeners. These scenes are the most interesting in the play. The scenes in which the two girls are together are characterized by what seem to be feminine touches, and this makes them especially attractive.

The outstanding character is, of course, García. He has imagination to a high degree, and we cannot but admire his resourcefulness. The other characters have very human characteristics, even such a minor character as "el Letrado." It would be hard to single out one of the minor characters as better drawn than the others. They all seem very real. Alarcón stands apart from other playwrights of the period for his ability in characterization, and this play is probably the most notable example.

Las paredes oyen.—In reading this play we should keep in mind what has been said earlier, that Alarcón was misshapen; that he came from a distinguished family, of which he was very proud; and that he had a better academic education than any of his rivals.

The play has only a slight plot. In many ways it is a pronouncement for the qualities that Alarcón considered characteristics of a true gentleman, and an object lesson for those who speak ill of others. In other places the author seems to be using the play as a vehicle for his own deeply felt sentiments.

At the beginning of the play the conversation between Juan and Beltrán seems inappropriate for the place they are in, Doña Ana's house. We should note that Beltrán, like the servant in *La verdad sospechosa*, has had some education, and the name "Juan de Mendoza" is also the name of the author. He is poor, and the description "feo y de mal talle," are as fitting for Alarcón as for the character, Juan.

In insisting on seeing Ana at this time, Juan is not very thoughtful of her, or even sensible about the timing of his visit. She is about to start on a trip and is busy getting ready. He ought to realize that she is in no mood to listen to a declaration of love. Furthermore, we must admit that Juan's pretending to be the bearer of an important letter is not a very good idea. Besides being "feo y de mal talle," Juan is evidently not very bright. In this play we have a most unusual sort of "hero."

As we continue, it would appear that Juan's first speech to Ana has been memorized. His second one, extemporaneous, is better, but not much better. When we see Mendo, we observe that he is good looking, a ladies' man who believes in having more than one girl on the string. He, unlike Juan, has a high opinion of himself. Ana likes him, and is ready to marry him as soon as she fulfills certain vows. The chances for Juan look pretty slim, especially when Mendo makes his pitch and Ana gives him considerable encouragement.

On the pretext of wanting to say goodbye, Lucrecia drops in and she, too, is inconsiderate. She stays on, though she can see that Ana is busy. Not only this, but she makes some catty remarks about Juan going with Ana to Alcalá. When Ana leaves, it is not likely that she would go out and leave her guests behind. Lucrecia gives Mendo "the works" for deserting her. Mendo rather lamely tries to defend himself and grabs wildly at a chance to get away when the Count arrives. The Count is not very loyal to his friend Mendo. And we can't help but wonder whether this is what we would expect from a person of his rank. He tells Lucrecia all the mean things Mendo said about her, but she finds it hard to believe what the Count says.

The crazy conduct of people on St. John's Eve is picturesquely described by Beltrán. The Duke is new to the place and to its customs and he wants his friends to advise him what to do. He takes occasion to express what appears to be the sentiments of Alarcón himself, when he says:

> ...el señor siempre es señor,
> Como Apolo siempre Apolo.
> Aunque en lugares indignos

Entren sus rayos hermosos.
Lengua honrosa, noble pecho,
Facil gorra, humano rostro,
Son voluntarios Argeles
De la libertad de todos.   ll. 832-39.

When they pass by the houses of various people Mendo makes mean cracks about all of them. When they stop at Ana's house — she has returned from Alcalá to please her servants — Juan speaks enthusiastically about her, but Mendo, fearing that the Duke will get too interested, says a number of things that would hardly be appreciated by any woman, much less by one a little advanced in years. Ana hears all this from the balcony (the *alto* again). In an aside Mendo quite characteristically tells the Duke:

Para entre los dos, don Juan
Es un buen hombre; y si digo
Que tiene poco de sabio,
Puedo, sin hazerle agravio.
Vuestro deudo es y mi amigo;
Mas esto no es murmurar.   ll. 1101-6.

The act ends rather abruptly, too abruptly, soon after this.

In Act Two it is not altogether clear why the author downgrades football and falconry. The scene is in Alcalá, and Mendo has distinguished himself as a bullfighter. He is certainly not effeminate, even though he is a ladies' man. The passages about bald-headed people are also difficult to interpret. Can they refer to some of Alarcón's enemies?

Juan's complicity with the Duke in dressing up like coachmen is hardly worthy of him, but his motive is more or less in line with his previous efforts. In this case they are about as stupid as they can be. Beltrán anticipates our thinking by saying it for us.

Lucrecia is certainly crazy about Mendo, for she has followed him to Alcalá, armed with a letter which on its face seems to be decidedly unfavorable to Mendo. She, characteristically feminine (some may think), shows the letter to Ana, who, wise woman that she is, does not commit herself. Juan has one good ally in Celia, whom Juan had impressed by his politeness to her. She, too, expresses the ideas of the author:

En el hombre no has de ver
La hermosura o gentileza;
Su hermosura es la nobleza,
La gentileza el saber.   ll. 1544-47.

Ana finds it hard, in spite of everything, to dismiss Mendo from her mind. In the scene with the "coachmen" we have a rather unlikely situation. There are too many people listening in (al paño) on the conversation between Mendo and Ana. In it she confounds him by repeating his unfavorable remarks (Las paredes oyen). Mendo has an evil-minded servant in Leonardo, as is seen when the latter suspects Ana of a secret love affair with someone beneath her in rank. Mendo, as a matter of fact, is not much better, as we see when he plans to do violence to Ana when she is returning from Alcalá. The act ends, as we expect, when Ana is properly rescued from Mendo.

In Act Three we have a fascinating scene in which Ana dismisses the "coachmen." Having Juan play dumb was a happy thought on the part of the author. At the end of it (Cf. "The Courtship of Myles Standish"), we have the following declaration from Ana:

> De mi consejo, dexad
> De terciar en esse intento;
> Porque mayor esperanza
> Puede, al fin, tener de mí
> Quien pretende para sí,
> Que quien para otro alcança.   2203-8.

From a practical point of view, this is the end of the play. The audience knows now how it is coming out. In a later scene we do learn a little more about Ana. She is not altogether averse to gossip, "la mejor salsa," but she will not tolerate it from servants. At this stage of the game this information is really not important to us. The rest of the play chiefly concerns Lucrecia in whom we are not particularly interested. There is an obscure reference to calvos and what seems to be a reference to some elderly man having an affair with a young girl. We do not know who these people can be.

Juan comes into the action to some degree, but the author downgrades him by making him so petty. This is certainly not what we would expect of him now. He must know where Ana stands and ought to be content with her obvious decision to accept him. Mendo makes another try, but his efforts are in vain, even with Lucrecia. And so, finally, the play ends.

The plot of this play, as we have seen, is not complicated. We know, of course, that walls do not have ears (Las paredes no oyen). Chance plays a large part in the outcome of the play. Ana happens to be on the balcony at exactly the right time; and although she is quite far away, she overhears all that the men below are saying. The element of chance also has a large part in her "rescue." The secondary plot sometimes gets in the way of the main plot, and toward the end of the play, it constitutes most of the action. All this is not very good drama.

The principal scenes of interest are the ones in which Juan and Ana appear. The one in which Ana identifies the "coachmen" by their hands is very ingenious. This is followed by Juan's playing dumb, and grunting when they ask him a question.

With regard to the characters, Juan is most unusual and for a strange reason — he is not very bright. It would be hard to find in any play a "hero" so little endowed with brains as he is. He is a "good man," and it is hard for any author to make a good man interesting. In this case, though, his self-depreciation is the feature that makes him stand out among the others. Indeed, one of the merits of the play is the complexity of the characters. Ana, for example, treats her servants with great consideration. She will not permit a person of low degree to spill any gossip to her, although she admits that gossip is the spice of conversation. She is able to discern people's intentions, and is careful to avoid any conduct that would attract unfavorable attention. She cannot suddenly change from her love for Mendo. She is the sort of person that Juan needs, although we must say that he might get pretty tiresome after a while.

Mendo is unscrupulous and so sure of himself that we turn against him right away. All the same, he is not a character to be despised — he shows that he is brave when it comes to fighting bulls. Even so, his attempt upon Ana seems considerably out of character. Lucrecia is typically feminine, suspicious and persistent. The two servants, Beltrán and Celia, are intelligent, loyal, and dependable at all times. They would be hard to duplicate in any play. They add greatly to its interest. They have originality.

RECOMMENDED READING

El Tejedor de Segovia, Part II. A melodramatic play, if there ever was one. There are such details as a mysterious weaver, a Kangaroo court, a big jail delivery, sympathetic bandits, treachery, hairbreath escapes, the King saved from the Moors, and much else along the same line. Needless to say, virtue triumphs.

There was a Part I by an unknown author. It is almost as exciting as Part II, which was written first.

SELECTED BIBLIOGRAPHY

Antonio Castro Leal, *Juan Ruiz de Alarcón. Su vida y su obra.* Mexico, 1943.
Julio Jiménez Rueda, *Juan Ruiz de Alarcón y su tiempo.* Mexico, 1939.
R. Monner Sanz, "Don Juan Ruiz de Alarcón: el hombre, el dramaturgo, el moralista," *Revista de la Universidad de Buenos Aires,* XXXI (1915), 5-31, 109-142, 433-478.

Chapter VII

GUILLÉN DE CASTRO. BALLAD ARTIST

Guillén de Castro y Bellvis (1569-1613)

Guillén de Castro was born in Valencia and is considered to be the best of numerous playwrights from that city. He was for ten years Captain in the Coast Guard of Valencia, which was supposed to keep off Barbary pirates, if there were any. He evidently had good friends among the aristocracy, for he was appointed Governor of Seyano, a city in Italy, by the Viceroy of Naples. After 1619 he made his residence in Madrid, where he also had many influential friends. Although he was a rival of Lope de Vega, their relations were friendly, something that did not always happen with Lope. In 1623 Guillén de Castro received the high honor of the Order of Santiago. He seems to have been very fortunate in his friendships. They paid off. The first part of his plays was published in Valencia in 1618, and the second in 1625.

Castro wrote some forty plays, of which the most famous is *Las mocedades del Cid, Primera Parte.* No little of the fame of this play is due to its adaptation in French by the eminent French dramatist, Pierre Corneille, but in our opinion, Castro's play is far superior to the French version, which follows it closely. In our opinion, too, the second part of this play has been unjustly downgraded. It deserves to stand with any play of the century. Castro is to be remembered especially for his skillful use of Spanish ballads. He was the first to draw themes from the *Quijote,* in plays entitled *Don Quijote de la Mancha* and *El curioso impertinente.*

Las mocedades del Cid (First Play).—The play begins very appropriately with an impressive ceremony in which a great historical character is the central figure. One may object that the whole business is an anachronism, but that would not mean anything to the audience of Castro's time. In the course of the proceedings certain motives come out that are important. These are the affection of Ximena and Doña Urraca for Rodrigo, the jealousy of the Conde Lozano; and the impetuosity of Don Sancho, the King's son. Sancho is too young yet to bear arms, but he is very prominent in the second play. In the ceremony we have an example of the use of the curtain in the back of the stage. It is used here to reveal a beautiful scene, rather than a scene of horror, as is often the case.

In the scene following the knighting of Rodrigo we should remember that honor is an all-important element in Spanish character. The blow struck by the Conde is a mortal offense. Furthermore, such violence in the presence of the King is a crime of the first magnitude. Even so, the King is rather a "weak sister," and his idea of keeping the whole thing secret is far from being a sensible solution.

The happiness of Rodrigo's brothers at this good fortune is rudely shattered by the appearance of the father, who to their mistification, sends them all away. Evidently, the back curtain comes into play again when the old man takes a sword off the wall and finds that wielding it is too much for him. This fact arouses profound sympathy in the mind of the audience.

The trial of the sons borders closely on the ridiculous when Don Diego tries out the youngest first and ends up by biting the hand of the eldest. It is interesting to compare what Corneille did at this point in his version of the play. What a violation of the French idea of decorum it would be to have one man bite another on the stage! The best that Corneille could do at this juncture is for the father to ask his son:

As-tu du coeur?

This is quite a come-down from what we have in Castro.

Corneille improves on Castro by saving until the last the name of the person who has insulted him. When left alone (this is the Spanish play now), Rodrigo analyses the situation, something that is rather out of the ordinary in Golden Age drama. The usual thing is for the characters to act rather than to reason why. In Corneille Act I ends with Rodrigo's monologue. It takes quite a while to recite it, but it makes a good ending to the act. [1]

Coming back to the Spanish play, we see Doña Urraca and Ximena on the *alto,* which here represents a window, and with them we witness the encounter of the Conde and the Cid. It is instructive to note that the Conde's philosophy of life is to try to do the right thing, but if he goes wrong, not to back down. This sort of private philosophy in a character is good drama. It stamps him with individuality. Castro handles the conflict between the Conde and the Cid in an admirable manner, but he closes the act rather ingloriously by having the Cid defy the servants and then

---

[1] Corneille's *Cid* has been the most popular of his plays on the French stage.

leave the stage for them to have the last word, and not a very dignified one, at that.

In the second act it would be difficult to find a more striking example of the grotesque than the bloody handkerchief of Ximena and the bloody face of Diego Laínez. This scene comes dangerously close to being ridiculous, which is certainly not intended.

When the Cid insists on seeing Ximena, her servant is quite right in saying that what he is doing is "locura y no gentileza." Not only this, but it is decidedly undignified for the hero to hide, when Ximena comes in. And this is not all, the whole scene with Ximena and Rodrigo is phony. What is Rodrigo there for in the first place? Can he think that Ximena would really kill him? If he does not think that, what is the point of his being there? Ximena is the one who has any sense when she tells him to leave and try not to let people see him go. Even at that, it takes him quite a while to make his departure.

An example of Castro at his best is the scene with Diego and his father. Diego is so proud of Rodrigo that he can hardly restrain himself and he must tell Rodrigo so. Rodrigo, on the other hand, is too moved for words. His few words are more expressive than any long speeches. How different this is from Corneille's version in which the Cid tells his father that he has avenged him, but that he has lost all — his "flamme." The trouble with this is that this is self-pity and what he says will make his father feel bad unnecessarily.

An excellent use of the *alto* is to be seen again when Doña Urraca is at a window *(alto)* and recognizes Rodrigo in the distance (really only a few feet away on the stage). It might seem that Castro had some appreciation of natural scenery when Doña Urraca speaks of the beautiful fields and the hills, but these sentiments on her part are probably derived from the Second Epode of Horace in the famous *Beautus ille*. Here again Castro shows fine feeling when Doña Urraca expresses her love for Rodrigo and Rodrigo cannot reply in kind. He simply changes the subject with such vague terms as "Mil años vivas," "Dios te guarde," and "Tú me animas." This is Castro at his best.

In the scene with the *pastor* the first words of the Moors "Li, li, li, li" may not be as ridiculous as they might seem at first sight. The author here is probably trying to imitate the war cry of the Moors. [2]

Still another good use of the *alto* is where the *pastor* climbs a "hill" (the *alto* again) and gives a blow by blow account of the battle between the Cid and the Moorish King. The *pastor*, of course, does not recognize

---

[2] Cf. The episode of the Duke and the Duchess in the *Quijote. Segunda Parte del Quijote,* Chapter 34.

the Cid, but in the mind of the audience who else can "El Cristiano," the bold warrior with the "penacho amarillo" be? Castro is not much given to humor, but the *pastor's* description of the battle has its humorous side.

The scene in which the fencing master and Doña Urraca appear has nothing at all to do with the play we are discussing, but the substance of it is extremely important for the second play. This should be kept in mind for when that play is studied. The principal things to remember are that Sancho's horoscope indicates that he will be killed with an "arma arrojadiza," and the cause will be "Muy propinqua suya." A statement of Doña Urraca is significant when Sancho says he will have a breastplate made to protect his heart. Her comment is that he may be killed from the back. Sancho, though, cannot possibly believe that he will not be facing the enemy. As we shall see, in the second play Sancho is facing the wrong way at the wrong time.

The Cid's prowess as told by the Moorish king is a little hard to believe, five hundred Christians against six thousand of the enemy. Corneille wisely tones this down to a considerable degree. In the French play the five hundred of the Cid's followers become three thousand before the battle takes place. This makes a lot more sense.

In the scene with the Moorish king it is very Spanish for the father to embrace his son, and for the Spanish king to do the same. Here we have an historic moment when Rodrigo is called the "Cid" for the first time. In the final scene of the act we learn three months have passed. Ximena has not forgotten her ideas of vengeance and in his reply to her complaints, the King exiles the Cid.

Early in Act Three we learn that a year has passed, that Ximena is still in love with the Cid, and Doña Urraca is being badly treated by her brother, Sancho. A very human touch is given when the King says he is sick and tired of having Ximena crying at his feet all the time. Rodrigo's father gallantly defends her and says he will prove that the two are still in love. When Ximena appears, Castro clumsily introduces a ballad, the details of which have little connection with the events of the play.

The scene in which Ximena is forced to show that she is in love with Rodrigo is a play within a play and is handled adroitly by Castro. In the preceeding scene Arias has a whispered and mysterious conversation with a servant. When the servant appears again, he gives himself away with his boisterous entrance, which is heightened by the exaggerated exclamations of Arias. All this makes it clear to the audience that the whole set-up is a trick. Ximena is deceived at the "news" of Rodrigo's death, but soon recovers sufficiently to ask the King to set a price on Rodrigo's head. She suggests that the reward should be none other than herself, if this person is equal in rank, plus other "fringe benefits." This the King reluctantly promises to grant.

The following scene with the leper has nothing to do with the main plot, but it reveals the Cid as a practicing Christian. He also turns out to be something of a preacher. This scene has elements of humor in spite of the frightful appearance of the leper. The leper turns out to be Saint Lazarus. The trouble is that Saint Lazarus actually stacks the cards against any opponent of the Cid. Now he is "un vencedor invencible." This is really not fair.

Don Martín, a regular giant of a man, takes up the cause of Ximena, but of course he doesn't stand a chance in the world against the Cid. The play closes with a rather cheap trick, in which a messenger announces that someone is coming with the head of Rodrigo. This individual, not altogether to our surprise, turns out to be Rodrigo. Now Ximena accepts him as her husband. The action of the Spanish play has covered over a year, so this decision on the part of Ximena is acceptable. The French play, which preserves the unity of time (24 hours) has the King give Ximena a year to dry her tears.

Before the Spanish play comes to a close, the author violates the all-important unity of action by showing Sancho, now grown up considerably, more intractible than before. He even tells his father that if he divides up his kingdom, among his children, he (Sancho) will take over all of it for himself. At this the King solemnly says:

¡Mis maldiciones te caygan,
Si mis mandos no obedeces!

This is preparation for the second play, also called *Las mocedades del Cid,* frequently spoken of as *Las hazañas del Cid.* As we shall see, neither of these titles is appropriate, for the Cid does not figure prominently in the play.

The plot of *Las mocedades* is principally an account of the early life of Rodrigo de Vivar, the Cid, with some extraneous details about the youth of Sancho, the heir to the throne. At the end of Act One the killing of Ximena's father gives rise to the events that follow.

There are many dramatic incidents, such as the conflict between the Cid and the Conde, the exile of the Cid, and the breaking of the news of his "death" to Ximena. It must be said that some of the scenes which Castro must have thought were dramatic are hardly that. We may cite as examples the Cid offereing his life to Ximena, and his bringing in his head at the end of the play.

The character of the father of the Cid is well drawn. Ximena's desire for vengeance may seem a little extreme, as it does to the King eventually. The Cid is shown as an heroic figure, highly sensitive at times, and at others, less so. In the main he lives up to our expectations.

Las mocedades del Cid (Second Play).—As we begin the second play, we should keep in mind that it is foretold that Sancho will be killed by a thrown weapon (*arma arrojadiza,* or *arma arrojada*), and that the cause will be very close to him (*muy propinqua suya*). In spite of this, Sancho feels safe, for he has a breastplate over his heart. We may put the case in other terms There will be a victim (Sancho), there will be an agent (one who will do the killing), and there must be a special instrument (*arma arrojadiza*). All these must be brought together for the prophesy to be fulfilled. We must add one more detail, his father's curse, if Sancho does not obey his father's last request. As the play works out, something from on high (*el cielo*) is involved. [3]

The play begins with plenty of action, a battle scene in which Sancho is engaged. So is Rodrigo, the Cid, who reminds us: "Al cielo ofende la causa." Things move pretty fast along here and the Cid is in the very thick of things. He saves Sancho, and then frees Sancho's brother, Alonso, from Sancho's men. After this last rescue, the Cid effects a sort of "Cease Fire" in order to bring us up to date on the situation, the father's curse and Sancho's disobedience. A good part of what he says is taken from traditional Spanish ballads. This is one of the important characteristics of the play, the use of ballads. It would be hard to find another play that makes a more effective use of these typically Spanish materials.

Sancho is unmoved by the Cid's reminder of the curse and, more serious still, not even by any possible intervention of heaven. Even now, something strange is going on, for Sancho is acting irrationally. He says he wants to drink the blood of his brothers and sisters. This sort of thing happens again and again. Sancho becomes irrational whenever he even thinks of going against his father's will. "El cielo" is in action.

We soon learn that Alonso has escaped, and Sancho is turning against Doña Urraca, to whom Zamora was bequeathed by her father. Rodrigo incurs the enemity of Sancho when he says that he will defend him anywhere, but that he will never draw his sword against Zamora.

In the city, Doña Urraca is dispirited by the turn of events, but Arias, with his five sons, offers to defend her and declares that Heaven is on her

---

[3] Sturgis E. Leavitt, "Divine Justice in the *Hazañas del Cid, Hispania,* XII (1929), 141-46. We have called the events leading up to the death of Sancho "Divine Justice." There may be a better term than "Divine Justice," but we don't know what it is.

side. We are never allowed to forget this fact. Heaven (Divine Justice) is really the moving force through half of this play. At this point Bellido de Olfos appears. He is the agent to whom reference is made above, but he is far away from Sancho and the instrument *(arma arrojadiza)* is nowhere in sight.

The scene now passes to Toledo, where the Moorish king cordially welcomes Alonso, addressing him as *"Tú."* Soon thereafter Princess Zaida appears with an impressive retinue. Alonso speaks of her as "Zaida, la que es maravilla del mundo." Right here it may not be amiss to assert that the actress selected for this part should possess two of the most alluring examples of "standard equipment" imaginable. And her Moorish costume should reveal, rather than conceal her charms. We should mention, too, that according to history, Alonso was a very handsome man. This romantic situation is a welcome change from the horrors of war.

Zaida has never seen Alonso, but she has heard of him and of his misfortunes, and has come to help him with all her jewels and other possessions. With the appearance of this luscious beauty the wheel of fortune has turned for Alonso. At the close of this scene we know that it is love at first sight that we are witnessing. And no wonder!

The scene now passes to the siege of Zamora, and Sancho is seen even more unreasonable than he was before. He wildly tells his soldiers to tear down the battlements with their bare hands and to bash the walls down with their heads. He pays no heed to Arias, who says "el mismo cielo" is on the side of Doña Urraca. Nor does he pay any attention to Doña Urraca's call to her dead father to protect her *(volver por* means to protect). At this juncture Sancho in his madness says:

> ¿Tu padre llamas? Para hacerme guerra
> Baxe del cielo, o salga de la tierra!   ll. 516-17.

In answer to this irreverent remark we have a most spectacular apparition. Sancho's father *does* come up from the ground with a bloody javelin in his hand, saying that this will be the weapon that will cause Sancho's death.

No one but Sancho sees this apparition, not even Doña Urraca, and Sancho withdraws just as Zamora was within his grasp. Shortly thereafter, Bellido de Olfos is seized by "algún impulso divino" that makes him feel that he is the one chosen to carry out the will of Heaven. This surprises him beyond measure, because he knows all too well that he is a base coward.

Doña Urraca is certain that a miracle has saved Zamora. So are we. Bellido tries to tell her that he can free Zamora with only one casualty, but Doña Urraca very cagily does not want to know how. What she doesn't know won't hurt her! Bellido takes her attitude, rather than her words, as implied consent, and the agent of vengeance is now activated.

Moved as he is by a mysterious force that he doesn't understand, Bellido dares to impugn the loyalty of such a staunch character as Arias Gonzalo. He is really putting on an act and doesn't realize what he is saying. Even Doña Urraca cannot comprehend what it is all about. Bellido, naturally enough, is set upon by Arias and his sons, and only a miracle (el cielo) saves him from death at their hands.

The next scene is really a throw-back. Part of it seems to take place as the same time that Bellido is in the city. Sancho is still terrified by the the vision and hesitates about continuing the siege. Diego Ordóñez gives him sage advice, and if Sancho had heeded it and desisted his wicked design, Bellido could never have escaped. But Sancho determines to go on with the siege. He even decides to arm himself with a javelin like the one he saw in his dead father's hands. The notes are wrong at this point. The javelin that Sancho arms himself with is not a symbol of office, but a frightful weapon, especially if thrown from close range. Now the instrument of destiny is in evidence.

Here is where Bellido appears, saved ironically by the determination of Sancho to capture the city. Now the three necessary elements — agent, instrument and victim — are close together, but not in the right combination. Sancho, not Bellido, has the weapon and he is in the midst of soldiers who can protect him in an emergency.

Sancho's determination is shaken by a voice from the walls (alto) of Zamora, and Bellido becomes the coward that he is in real life. The voice is that of Arias Gonzalo. Even though he wants to protect the city, he cannot bear to see Sancho deceived by such as a scoundrel as Bellido. He warns Sancho against him in no uncertain terms.

When Sancho fails to heed this most unusual warning, Bellido recovers his divine frenzy and defies no less a person than the Cid. Rodrigo is most indignant, and the King summarily exiles him. This exile turns out to be important later on, when Sancho is in danger far from his men and the Cid is within hailing distance.

When the Cid has departed, Bellido's courage is again restored and he tells Sancho that he can show him a gate that is never closed. Sancho is imprudent enough to go with him into no man's land. It is really Divine Justice that is leading him on.

Out in the desolate terrain the Cid is near enough to help Sancho, if he is called upon to do so. Even this slight possibility makes Bellido cringe. At one moment he thinks he has his opportunity when he stands behind Sancho, ready to plunge a dagger into his back. But some mysterious force restrains him. He does not realize that Sancho can only be killed with an "arma arrojadiza."

Shortly after this, Sancho says that he has to step aside for a "cierta necesidad que a los reyes no perdona." This is not an ordinary call of nature, it is "el cielo" setting up a sequence that will have a tragic outcome. As Sancho is descending a slope to a place pointed out by Bellido, he slips and quite naturally drops the javelin. Bellido tells him not to worry, that he will hold it for him.

Now the combination — agent, instrument, and victim — are in the right order. Bellido has the javelin and Sancho is in the most defenseless position imaginable. He believes himself protected by a breastplate, but this is no good now. Even as he is "busily engaged," he is facing the city, intent on its capture, and his back is toward Bellido. Bellido cannot miss.

Bellido is now ready to hurl the javelin, but Heaven is giving Sancho one last chance to repent. For some reason which Bellido does not understand, he cannot throw the weapon. This tense moment passes, and with a running start Bellido hurls the javelin downhill (off stage) with all his might. We hear a dull thud as it strikes. It would be impossible to find a more dramatic moment anywhere

But Divine Justice (*el cielo*) has not finished with Sancho. Under ordinary circumstances Sancho would be killed instantly. It is not fair for Divine Justice to stop here, though. Sancho must live long enough to confess his sins and forgive his enemies. And from a dramatic point of view, at least in Golden Age practice, the audience ought to have a chance to see what Sancho looks like now. From a practical point of view, enough time must elapse for the make-up artists to fix Sancho up and show him pierced through and through by the javelin. Eventually, Sancho is brought in and he lives for an extraordinarily long time, during which it is made abundantly clear that he makes amends with "el cielo." He had a fair deal, and only he is responsible.

Bellido makes his escape to Zamora in the course of a rather dubious effort on the part of the Cid to overtake him. Doña Urraca hears an uproar and naively asks:

¿Si fué algún atrevimiento de Bellido?   ll. 1418-19

Doña Urraca is rather an enigmatic character, especially in her relations with Bellido. An example is her indecision about what to do with Bellido.

The funeral services of Sancho is made impressive in a rather ingenious way. The mourners pass across the stage, go out by one door, and come in by another in an endless procession. It is interesting to note that the fatal javelin is still sticking through Sancho's body. The audience certainly has plenty of opportunity to see it. This last time is almost too much for us.

The challenge of Diego Ordóñez may seem rather odd, including as it does, birds, fish, and a whole lot more, but we should note that this is a ritual that Castro takes from the ballads (Durán, 786). [4] The most important detail is that the challenger obligates himself to fight with five men, one after another.

A pleasant change from the violence and its consequences is an opportunity to see Alonso and Zaida again. Alonso is not only good looking, but he can make nifty love speeches. A Spanish audience would be gratified to learn that Zaida of her own free will has decided to become a Christian. Right along here Castro becomes rather naïve when Zaida reports that the Moorish king is beginning to suspect that she and Alonso are in love. He would be blind, if he didn't.

Castro comes to the brink of the ridiculous in the "sleep" scene. The drooling of Alonso, his asides while he is "asleep," and the hair-raising sequence are anything but heroic. But Castro is following the ballads again (Durán, 767), evidently thinking that anything from the ballads must be appropriate and dramatic. He was wrong in this instance. In the ballad and in this play even the Moorish king is downgraded when he says he will imprison Alonso.

The third act presents scenes that are truly heroic. Arias wants to be the first to fight not because he has any hopes of winning, but under the illusion that his sons may stand a better chance if he blunts the sword of Diego Ordóñez. As in the ballads (Durán, 795), Doña Urraca eventually dissuades him from such a rash act.

Then follows the trial by combat. This is an extraordinarily successful effort on the part of Castro. He brings upon the stage the contestants, the officials and two groups of spectators. Those from Zamora are on the walls (the *alto*) and Sancho's men are at the side of the field. The conflict is decidedly unequal — one man against five — and a natural tendency would be to side with Diego Ordóñez, but this must not be. Our sympathy should be with Arias and his sons. This is attained by Diego Ordóñez's attitude. He is so cocky that we cannot help but turn against him.

We cannot see the actual conflict (This would be possible in a movie or on TV), but we get a blow by blow description of it, and this is just as good. Something should be left to the imagination. The first son loses because he is too impetuous and, besides, he lacks experience. The father solicitously coaches his second son and tells him to take his time and watch for the "breaks." This makes good sense, but in the battle this son has bad

---

[4] Agustín Durán, *Romancero de romances* ..., Madrid, 1832. 2 vols.

luck. He loses a part of his armor and Diego Ordóñez cooly and merciless-ly takes advantage of it. The good counsel of Arias is all in vain.

When the time comes for the next contestant, Arias goes down to ground level to be the "Padrino." This act makes it possible for the father to be close to his son in the final moments. In this conflict strange things happen. Arias' son is mortally wounded, but in desperation he succeeds in slashing the reins of Diego Ordóñez's horse and severely wounding him. The horse in his madness runs out of the ring. But just as he does, Diego Ordóñez jumps off and has one foot on the line. Is he out of the ring or in it? Has he lost the fight? This is a question of technicality, interpretation of the rules. Only the officials can decide.

A most pathetic moment is where the son, right at death's door, is only interested to know if he has won. Even though the officials have not yet rendered their decision, the father assures his son that he is indeed the winner. A most pathetic detail is that he dies without being really sure.

The rest of the play is, necessarily, something of an anti-climax. The officials render their decision; Diego Ordóñez is violently upset by the ac-cident, even to the extent of childishly throwing down his arms. Bellido is disposed of (fortunately off-stage). Alonso returns from exile with Zaida and is greeted as king. Zamora is now free. At this point the play could well come to a close.

But the author seems to have been so carried away by the ballads that he introduces one more, the strange oath (bolt and crossbow) that Rodrigo demands. This ceremony rather demeans both Alonso and the Cid, and is quite unnecessary to the plot. Compensation of a sort brings the play to a close when the Moorish princess changes her name to María.

At first sight there seems to be three plots to this play, the events lead-ing up to the death of King Sancho, the love affair of Alonso in Toledo, and the trial by combat of the city of Zamora. But further consideration will show that they are all the consequence of Sancho's disobedience of his father's will.

Castro can be very skillful in the construction of dramatic situations. He can also be quite inept, as is to be seen in the scenes where Alonso pretends to be asleep toward the end of the second act. But here Castro is following the ballads. In his use of these *romances* he is superb for the most part. As a matter of fact, the play abounds in unusually dramatic situations, and some are to be found in each act. Perhaps, the most emo-tional is the death of Arias' third son. It is profoundly moving to have him die, not knowing whether he has won or not.

The characters in the play are well depicted, but one stands out from all the rest. This is Arias, with his high sense of duty, his loyalty to Doña Urraca, and his love for his sons.

French critics have praised this play highly, but it has been severely criticized by English and American scholars who have been shocked by the "cierta necesidad." This detail is very important in the sequence of events, and it is not an invention of Castro. It occurs in Juan de la Cueva's version and, more important, it is found in the ballads. Castro follows Cueva's play rather closely, but he improves upon it greatly. [5]

SELECTED BIBLIOGRAPHY

Otis H. Green, "New Documents for the Biography of Guillén de Castro," *Revue Hispanique,* LXXXI (1933), 248-60.

Courtney Bruerton, "The Chronology of the Comedias of Guillén de Castro," *Hispanic Review,* XII (1944), 89-151.

---

[5] In an article to be published in a homage volume to William M. Fichter, a recognized authority on Golden Age drama in Spain, we have called Castro's play a "*Comedia* sin paralelo."

CHAPTER VIII

AGUSTÍN MORETO, INDEBTED TO OTHERS

AGUSTÍN MORETO Y CAVANA (1618-1669)

Moreto was born of Italian parentage in Madrid, but he passed most of his life in Toledo. After studying at the University of Alcalá de Henares, he became a priest. In 1657 he was put in charge of a charitable institution in Toledo, where he enjoyed the favor of the archbishop. He was buried along with the poor that he had cared for.

Moreto was the author of about a hundred plays, some of which were written in collaboration. His plays deal with historical, religious and everyday subjects. He had the reputation of lifting material from other authors. He was depicted, for example, as going through old manuscripts and plays, saying "Este no vale nada. De aquí se puede sacar algo, mudándole algo." *El lindo Don Diego* is derived in part from *El Narciso en su opinión* of Guillén de Castro, and *El desdén con el desdén* from *La vengador de mujeres* by Lope de Vega. Moreto generally improved on his models. In this connection, we must remember that in those times there was no copyright, and plays were more or less common property.

El lindo Don Diego.—This play is an example of a kind of play we have not seen before, a *comedia de figurón*. This is a play in which the principal character is grotesque, eccentric, somewhat "cracked." He usually comes from the "sticks." He looks funny and he acts funny. [1]

Moreto is fond of giving his *graciosos* queer names and the one in this play is no exception. Mosquito is given to saying funny things, and the author seems to think that every time he opens his mouth, he must make some comic remark. He is addicted to puns, and unless one is pretty familiar with the Spanish language, the puns are not always very intelligible.

---

[1] Edwin B. Place, "Notes on the grotesque: the *comedia de figurón*," *PMLA*, LIV (1939), 412-21.

Some of them are far-fetched. It has been said somewhere that puns are the lowest form of wit.

We may note in passing that Moreto is over-fond of the word "empeño" and its verb form "empeñar." Some of the readers of *El lindo* may want to have fun keeping track of the number of times these words are used in the play. They would add up to quite a total.

At the beginning of the play we get an unusual touch, an explanation of the friendship between Don Tello and Don Juan, both having been passengers on the same ship from Mexico to Spain. When we consider what a long voyage it was in those times and the little space that was available on the ship, we must conclude that passengers either became close friends, or mortal enemies during the trip. [2]

Another interesting detail is the attitude of the two girls toward their father. They are not disobedient, but they feel that they should at least be consulted about marriage. This seems reasonable enough, but their father is adamant. As a consequence, we side with the daughters and not with him.

The decisión of Inés and Leonor to fix themselves up "Apelar al artificio: mucho moño y arrancadas," and thus become unattractive to the suitors is a false lead. Moreto is not doing very well at this point. And neither is he at his best when he has Inés agree to take back Beatriz on condition that she (Beatriz) will not be seen by Tello. She could not possibly keep out of his way for very long.

Mosquito gives a colorful description of Don Diego before his appearance, and this is all to the good, provided Don Diego lives up to this advance billing. Needless to say, he does — and to a high degree — first in the scene with the mirrors, and later when he arrives at Tello's house. The pantomime that the actor would introduce on these occasions would be a delight to the audience. And so would his first remark when he meets Tello and the family:

¡Buen lugarillo es Madrid!   l. 803.

It would be difficult to find a more ludicrous situation than the one in which Don Diego thinks that everyone, both male and female, fall victims to his "charms." From time to time Mosquito makes comments, not always, it must be said, in perfect taste.

---

[2] This trip was rather complicated. Vessels from Mexico would stop first at Santo Domingo, then usually at the Azores, and thence to San Lúcar and Sevilla. Oviedo (*De la natural historia del las Indias*. Toledo, 1526.) estimates that the voyage would take approximately sixty days. It may have been a little shorter in the seventeenth century, but not much.

The act closes with uncertainty. Nothing is decided. All we have to look forward to is more of Don Diego, and after all we have seen of him, we can hardly expect him to surpass himself. Even if he doesn't, it will be great to watch him in action again.

In Act II it is not altogether dignified of Don Juan to put himself in the hands of Mosquito in working out a scheme to deceive Don Diego. We should observe here that Mosquito is still full of puns and is even enriching the Spanish language with words of his own manufacture. Don Juan's dealings with Mosquito do not heighten his character any. Don Juan is not an outstanding personage.

Don Diego lives up to our expectations when he explains why he praises himself so much. It makes no sense to have any false modesty, if a person presents such a devastating appearance as he does. Mosquito now has evidently told Don Diego about the "Countess," and Don Diego takes the bait, hook, line and sinker.

It is not amusing to see Don Diego believe that Leonor wants him for herself, when she tries to explain that Inés does not care for him. But we can't have comic scenes all the time, and Don Diego is perfectly in character when he reacts as he does.

It might be admitted that Inés has a terribly long speech when she asks Don Diego to give up thought of marrying her, but we must remember that the actress who has the role of Inés would naturally expect to have a prominent part. The author is giving her some extra lines to keep her satisfied. Incidentally, though, the actor who plays the part of Mendo in this scene has to stand around all the time and not have anything to do or say.

Don Diego listens intently to this long speech of Inés because he is the subject of it and, not altogether to our surprise, he misinterprets it completely. When pressed for a decision, he says that he must sleep on the matter and will let Inés know later.

The stage directions in brackets explain the change of scene to the house of the real countess. We must keep in mind that notations in brackets are not indications by the author, but have been added by the editors. Normally, we would expect some remark on the part of the characters that would indicate where the action is taking place, if the scene changes. There is none here.

It would seem at first sight that it is unworthy of Don Juan to listen in on the scene in which the "Countess" figures, but, as we shall see later, he is in on the plot. We have said that the author would find it hard to duplicate the scene in Act One where Don Diego comes to Tello's house, but here he does just that in a totally different manner.

We can only imagine the "get-up" of the "Countess," but we can be sure that it was impressive. It certainly is to Don Diego, when he says:

> No he visto en toda mi vida
> mejor bulto de señora.   ll. 1655-56.

The dialogue right along here is most interesting. The "Countess" has a vocabulary that is somewhat unusual for a servant, but we can overlook this. Don Diego replies in kind and is proud of his own ability along this line when he says, aside, to Mosquito:

> Bravo pedazo de prosa.   l. 1696.

Later on, the "Countess" gets so "far out in left field" that what she says is unintelligible even to Mosquito, and he has to ask Don Diego to translate for him. Finally, Don Diego makes his proposal and it is fitting for him to receive substantially that same reply that he gave to Inés:

> Cogitación habrá en eso.   l. 1748.

The pleasant conversation between Don Diego and the "Countess" is interrupted by the appearance of Don Juan, who demands to know what Don Diego is doing in the house of his cousin, the "Countess." Don Diego has a hard time finding an excuse, but he finally hits upon one that fits the case.

The scene passes to the house of Don Tello, although no line in the play so indicates. Don Diego catches Mosquito and Beatriz in an embrace and this is something Mosquito had not counted on. This time it is Beatriz that has the bright idea, and all seems well until Don Juan appears. Here the author shows his ingenuity by really complicating things. The act ends with a misunderstanding which, if examined closely, is not really serious.

Act Three takes place in the street and the problem is for Beatriz to get away from Don Juan. This complication Moreto handles very well. In this scene we get a rather surprising definition of honor (opinión):

> Que la opinión no es lo que es,
> Sino lo que entiende el pueblo.   ll. 2291-92.

In the conflict between Don Juan and Don Diego the latter appears as a rather different person from what we have seen before. He is keener in mind and bolder in spirit, ready to defend the "Countess" even against el Armada del Inglés. He skillfully takes advantage of the arrival of Mendo to make his escape from Don Juan.

The misunderstanding now involves Don Juan and Mendo, and a duel between the two is only averted by the arrival of Tello. At this point the play becomes more of a "comedia de enredo" (comedy of intrigue) than a "comedia de figurón."

Inés is so convinced that Don Juan has other interests that she tells her sister that she will avenge herself by marrying Don Diego. Parenthetically, this attitude is too extreme for us to sympathize with her. Furthermore, from the point of view of the play, we are almost on the point of forgetting about Don Diego, and this is bad. Indeed, the situation becomes almost too complicated for us to follow until Inés, in an unduly long speech, tries to set things right. In acting in this manner, however, she seems so unreasonable that we almost lose interest in her.

Beatriz now shows up and persuades Inés to hide and see what Mosquito has to say to Tello. Really, it is almost too much to have so much hiding (al paño), especially since the hidden characters have a good deal to say to each other that is not "heard" by the other actors. We have by now nearly forgotten about Don Diego, for here the interest is centered on Mosquito. The story he tells is a gem, and with it he almost becomes more important than Don Diego.

The play closes with everyone on the stage, or hiding close by. Fortunately, Don Diego is once again the center of attention and he remains so to the end of the play. One curious detail that might easily be overlooked, is where the action of the play actually stops and Don Diego speaks directly to the audience: [3]

> Señores, ¿qué es lo que escucho?
> Mil cruces me estoy haciendo.
> Y dirán que no me alabe!
> Un testimonio de aquesto
> Tengo de enviar a Burgos.   ll. 3027-31.

He does this again a little later. This sort of thing is some compensation for his having been off the stage for so long. Mosquito also directs himself to the audience in the same manner.

The play closes happily for all concerned, for all except Don Diego.

The plot of this play is simple enough, dealing mainly with the "adventures" of Don Diego. He is the most interesting character, though of course he is exaggerated. The other characters are principally foils for him, and the scenes in which he appears are the ones that stand out in the play.

---

[3] Sturgis E. Leavitt, "The gracioso Takes the Audience into his Confidence," Bulletin of the Comediantes, VII (1955), No. 2, 27-29.

El desdén con el desdén.—The principal characters in this play are all high-class people, all except Polilla. Like the usual *gracioso* of Moreto, he has a strange name. No explanation is given for his arriving late in Barcelona where his master now is. He just arrives late, and that is that. Again, we call attention to the author's propensity to use the words *empeño* and *empeñar*, which have a variety of meanings for him. One last word about Polilla. He is not a punster like Mosquito, but something better. His thoughts run to things to eat. It is remarkable how the author introduces so many colorful references to eating.

It takes a long speech by Carlos to bring Polilla up to date on the situation he is in. One cannot but wonder whether any actor could memorize so many lines. This speech is very important, though, because it establishes beyond all doubt that Carlos is madly in love with Diana. We must be absolutely sure that this is the case when later he pretends that he is not.

The substance of his speech is as follows: his love for Diana is not love at first sight, she is no startling beauty, he has stood out among the other suitors, but apparently has made no impression upon her. She is a sort of bluestocking, an intellectual. Her very disdain for men is what has kindled an all-embracing love in Carlos. In telling Polilla about it, he gets so carried away that he talks to himself, asking questions and answering them himself. When he finishes his long story, Polilla surprises him (and us) by saying that this sort of thing happens every day. He gives appropriate examples — grapes in abundance and grapes out of reach. He follows this up by a parable about figs, and this is altogether fitting, as we shall see in the course of the play. Similarly, he suggests an effective way to make Diana pay more attention to her suitors. It is noteworthy that Carlos' idea of winning over Diana is his own, and not the *gracioso's*. Usually, it is the other way around.

When we first see Diana it is in a pretty scene, with her girl friends all dressed up nice, and musicians playing. Polilla, we find, is no ordinary *gracioso*. He socializes freely with the princes and with Diana. In his conversation with her he has one of the best lines in the play:

> El beso es el queso
> De los ratones de amor.   ll. 693-94.

Polilla is now a spy in the camp of the "enemy" and he can keep Carlos posted on the results of his campaign. Diana is not a disobedient daughter, any more than the girls in *El lindo*.

After some word play Carlos surprises Diana by going her one better:

Yo señora,
No sólo no quiero,
Mas ni quiero ser querido.   ll. 969-71

Diana's pride is now aroused and she decides to bring Carlos to her knees and humilitate him. This makes an appropriate end to Act One. Important motives are now in action.

At the beginning of Act Two Polilla makes a "progress report." Diana is now definitely interested and she stacks the cards against — really for — Carlos in the game that they are to play that day. She makes one pass at him when she says that if she ever should fall in love with anyone, it would be with him. Carlos does not fall into the trap, but puts up a long argument against falling in love. Diana cannot say much against this without going over to the other side.

The play almost becomes an opera when the game for the day begins. Musicians are playing, the girls are beautifully dressed, the men appear at their best. The scene has a special attraction because we know in advance how the most important choice will come out. We should note the color symbolism here and the dancing after each choice.

One of the two capital scenes of the play follows. The actor who plays the part of Carlos should with the utmost sincerity recite the lines about the fish and at this point passionately declare himself. This is no pretense. It is the real thing. Diana falls into her own snare and as the scene develops, she becomes more and more entangled. Moreto has done himself proud in developing this situation. A comic touch is introduced when Polilla learns of her indisposition and prescribes a remedy. It is one that would either kill or cure. Kill, more likely.

Diana now decides to make another try. And here Polilla speaks directly to the audience (ll. 1775-82), with the introductory word "Señores." He is, as usual, in character with his reference to eating.

As a rule where a change of scene and costumes is required, we have intervening scenes, or many lines, to allow time for the actors to effect the necessary changes. Not much time is needed here, for all the girls have to do is take off some of their clothes.

The garden scene is a gorgeous affair. The girls are in a state of undress that heightens their physical charms, they are singing, and we are to imagine that they are in a beautiful garden. Talk about strip tease! This is it. [4] Carlos enters the garden and doesn't look at anything but the

---

[4] Sturgis E. Leavitt, "Strip Tease in Golden Age Drama," *Homenaje al Profesor Rodríguez Moñino*, Madrid, 1966.

flowers. He doesn't look at Diana, not even when she thusts herself before him making her attractions, "standard equipment," as visible as possible. When he leaves abruptly, the finishing touch is put on, when Polilla reports that he said the girls were singing like school children.

The Third Act introduces an unexpected note — the other suitors have decided to show disdain for Diana. Carlos agrees that this might be a good idea. We have more music and this does not please Diana at all, because it is all in praise of other girls. Observe that Polilla (ll. 2205-28) again takes the audience (Señores) into his confidence.

Diana now tries another tactic — to make Carlos jealous by consulting him about her marrying another, the Prince of Bearne. He counters this declaration by telling her that he, too, has become enamored. It is with a beautiful girl, whom he praises highly. Diana thinks he is referring to her, and is overcome when she finds that it is Cintia that Carlos is talking about. Diana can only reply that she doesn't see anything attractive about Cintia. Some people might say that this spitefulness is truly a feminine touch!

The play closes without anything happening that is especially notable. The actress that plays the part of Diana comes in for her share of the dialogue and is the center of attention. This is right and proper.

The plot of the play is straightforward and easy to follow. We have called attention to the unusual construction of Act One, when special emphasis is given to the sincere love of Carlos for Diana. This emphasis is important so as to make it clear that in the rest of the play he is only pretending not to love her.

The scenes between Carlos and Diana are all interesting, but the capital scene is of course in the third act where Diana is in a state of partial undress.

Of the characters one of the most notable is Polilla, with his preoccupation with food. Carlos is well drawn, but the prize goes to Diana, who is plenty smart, but not smart enough to see through the pretense of Carlos.

SELECTED BIBLIOGRAPHY

Frank P. Casa, *The Dramatic Craftsmanship of Moreto.* Cambridge, Mass., 1966.
Ruth Lee Kennedy, *The Dramatic Art of Moreto.* Philadelphia, 1932.
Charles David Ley, *El gracioso en el teatro de la Península: Siglos XVI-XVII.* Madrid, 1954.

Chapter IX

FRANCISCO DE ROJAS, UNEVEN IN PERFORMANCE

Francisco de Rojas Zorrilla (1607-1648)

Rojas was born in Toledo, but his parents soon moved to Madrid. There he joined with others in celebrating such important (!) events as the King's killing a bull, not in the usual way, but with an arquebus. In another of these ventures, this time satirical, he so incensed one of the contributors that he was wounded by him in a brawl. These exploits were pretty trivial, but the honor of the Order of Santiago, granted him in 1634, was not. This honor came after the committee waived one of the requisites. It seems that Rojas' father was an "escribano."

Rojas wrote some sixty plays, only one of which is a *comedia de figurón*. The others are religious or historical plays, and plays of customs.

Del rey abajo, ninguno.—At the beginning of the play the most prominent thing that we see is the *banda roja*. This is altogether appropriate since the principal action of the play centers upon it. Right away, Mendo antagonizes us by his insistence on being awarded the honor symbolized by the *banda*. He is deserving of it, though, as we learn from El Conde. Among the offers of help in the crusade undertaken by the king, that of García del Castañar attracts particular attention on account of its practical nature. This and the Conde's praise of García makes the King want to see him. According to the Conde, García leads an ideal life. One detail is particularly emphasized — he has never seen the King.

The author is not very ingenious in having García in soliloquy tell who he is and who his wife is. The principal point is that they are both of noble birth. Neither is it natural for them to declare their love so openly with other people present. If a married couple feels this way, they do not have to say so all the time, and certainly not with other people around.

García learns that the King is planning to visit him and here the *banda* become important. When the King and his men appear, it is Mendo who is wearing the *banda*. He has finally got what he wanted. When the

King offers to take García along with him to fight Moors, we get one of the most alluring descriptions of hunting to be found anywhere. And the meal that Blanca has prepared would rank high, too.

In spite of being a guest, Mendo, not altogether to our surprise, starts to make passes at Blanca. García is smart enough to suspect it, but all is well when the King and his men depart. All if well, that is, unless Mendo returns to make love to Blanca.

In Act Two the way the author arranges for Mendo to see Blanca again is unlikely and, worse than that, rather shocking. It is hard to believe that Bras, simple minded though he may be, would betray his mistress. Upon this point the rest of the play depends.

It seems strange indeed that García should do his hunting at night, but he has to do so in the play, regardless of its improbability. And what could be more improbable than Mendo having a servant with him carrying a ladder! Mendo, of course, would not do anything as undignified as this, and carrying a ladder through the woods would be quite an operation. But how is Mendo going to get into Blanca's bedroom without it?

There is not much chance for García to find any game around with Mendo hollering the way he does, and quite properly García decides to call it off and go home. At this point we get a series of improbabilities. One is Blanca's custom of sitting up for her husband until he returns from his hunting. The servants stay up, too, and they seem to have nothing to do but play stupid games. When García gets home, instead of going to bed, he makes another long love speech to Blanca; and Blanca, late though it is, decides to lay out some clothes for García. The author is having a real hard time setting up the encounter between García and Mendo. It is a dramatic moment, though, when Mendo appears at the balcony and draws aside his cloak, revealing the *banda roja*. And so are other details, such as García dropping the blunderbuss (Is it loaded?), his allowing Mendo to pick it up, and his holding the ladder so that Mendo (the "King") will not fall.

It is unusual in plays of this period for a character to analyze his situation as García does at the end of this act. Usually, the characters act, rather than reason things out. It may be unlikely for García to have so much to say at this point, but the actor who plays the part is given an opportunity to do some emotional acting, and bring Act II to an exciting close.

At the beginning of Act III the Conde, for reasons that are not very clear, happens to take the same road and at the same time that Blanca does when she is fleeing from her husband. At this point the author gives the audience something of a treat, because Blanca does not have many clothes on. Not only this, but the author gives the actress who plays the part a long speech describing what has happened. The lines are too fancy to sound sincere, but the actress does have a chance to do some emotional acting, just as the actor who plays the part of García did at the end of Act II.

Soon after this the Conde provides a motive for García to go to Court. There Blanca learns of her noble origin. Mendo, the "stinker," is still around and strangely enough, the Queen has told him to "guard" Blanca. Just what this entails is not at all clear but, whatever it is, it is a strange assignment.

It is quite a coincidence for García to show up at the right moment and overhear Mendo, the "King," make love to Blanca. García is clearly in a bad spot. Blanca is in the palace and how can she resist the advances of the "King"? The situation becomes critical when the "King" orders her to remain in the palace. Mendo is doing all right in carrying out the orders of the Queen! There seems to be no remedy for García as he discusses his plight with Blanca, who now understands why he tried to kill her.

It is a dramatic moment when García learns that Mendo is not the King. He takes his vengeance off-stage, and this is the proper thing from a dramatic point of view. Mendo has nothing to defend himself with and for García to murder him, for that is what it is, before our eyes would prejudice us against him.

The play closes with a terribly long speech in which García gives in great detail the romantic antecedents of his life and that of Blanca, but this concludes with a declaration that must have had a special appeal to a Spanish audience:

> Aunque sea hijo del sol
> ....
> No he de permitir que me agravie
> Del rey abajo ninguno.

The plot of the play, as we have seen, depends a good deal upon chance. Mendo gets the *banda roja* that he has sought for so long, just before the visit to García. He seems to be wearing it all the time, rather than on special occasions, as we might expect. On his way to see Blanca, his shouting in the woods is heard (by chance) by García, who is hunting at night. The Conde happens to meet up with Blanca when she is wandering around in the early morning. And so it goes.

The really dramatic scenes are not numerous. The most spectacular — and incidentally the least probable — is the entrance into García's house with the *banda roja*.

The characters in the play are hardly believeable, all except García, whom the author presents as one of nature's noblemen. It is hard to believe, though, in his attack upon Blanca. If we had seen it on stage, it would have seriously prejudiced us against him.

Entre bobos anda el juego.—The title of this play is hard to translate. Perhaps, one version might be: "The dice are loaded, and these hicks are really sharpers."

The play starts off as a *comedia de figurón,* but it turns out to be rather more of a comedy of intrigue. At the very beginning we have an argument between Isabel and her servant Andrea in which Isabel contends that persons in love do not need to be telling each other so all the time. If we recall García and Blanca in *Del rey abajo ninguno,* such sentiments from the author come as something of a surprise. In the same scene we have adverse criticism of *culto* language. We may note in passing that the words that Isabel cites as *culto* are in common use today.

As in the case with the usual *comedias de figurón,* the *figurón* person is described before we get a chance to see him in action. We must say that Lucas will have a hard time to live up to the advance notices. Over against Lucas is Pedro, who has all the good qualities one could possibly desire. And there is Doña Alfonsa. She is what we might call a *"figurona,"* if there were such a word. She is just as eccentric as her brother Lucas. This play is full of crazy people.

The first sample of Lucas is the letter he has sent in advance to Isabel, which closes with the startling statement, "Dios os guarde y os dé más hijos que a mí."

Pedro, who comes along with Lucas, finds that Isabel is the girl he is in love with. We find out later how this happened. Lucas shows his practical spirit when he tells Isabel's father why it is not necessary for him to go along to the wedding. He has a receipt made out in due form. In it the description of the girl is more like that of an animal than a human being. The case of eccentric characters is complete with Luis, whose extravagant language does not dissappoint us.

A scene with unknown people hollering off-stage and mentioning Don Quijote and Dulcinea makes a fitting entrance for Lucas and his sister. Lucas gets into a fight right away with Luis' servant, Carranza (There was a famous swordsman of the time by that name). So it is that when Lucas finds out who his opponent really is, he makes a remark that corresponds to what might be appropriate today in a similar situation: "I thought I was fighting with Muhammad Ali."

Lucas has difficulty saying anything nice to Isabel and she replies in a way that may be taken as either complimentary or uncomplimentary. Lucas finally asks Pedro to speak for him, and this is good drama, for here Pedro really outdoes himself, speaking as he does for Lucas and more especially for himself. The act closes with a promise of more of the same. It is something to look forward to.

The second act is a radical departure from customary practice in that the action takes place in the dark, beginning at two in the morning. Brief darkness scenes are fairly common on the stage of the Siglo de Oro, but a whole act in darkness is unique. This act has to do with mistaken identity, failure to recognize voices (except in some cases), and misunderstandings regarding who is who.

The principal fact brought out at first is that Pedro has saved Isabel's life under strange — and, let it be said, unlikely circumstances. In spite of the author's satire of *culto* language, even Pedro speaks in this manner. Through this whole act and into the next, Isabel surprises us by being unconvinced by what seems to be clear evidence of Pedro's affection.

One of the highlights is where Lucas shows his good sense by standing at the door with his arms outspread to intercept anyone trying to escape from Isabel's room. Lucas may be eccentric, but he is pretty sly.

Another interesting detail is the remedy suggested to bring Alfonsa out of her swoon.

In Act III Lucas gives a fascinating account of himself. He is indeed quite a guy after all. He doesn't like to have Isabel palmed off on him:

> ...hallo que con vuestra hija
> Me dis[t]is por liebre gato.   ll. 1831-32.

He makes a good case for calling the whole thing off, but if this comes about, he demands to have his receipt returned. This is only reasonable, after all! Somewhat later the author stages a highway accident and we get further misunderstanding, principally on the part of Isabel. It seems to be terribly hard for her to see the light in spite of what seems to be convincing evidence of Pedro's affection.

Luis is still in the picture and we have more *culto* from him. His account to Lucas complicates matters and gives the actor who plays the part of Lucas some good lines. This is also the case with Alfonsa, when she gives her version of what happened.

The play ends happily — in a way — but the ending is quite out of the ordinary in that Lucas gets his revenge, even though he never does get back that important receipt!

It seems unnecessary to discuss plot, scenes, of characters in a play in which everything is so exaggerated. We cannot take any of these features seriously. The play has been enjoyable, though. What more could we ask for?

SELECTED BIBLIOGRAPHY

Emilio Cotarelo y Mori. *Francisco de Rojas Zorrilla, Noticias biográficas y bibliográficas*. Madrid, 1911.

Raymond R. MacCurdy, *Francisco de Rojas Zorrilla*. New York, 1968.

Chapter X

PEDRO CALDERÓN DE LA BARCA, FAIR-HAIRED DRAMATIST

Pedro Calderón de la Barca (1600-1681)

Pedro Calderón de la Barca, or Pedro Calderón de la Barca Henao de la Barrera y Riaño, to give him his full name and do him justice, was the fair-haired boy of the Spanish court during the reign in Felipe IV. More than any playwright of his time he seemed to get what we call the "breaks" during his lifetime and even after his death. He came upon the theatrical scene when a young king, tremendously interested in the theater, was on the throne, and when the king's favorite, the Conde-Duque (fancy title) de Olivares was eager to fulfill the King's desires.

As an example of the "breaks" that came to Calderón, we cite an incident that turned out happily for him, but which might well have ruined his career forever. In some sort of a brawl a brother of Pedro was wounded and the agressor took refuge in a convent, customarily a safe place for anyone. It was not on this occasion. Pedro and others forceably entered the convent and in the course of their search for the culprit, they roughhoused some of the nuns. This caused a tremendous scandal, and the court preacher, a certain Paravicino, condemned the occurence and Pedro in a sermon honoring the father and mother of the King. Thereupon, Calderón made a derogatory reference to the man of God in one of his plays, *El príncipe constante*. He inserted these verses after the play had been passed by the censor. Clearly, this was a rank infringement of the "rules," and Paravicino made the most of it in a complaint to the King. Calderón, he said, had brought dishonor upon God, the King, and the King's father and mother, as well as dealing a mortal affront to him, a highly respected man of the cloth. The King, who was probably sick and tired of Paravicino anyway, "passed the buck" — and probably a good word — to the Cardinal, President of the Council of Castile, who was to investigate the case. All Calderón got was a mild reproof. He got off easy, because he had friends in the right place.

Philip IV was fond of spectacular shows, and in this he was encouraged by Olivares, who had a park, El Buen Retiro, fixed up for these and other forms of entertainment. It seems pretty sure that Calderón contributed to the "new deal" with *Los encantos de Circe*. This play was full of *encantos,* the capital scene presenting Circe (probably in a state of partial undress) being drawn across a pond by dolphins and performing a series of enchantments. These enchantments, not to mention Circe, must have been something to see. No doubt the King put in an order for more, and Calderón could be counted on to deliver the goods, the "real McCoy." We do not know what monetary reward Calderón received for his efforts to please the King, but we may be fairly sure that he did not go unrewarded.

Another great triumph for Calderón, in addition to the many *comedias* presented at court and in the theaters downtown, was in the composition of *autos sacramentales,* of which he wrote about seventy. He seems to have been the favorite dramatist in writing these spectaculars, for that is what they were. The pay for these *autos* was splendid, more than five times as much as would be brought in by a *comedia*. It was public money and the committee in charge wanted to put on a good show. They could be certain that Calderón "had a better idea," indeed the best.

In the case of most of the playwrights of the time we do not know for sure just what plays they wrote, or how many. Not so with Calderón. During his lifetime he published four *partes* of twelve plays each. Toward the end of his life he sent an admirer a list of all the plays he had written, supplemented by a list of those he had not written, but which had appeared under his name.

Calderón's good fortune did not stop with his death. A certain Juan de Vera Tassis, who styled himself "su mayor amigo," proceeded to publish his plays in nine volumes (1682-1691). He said he took the text from the "originales." It is not clear what he meant by "originales." Up until recently the *comedias* of Calderón that were published derived from the Vera Tassis edition which, it must be said, is none too good. There was another edition in the eighteenth century. And there were in all three editions of his *autos*. There were numerous *sueltas* (single copies) in that century. So it was that he was better known through the eighteenth century than any of his rivals. The German romanticists "discovered" him in the early nineteenth century and lauded him to the skies. His fame still continues.

La vida es sueño.—The Vera Tassis edition of Calderón's plays states that this play was a "Fiesta que se representó a sus Majestades en el Salón de su Real Palacio." In the *Primera Parte* where the play first appeared, there is no such statement, but even so, the highly figurative language of the play and other evidence lends support to Vera Tassis' assertion. For example, we may note the very first word of the play, *hipogrifo*. If the play was intended for the audience downtown, who in that motley assembly would have the slightest idea what a hippogriff was? And who of them would understand the second line, "que corriste parejas con el viento?" One could make quite a long list of similar words and expressions elsewhere in the play.

Rosaura, it should be noted, is dressed as a man, not an uncommon practice in plays of this period. Of course, it must have taken some imagination on the part of the audience to accept this, just as it did to believe that the raised place in the back of the stage was a rugged mountain. Clarín, as a *gracioso*, has rather an unusual name, "trumpet," and we expect him to say funny things. Somethimes he does, but all too often his remarks fall rather flat. [1]

By a strange coincidence Rosaura has been carried away by her runaway horse to no less a place than where Segismundo is confined in a cave. This "cave" is the place in the back of the stage behind the curtain. Segismundo is quite a sight to behold, dressed as he is, in skins. He is supposed to be surrounded by guards under the command of Clotaldo, but for some strange reason they are off-duty at this moment. The actor who plays the part of Segismundo would undoubtedly come out of the cave to recite his lines about liberty, one of the notable parts of the play. From a practical point of view he might be somewhat hindered by his chains.

A truly thought-provoking moment is where Segismundo grabs hold of Rosaura. He has never seen a woman in his life. In such a case would a man sense that the person in his arms was a different sort of person from those he had known before?

When the guards do show up from their "coffee break," there is no explanation for their being masked. What difference does it make if anyone recognizes them? And Clotaldo, the most important of the guards, strangely enough, does not have a mask. Clotaldo makes a rather cryptic remark about why Segismundo is locked up, and the audience has certainly seen enough to wonder, too.

The sword that Rosaura surrenders has more significance than at first appears. Clotaldo recognizes it as one that he left with a certain Violante as a means of identification. It is therefore clear to him that the person

---

[1] Sturgis E. Leavitt, "Did Calderón have a sense of humor?" *Studies Presented to William M. Dey, Studies in the Romance Languages and Literatures*, Chapel Hill, 1949.

he has arrested is his son. This knowledge puts him in a state of anxiety. Shall he follow his paternal instinct and liberate his "son," or shall he do his duty to his King and take his son captive? Perhaps, it is not altogether fair to ask along here — just what was Clotaldo's affair with the said Violante? It looks as though he left her in the lurch when he found out that she was in "an interesting condition." If this is the case, Clotaldo can not rate very high in our esteem.

When the scene changes to the court, the lines of Astolfo about "excelentes rayos" are not altogether easy to understand. They were probably intended to impress the aristocracy in the audience, and they perhaps did. The notes explain that Astolfo is really explaining things to the audience, rather than to Estrella. This, let it be said, is hardly good dramatic practice. We might add that it is rather stupid for Astolfo to make love to one woman while wearing about his neck the picture of another.

We have had examples of long speeches in this study of the Spanish theater, but, we believe there are none as long as that of Basilio. A good part of it is praise of himself, and there are places where it seems as though his listeners are not paying close attention to what he says. He has to call them to order. In this speech we have mention of the possible influence of the stars. It is asserted that the stars may incline, but not force, a person to a certain action. It will be well to keep this in mind, because there will be further reference to it later.

Clotaldo appears with his captive, and his mysterious remarks are not heeded by Basilio, who seems to have no sense of curiosity. He is thinking his own thoughts. Neither does Rosaura have any curiosity when Clotaldo makes a slip, and says that the sword was his.

In the final scene to this act we learn that the mother of Rosaura has never told her the facts of life. If she had, perhaps Astolfo would not have done her wrong. Anyway, Clotaldo is once again in state of moral conflict. From a dramatic point of view it is not good to close the act with a secondary character. We are really not that interested in him.

Clotaldo's report at the beginning of Act Two is just as flowery as the speech of Basilio in Act One, but happily it is not as long. In it we have the "trademark" of Calderón, the expression "vivo cadáver," and a surprising line "No tenemos que argüir." Who is going to argue, anyway? Certainly not Basilio. He knows a lot more about science than Clotaldo.

It seems as though Clotaldo had not given Segismundo a fair break when he administered the sleeping pill. Segismundo was in a frenzied state of mind, and is it not likely that this will carry over into his waking moments? In his explanation to Clotaldo, Astolfo changes his previous statement about the influence of the stars to a positive assertion "el hombre predomina en las estrellas." Calderón seems to be playing it safe, but we should wait until later and see this subject discussed again.

It is hard to believe that Clarín could "crash the gate" and get into the inner sanctums of the palace, but how else could the audience be informed that Rosaura has changed her clothes and will now appear as Clotaldo's niece?

The awakening of Segismundo is very impressive. His remarks are straightforward and there is little trace of *culto* in them. It is, however, "far out in left field" for him to say he only likes military music. Where has he heard any military music? And we cannot agree with him that Clotaldo has mistreated him. He has no cause to say this.

Segismundo is naturally confused by what he sees around him. He has had no experience with women and yet he makes a very fancy speech to Estrella playing on the word "parabién." This sort of language is out of character. And even if Segismundo's attitude offends her, she should have a better line than "Sed más galán cortesano."

We should take particular note of the conflict between Segismundo and the servant, because we shall have a similar incident in *El alcalde de Zalamea,* to be studied later. Calderón gives Segismundo a good line when the King asks what is going on, and Segismundo replies with a splendid understatement:

> Nada ha sido
> A un hombre que me ha cansado,
> De ese balcón he arrojado.   ll. 1440-42.

We must admit that Segismundo has considerable reason to ask Basilio if he has done right by him, treating him like a "monstruo." Basilio's reply does not help matters any.

Even if it is unlikely for Clarín to be in the palace, we can overlook this fact when he asks Segismundo what he has liked best in his new situation. Segismundo's reply is almost free from *culto* and is most appropriate and impressive. Not quite so effective is his speech to Rosaura, though his figures of speech are drawn from his experience in the wilderness. We find no fault with the timely arrival of Astolfo and Basilio, as it avoids bloodshed. The portrait which Astolfo has finally decided to leave at home gives rise to some confusion and here the play becomes more a comedy of intrigue than otherwise. From a technical point of view it serves a purpose by providing a lapse of time, during which Segismundo is to be drugged and returned to his cave.

Basilio's reason, "necia curiosidad," for being present at the awakening of Segismundo is not praiseworthy, and neither, as the notes explain, is his departure just when Segismundo shows signs of repentance. There has been criticism of Segismundo's sudden "desfallecimiento," but if we study the lines carefully, we can see that from the very moment of awakening he is a changed man. One criticism that does seem valid is that he generalizes, and includes all mankind in his final statements. His experience has been too limited for him to come to such a conclusion.

The account that Segismundo gives about his "dream" is couched in fairly simple language and is deeply affecting, and, so with some reservation, is his soliloquy closing with:

> Que toda la vida es sueño,
> Y los sueños sueños son.   ll. 1199-1200.

There is one passage, though, that reaches a high degree of emotion and is as moving as anything in Spanish literature:

> Sólo a una mujer amaba...
> Que fué verdad, creo yo,
> En que todo se acabó,
> Y esto solo no se acaba.   ll. 2134-37.

At the beginning of Act Three it is hard to find much humor in the remarks of Clarín, but his thinking that it is the custom of the country to have a "king for a day," and his effors to live up to his new position partially make up for his feeble efforts at humor elsewhere.

When Segismundo learns from the soldiers that he is King, Calderón wisely refrains from flowery language and presents a highly effective scene in which Segismundo refuses, hesitates, and finally accepts with one reservation. Basilio adopts a totally fatalistic attitude:

> Poco reparo tiene lo infalible.   l. 2452.

It is hard to imagine that a war is going on as Rosaura and Clotaldo debate at great length on whether it is better to give than to receive. We have seen Segismundo win a victory over anger and now we see him conquer his pride. His third test, over passion, is soon to present itself. The trouble is, though, that it takes so long for Rosaura to tell her story that Segismundo could well lose his interest in her, just as we do. We know most of her history anyway. The only excuse for such a long speech is, perhaps, the author's desire to give the actress who plays the part of Rosaura the center of the stage for a good long period. If she had to memorize all those lines, she would have quite a task before her. To return to the play itself, it is ridiculous to think that Rosaura, if she fights on the side of Segismundo, could be "un escándalo del mundo."

Basilio speaks a true word when he says:

> En batallas tales,
> Los que vencen son leales,
> Los vencidos, traidores.   ll. 3065-67.

We should note that the only casuality in the conflict is Clarín. Not only did he try to escape danger, but he defied death. And this brings up again the idea of predestination. Basilio takes Clarín's death as a sign of fatalism, but Clotaldo takes the other side!

> El prudente varón
> Victoria del hado alcanza.   ll. 3118-19.

Astolfo backs him up in this statement. We are not left with this lesson, however, because Segismundo gives a different interpretation of fatalism (ll. 3164-70) and cites himself as an example. Take it all in all, it is more than difficult to figure out just where we stand in this business of predestination. Before we can do so, the play comes to a conclusion.

Evidently, there was not enough material for a three act play with the story of Segismundo as the only plot. A secondary plot was therefore called for. Neither of these two plots is complicated, and Calderón makes them mesh together in a rather satisfactory way. Even so, it would seem that the two plots turned out to be less than enough, and some padding was needed. This filling takes the form of a number of excessively long speeches.

At the very end of the play the two plots fail to fit together perfectly. This happens so near the conclusion that it would probably pass unnoticed. We must spell it out, however. In the first cave scene we have noted that Segismundo is mysteriously moved when he makes physical contact with Rosaura. Later, he recognizes her in the palace and makes love to her. His impression is so vivid that he calls particular attention to it when he gives an account of his "dream," "Sólo a una mujer amaba."

If he was so deeply in love with this woman, why did he forget all about it at the end of the play and marry Estrella? But it cannot be otherwise because the exigencies of the secondary plot make it necessary for Astolfo to "make an honest woman" out of Rosaura.

The play has a number of dramatic situations. Among these are the first meeting of Rosaura and Segismundo, the awakening of Segismundo in the palace, his reaction after his return to the cave, and his rescue by the soldiers.

The characters in the play seem more symbolic than otherwise. Of course, the scene takes place in a far-away country and we naturally expect things to be different. As it is, the characters have few characteristics that make them stand out as individuals.

Notwithstanding all this, the play is not one to be easily forgotten. For the audience of Calderón's time, the theme was very much in the air. The introduction to this edition mentions the Marco Polo story, and the one in *El Conde Lucanor*. Calderón himself composed an *auto sacramental* on the same subject, and the *auto, El gran teatro del mundo,* deals essentially with the same theme. In itself, the idea that this life is a dream captivates the imagination. Dreams sometimes are so real that they seem to be true, and events in real life are at times so extraordinary that what has happened seems altogether unreal.

It may be that this play was a command performance, written hurriedly at the request of the King or someone high in authority. If this is so, one cannot but wish that Calderón had had more time to compose it. We would then have had an even more remarkable play.

El alcalde de Zalamea.—The play begins in a striking manner — with a curse. This is followed by the soldiers griping at the treatment they receive. A better introduction to scenes of army life could hardly be found. The soldiers are walking back and forth across the stage, and this suggests that they are travelling along a road. Among them is Rebolledo, who is clearly a troublemaker. He threatens to go AWOL, but one of the soldiers reminds him that they have a general that will tolerate no breach of discipline. In the group is Chispa, a camp follower, who enlivens the whole group by her gaiety and song. She is quite a "cookie."

In the same spirit of army life the Captain makes the most of an order from higher up to get the soldiers in a friendly mood. Similarly, the sergeant does what he can to get on the good side of the Captain by billeting him in the best house in town. He is more than a little disappointed to find that the Captain doesn't appreciate the fact that in this house is the best looking girl in town. The Captain's disparagement of country girls is actually a tip-off to what will happen when he sees the girl. The audience now has something to look forward to.

The reason for the overlong scene with Don Mendo and Nuño is hard to figure out. Neither one of them is important to the play, they are not interesting, and the humor of Nuño is pretty ghastly. In a recording of the play the whole business of these two "tipos" is omitted "… se suprimen los personajes del hidalgo Don Mendo y su criado Nuño, por considerar que su intervención [es] ajena a la linea directa del drama…" Perhaps it was only intended to be padding, so as to fill up time. Otherwise this act might be too short.

The conversation between Pedro Crespo and his son Juan is revealing. Pedro Crespo is concerned about his farm, and Juan has taken a turn at gambling, something quite out of the world of his father. The old man's advice is good, but his son counters with an apt remark. We can see from Pedro Crespo's reply that he is fond of Juan and perhaps over-indulgent. Pedro Crespo's reply, "Bien te vengaste" may perhaps be translated, "You win."

What follows is a logical series of events. Pedro Crespo welcomes an opportunity to serve his King by billeting the soldiers, but he does not want Isabel to be subjected to rough army talk, and he has her secrete herself upstairs. This very fact arouses the curiosity of the Captain and he dreams up a way to go up and see her.

Here we have a play within a play, always an effective dramatic device. The Captain and Rebolledo pretend to quarrel, and Chispa, who is not in on the deal, thinks it is the real thing and gives the alarm. In this she is joined by the sergeant who is also unaware of the true situation.

And this brings us to one of the capital scenes in the play. A tragic conflict between the Captain and Pedro Crespo is only averted by the appearance of Lope de Figueroa. The two men, Pedro Crespo and Lope de Figueroa are both tough "hombres," eccentric, stubborn, and each a match for the other.

One detail of this confrontation must not be over-looked. The cruel sentence meted out to Rebolledo is too much for him to bear and, in spite of the Captain's whispered assurance, he refuses to take the rap. At the end of the act everything seems settled by Lope's decision to lodge in the house of Pedro Crespo and for the Captain to stay elsewhere. Usually, in a play, some conflict develops at the end of the act. There is none in this play. Some critics might call this a flaw.

We have seen that everything seemed to be satisfactorily settled at the end of Act One, and we can only have a suspicion that the Captain will persist in his intentions toward Isabel. The very first line in Act Two indicates that he will — he already had made attempts to see her, but to no avail. What he is doing may turn out to be fraught with danger, because Lope is in Isabel's house and he is not a man to be trifled with.

Rebolledo is still around, and here we get one of the most unlikely situations in the play. [2] After his refusal to take the blame for the Captain's invasion of Isabel's privacy, we would normally expect the Captain to make his life miserable from then on. This, greatly to our surprise, is not

---

[2] We have written a brief article, "Cracks in the Structure of El alcalde de Zalamea," Hispanic Studies in Honor of Nicholson B. Adams, UNC Studies in the Romance Languages and Literatures, Chapel Hill, N. C., 1966. Since this book may not be readily available, we shall incorporate in our analysis of the plot the criticism contained in the article.

the way things are. The two are actually chummy to the extent that Rebolledo says he will assume responsibility, if Lope is angered by the serenade. Did he do it before? The improbability of all this is further heightened by the statement that Lope cannot sleep well at night. Calderón makes it clear that the Captain is madly in love with Isabel. Even so, it does not seem likely that he would risk offending the general. He has too much to lose.

The dinner scene in Pedro Crespo's house is marked by courtesy, expressed to a charming degree by both Pedro Crespo and Lope. It is evident that they have a high regard for each other. And here we get a statement about the private philosophy of Pedro Crespo; he swears with those who swear, and he prays with those who pray. This whole scene is one of the finest parts of the play.

The pleasant scene is rudely interrupted by the serenade. This is a situation that could not be presented on the modern stage. Outside the house everything happens in the dark. Pedro Crespo and Lope are face to face and yet they cannot recognize each other.

Lope de Figueroa's farewell, especially the part dealing with the locket, gives evidence of the fine feeling characteristic of the old soldier. Likewise, Pedro Crespo's advice to his son shows a lot of common sense and at the same time it tells us how fond he is of him. It is interesting to see how Pedro Crespo tries to cover up his feelings by saying that Juan would be only a ne'er do well, if he stayed at home.

The turn of events is now altogether in the Captain's favor. Juan is on his way to join the army, Lope has gone off with his detachment, and Pedro Crespo and Isabel are outside the house enjoying the cool of the evening. At the end of the act there seems to be some possibility of Juan's rescuing Isabel. He hears cries from opposite directions and goes off to help his sister. The audience rightly fears he will not succeed.

In Act Three we find immediately that Juan has been unable to rescue his sister, and as a consequence we have a rather unusual scene. The actress who plays the part of Isabel has so far acted the part of a meek person, obedient to her father, and never in a situation where she could show any emotion. This sort of thing will hardly satisfy an actress who wants her share of the attention (and applause) by way of emotional acting. She gets it now. She could tell her sad story in four lines, if not four words, but instead of that she has 67 lines of soliloquy and 175 more lines when she talks to her father, who, conveniently for her, is tied to a tree. The actress could take her time telling her story and surely would be satisfied with her part now.

On their way back to town Pedro Crespo is surprised to learn that he has been elected *alcalde*. Incidentally, it comes as rather a surprise to us that he has had no inkling of this election, being a man of such prominence in the town. It is ironic for him to learn that he has an important trial case awaiting him. A captain in the King's army has been brought into town, wounded. If Pedro Crespo can find out who did it, his reputation is made.

The business of the Captain's wound is a rather tricky one. He must have been wounded severely enough for the soldiers to have to bring him to town and yet he cannot (dramatically) be so badly wounded that he will not be able to face up to Pedro Crespo when that time comes. The author must see to it that our sympathy rests with the right party.

Facing the Captain the new *alcalde* puts aside his staff of office and speaks not as a man of authority, but as a private individual. At first sight this seems like a true confrontation in which Pedro Crespo offers the Captain everything possible in an effort to persuade him to marry the girl. Some may think that this scene is not phony, but in a previous article [3] we have tried to show that it is just that. Pedro Crespo certainly can see from the outset that the Captain will not consent to any arrangement whatever. The Captain insists that Pedro Crespo has no jurisdiction over him, that if he is to be tried, it should be by a military court. His soldiers are not far away and, neither is Lope de Figueroa. There is a good chance that he can be rescued. What we have tried to show in the article is that Pedro Crespo can offer the Captain the proverbial pie in the sky, knowing all the time that what he offers will not be accepted. We contend that Calderón is "conditioning" his audience to accept eventually and without protest the punishment of an officer in the King's army at the hands of the civil authorities.

There are some highly dramatic moments along here, where the Captain says that Pedro Crespo cannot arrest him (This recalls the scene in *La vida es sueño* where the servant defies Segismundo.), and where the Captain insists on being treated with respect. At this point, Pedro Crespo shows his human side as he gloats over the Captain with sneering remarks. In the same vein we consider his locking up his son, ostensibly to punish him, but in reality to keep him out of the hands of the soldiers.

After these tragic moments it is high time for a let-down, and we get it when Pedro Crespo threatens to put Chispa to the torture. She, we remember, is dressed as a man. When she counters the threat by saying he cannot do that to her, because she is pregnant, we can imagine Pedro Crespo's reaction and his saying to himself, "What the hell kind of an army is this."

---

[3] Sturgis E. Leavitt, "Pedro Crespo and the Captain in Calderón's *Alcalde de Zalamea,*" *Hispania,* XXXVIII (1955), 430-31.

We cannot say enough in praise of the scene in which Lope de Figueroa demands that the Captain be released. We have seen the two old men in conflict before, but this time it is a matter of life and death. Lope is almost beside himself with rage, and Pedro, who holds all the high cards, is calm and quiet. This, even though he knows full well that his life, and perhaps that of the whole town, is in the balance. Here we have the capital scene of the play and, in our opinion, in the whole repertory of Golden Age drama.

Mention has been made from time to time in the play of the presence nearby of the King, and therefore his timely arrival on the scene is not altogether a surprise. The King, as we have a right to expect, makes a wise decision. The prisoner is to be released.

When Pedro Crespo says it is too late, the curtained-off alcove is brought into play and we are presented with a scene of utter horror. There is the Captain dead, with a garrote about his neck. The writer of this account has seen this play on the stage in Madrid, and no such horrible sight was presented to the audience. What the audience saw was a form in the shape of a man stretched out on a bench and covered with a sheet, or something like that, with burning candles at the head. It seems quite clear that the present day audience cannot stomach the "red meat" that was fairly common in seventeenth century Spain.

The ending of the play is another remarkable feat of Calderón. Lope asks where Juan is, and Pedro Crespo replies that he has been locked up, awaiting punishment for wounding the Captain. Lope knows full well that this statement is not true, that Pedro Crespo will do no such thing. All Lope says at this juncture is "Bien está. Llamadle." which can be freely translated "You win. Tell him to come on out." Lope is generous in defeat. As a final touch Pedro Crespo, knowing very well what Lope is going to say, has Juan ready at hand.

Except for the unlikely "chumminess" of Rebolledo and the Captain at the beginning of Act II, and the unlikelihood of Juan's wounding the Captain and not being set upon by the Captain's men, the plot of the play is straightforward and logical. Interest in the characters is sustained up to the very last line.

The most important scenes are those in which Pedro Crespo and Lope de Figueroa are in conflict, but there are others that are worthy of note, for example, the hospitality of Pedro Crespo and his farewell to his son in Act II. The confrontation of Pedro Crespo and the Captain has been highly praised in some quarters but, as we have tried to show, is really hollow.

Of the minor characters in the play, Chispa is the most interesting. She is happy-go-lucky, quick witted, and loyal to Rebolledo. Were it not for the unbelieveable change of attitude mentioned above, Rebolledo would be the embodiment of a typical soldier. Juan is not especially well drawn, and neither is Isabel. The Captain's persistence with Isabel is hard to accept in view of the circumstances. His refusal of Pedro Crespo's offer is what we would expect of an officer in the King's army, but Calderón cannot afford to make him sympathetic even here.

The great merit of the play lies in the creation of the two old men, Pedro Crespo and Lope de Figueroa, one from country life and the other from the military. They are both stubborn, with a high sense of honor, and yet with a subtle sense of humor. They are unforgettable: One of the two, Pedro Crespo is a little sly, as we might suspect of the rustic that he is when he locks Juan, his son, up, ostensibly to appear as a sort of Roman father, but really to protect Juan from the soldiers.

AUTOS SACRAMENTALES

An *auto sacramental* is a one-act play in verse, every feature of which is allegorical, leading up to the mystery of the sacrament. These plays were given in a public square, the parts were taken by professional actors, and no admission was charged. It was a highly spectacular show, which began with a circus-like procession of floats through the streets. These floats were lavishly decked out, and the settings were suitable for the action of the play after they had moved into place in the square.

There were no loud speakers in those times, and no doubt many in the audience could not understand all that the actors said, especially since it was usually couched in flowery language. They could get an idea, though, of what it was all about from the setting, the costumes, and the gestures of the actors. These plays were an important part of the celebration of Corpus Christi Day (The Thursday after Trinity Sunday). [4]

Calderón had a contract to present two of these *autos* each year. Even after his death, his *autos* were the ones that were most popular. Presentation of the *autos sacramentales* was prohibited in 1763, and the reason for this was, in part, the fact that sometimes the loose life of the actors was in sharp contrast to the virtuous characters they represented.

La vida es sueño.—The reader will find it difficult to follow the intricate reasoning in the opening scenes. And no doubt the audience of the time was puzzled to figure out just what it was all about. Even so, there was

---

[4] In the *Quijote* Part Two, Chapter Eleven, Don Quixote and Sancho meet up with a company of actors who are on their way to a neighboring town, dressed up for a performance of an *auto sacramental.*

compensation in the fancy costumes, the dancing patterns, and the music that accompanied a good deal of the action.

After something over 350 lines we get to the main action: the creation of man in his environment. How he will act is the question. It takes quite a while to get certain ideas across, but finally, we see man dressed in skins in a cave. In the *comedia* of the same name it took much less time to show Segismundo in similar dress. As in the *comedia*, we first have a long monologue about liberty. In the *comedia* the actors who play the parts of Rosaura and Clotaldo have a chance to retire from the stage and sit down during this long speech. In the *auto* the actors who play the parts of Sombra, El Príncipe de las Tinieblas, Luz and La Gracia do not have any chance like this to rest their feet.

In lines 727-28 we are somewhat surprised to have the Príncipe de las Tinieblas quote from the Psalms: "What is man that thou art mindful of him?", but taken in the context of the *auto* the quotation is quite appropriate.

In a colorful scene the various elements clothe man in a way that corresponds to the place in the *comedia* where Segismundo wakes up in the palace. In the *auto*, however, the edge is taken off the situation by having him really "wake up" before this in order to discourse about liberty. In the clothing scene, as well as at other appropriate moments, we have music.

Two of the most important characters, Albedrío and Entendimento, are introduced to El Hombre — and to us — in a straightforward manner. It is manifestly essential to El Hombre — and to us — to know exactly who they are and what they stand for

There is a striking scene where Sombra and El Hombre are brought face to face with the elements: Agua (a mirror), Fuego (a sword), Aire (a plumed hat), and Tierra (flowers). From here it is a natural transition to the fatal apple. At this point we note what was visible to the audience all the time — La Sombra is a "bella zagala." It may seem a little strange that El Hombre has not been aware of her beauty before. What were his eyes for, if not to gaze upon a sight like this?

We are gradually led up to the climax of the *auto* as Albedrío and Entendimiento advise him what to do with the famous apple. The moment becomes doubly dramatic when El Hombre throws Entendimento off a "cliff," and then eats the forbidden fruit (Eve does not seem to be in on this). The resulting earthquake brings about dire consequences. El Hombre is indeed in a sad plight. Like Segismundo in the *comedia*, he is worse off than he was before, because he now knows who he is.

The rest of the *auto* follows out, as we expect, with the proper allegorical significance, which by now must be evident to all. The ending of the *auto* is, as it should be, phrased in clear and unmistakable language. The lesson to be learned is orthodox and crystal clear. The afternoon has been well spent.

La cena del Rey Baltasar.—In reading this and other *autos sacramentales* we should remember that the action and the characters are allegorical. Pensamiento, for example, has a cloak of many colors to show how scattered anybody's thoughts are. He is in constant movement, indicating how quickly one's thought changes from one thing to another. This idea is repeated again and again early in the play, so that even the most inattentive person in the audience cannot fail to get the idea. In this play, as he explains, he is the thought of Baltasar "que no cabe en todo el mundo." Pensamiento has some funny lines from time to time. [5]

Baltasar represents a sort of superman, a law unto himself, unanswerable to any law or authority, even to that of a supreme being. Daniel is the power of God, divine destiny. Vanity and Idolotry identify themselves. Death shows who he is by his mantle covered with skull and bones. He is not ugly or repellant, and yet there is something about him that inspires fear, even in Daniel who has authority over him.

The long speech by Baltasar at the beginning of the play might, one must confess, be pretty boring to an audience. It reminds one of the long speech in the first act of *La vida es sueño,* but here there is no chance for the listeners to sit down! In this speech the author gets mixed up a bit when he speaks of "los dioses" causing the flood and later a "Dios" bringing it about. The description of the flood, in spite of its length is interesting. The deluge does not begin all at once, but starts with dense clouds, followed by gentle rain which soon becomes a downpour, a disaster which Calderón describes in picturesque detail.

There are numerous striking scenes in the *auto*. The places where Baltasar and the luscious "queenies," Vanity and Idolatry, appear would be quite a sight to see. The tricky business of the *apariencia* might have been all right in the seventeenth century, but it is really not very spectacular. The scenes in which Death participates, however, are all impressive, and the stage business of the handwriting on the wall, crude as it must have been, is still startling enough.

Take it all in all, this *auto,* once seen, would not easily be forgotten.

El gran teatro del mundo.—This auto is, in our opinion, by far the best of the *autos* of Calderón. It has as much plot as one could reasonably

---

[5] Sturgis E. Leavitt, "Humor in the *autos* of Calderón." *Hispania,* XXXIX (1965), 138-44.

expect from a one-act play, it has many interesting scenes, the characters have distinct personalities, and it has humor of a rather high order.

Calderón has done a daring thing in having an allegorical figure, El Autor, represent the Creator. Not as daring, but almost as surprising is the character, El Mundo. The dramatisation of the idea "Life is a Stage" is most effective, carried out, as it is, in three parts: selection of the actors, their playing their roles, and receiving their reward. As we might expect from what we have seen in *La cena del Rey Baltasar*, we have early in the play a long speech — this time by El Mundo — in which is given the history of the world. The narration, as is characteristic of Calderón, is picturesque, especially the part dealing with the stage on which the play is to be performed. We are attracted by the concept of only two doors, the cradle and the grave. Before the actors are chosen, we learn what stage properties are to be given them. This makes for economy, when they finally appear.

The *auto* has a special interest in that it gives considerable information about the staging of plays at that time. There is, for example, mention of the *loa*, an introductory piece that probably served to quiet the audience down before the main performance began. Then there is the audience, El Mundo, who makes appropriate comments on the play from time to time. There is even one place where one of the actors speaks directly to the audience. Several of the actors stress the importance of rehearsals, even though the play to be performed may be one that has been given before. In records dealing with dramatic companies there is ample evidence that rehearsals were a very important part in the life of an actor.

SELECTED BIBLIOGRAPHY

Emilio Cotarelo y Mori, *Ensayo sobre la vida y obras de D. Pedro Calderón de la Barca*. Madrid, 1924.

Everett W. Hesse, *Calderón de la Barca*. New York, 1967.

Sturgis E. Leavitt, "Humor in the *autos* of Calderón," *Hispania*, XXXIX, 138-44.

Marcelino Menéndez y Pelayo, *Calderón y su teatro*. Buenos Aires, 1946.

A. A. Parker, *The Allegorical Plays of Calderón. An Introduction to the autos sacramentales*. Oxford-London, 1943.

Albert E. Sloman, *The Dramatic Craftsmanship of Calderón. His Use of Earlier Plays*. Oxford, 1958.

Ángel Valbuena Prat, *Calderón, su personalidad, su estilo y sus obras*. Barcelona, 1941.

Bruce Wardropper, *Introducción al teatro religioso del Siglo de Oro*. Madrid, 1954.

Chapter XI

THE *COMEDIAS* LOSE THEIR IDENTITY

After the accesion of Felipe V to the Spanish throne in 1700, a flood
of French influence descended upon Spain, affecting principally the intellectual life of the country. The most notable examples of French influence
were the establishment of the Biblioteca Nacional in 1712 and the Academia Española in 1713.

The first work of the Academia was the publication of a dictionary in
six volumes (1726-1739). This is commonly called the *Diccionario de Auto-
ridades*, because it gave not only the definition of words, but also quotations
illustrating their use. Later (1780) the Academia issued a one-volume
edition, omitting the quotations. The first edition is rather rare.

The theater of the early eighteenth century continued in the tradition
of Lope de Vega and Calderón, but the practitioners lacked the talent of
their predecessors. The plays of the Golden Age continued on the Spanish
stage, along with the productions of the newer writers, and evidently gave
pleasure to the spectators. Those who found fault with the Golden Age
plays were the erudite members of Spanish society. It was easy for them
to see that these plays did not conform to the unities (time, place and
action), as the French plays did, and it was this lack that particularly attracted their attention,

The most notable critic of them all was Luzán, who in 1737 published
his *Poética*. His full name is quite a mouthful — Ignacio Luzán Claramund
de Suelves y Gurrea (1702-1764). His book is a horrible example of what
can be perpetrated by a critic who wants to show off his erudition. It is
full of Latin quotations and learned pronouncements from Aristotle. He
does not altogether condemn Lope de Vega and Calderón by any means,
as will appear from the following quotation:

> "...en particular alabaré siempre en Lope de Vega la natural fa-
> cilidad de su estilo y la suma destreza con que en muchas de sus
> comedias se ven pintadas las costumbres y el carácter de algunas
> personas; en Calderón admiro la nobleza de su locución, que sin

ser jamás obscura ni afectada, es siempre elegante; y especialmente me parece digna de muchos encomios la manera y traza ingeniosa con que este autor, teniendo dulcemente suspenso a su auditorio, ha sabido enredar los lances de sus comedia, y particularmente de las que llamamos de capa y espada, entre las cuales hay algunas donde hallarán los críticos muy poco o nada que reprehender y mucho que admirar y elogiar..." *Poetica,* II, 124.

Luzán mentions seven plays of Calderón, as well as a good many by other writers of Calderón's time that fall into the category of excellent. He does point out a considerable number of the *comedias* of Lope de Vega and others that did not measure up to a high standard. In the second edition of the *Poética,* published in 1780 after his death, and emended by others, Lope de Vega is highly praised:

"La extensión, variedad y amenidad de su ingenio, la asombrosa facilidad, o por mejor decir, el flujo irrestañable con que produjo tantas obras de especies tan diversas, y la copia y suavedad de su versificación, la colocan en la clase de los hombres extraordinarios..." II, 305.

Luzán follows this by saying that it was a "desgracia" that Lope did not live at a time when "la buena crítica" was operative.
Of Calderón he says, in this second edition:

"[El] ... se formó un lenguaje tan urbano y seductivo, que en esta parte no tuvo competidor en su tiempo, ni mucho menos después... [Calderón] sirvió y sirve de modelo; y son sus comedias el caudal más redituable de nuestros teatros." II. 309-10.

Following this statement, in the same second edition, he waxes even more eloquent in praise of Calderón than he did in the first edition.
The most interesting modification of Golden Age dramatic practice in the eighteenth century was the play, *Raquel,* by Vicente García de la Huerta. This play deals with the tragic life of a Jewess who had great influence upon King Alfonso VIII (d. 1214). This theme had been dealt with by several playwrights of the seventeenth century, including Lope de Vega (*Las paces de los reyes, y Judía de Toledo*).
García de la Huerta's play is in three acts and in assonance. It adheres to the unities, and there is no mixture of the tragic and the comic. Put on the stage in 1778, it became immensely popular. [1]

---

[1] The really bright light of the century was Ramón de la Cruz. His best work is in his *sainetes,* one act comic plays, of which he wrote 475. They present characters and customs of the time in an inimitable manner.

A far-reaching, and extremely important change in Golden Age plays occurred toward the end of the eighteenth century. This was what is called *refundiciones*. Relatively little has been written about what these *refundiciones* were, but a dissertation by Edward Vincent Coughlin, "Neoclassical *refundiciones* of Golden Age *comedias* (1772-1831),[2] makes up for this neglect. He records the statements of various critics up to the present, and discusses at considerable length Luzán's objections to Golden Age plays from such points of view as verisimilitude, poetic justice, character portrayal, propriety, and the unities.

Coughlin studies twenty-two representative *refundiciones* of the period 1772 to 1831. He considers "only the works of those recasters who openly acknowledged their sources and in many instances indicated their goal of modifying the Golden Age *comedias* under the influence of the neo-classical "rules."

In his conclusion he states:

> "Undoubtedly, certain revisions executed by the neo-classical recasters resulted in minor improvements in the *comedias*. All too frequently, however, the plays were divested of their vitality and color ... As a result of their insistence upon verisimilitude the neo-classicists were often obliged to sacrifice some of the intrigue so essential to the Golden Age plot and character development. Numerous didactic passages...imparted a platitudinous quality which had not been present in the source plays. In addition, the neo-classicists narrow conception of what constituted "good taste" prompted many revisions in the diction of the Golden Age *comedias* whereby vivid dialogues were replaced by prosaic passages." p. 139.

In connection with these *refundiciones* there is one consideration that has received no comment whatsoever from any critic at any time, namely, the introduction of a front curtain on the Spanish stage. This probably occurred late in the eighteenth century. Coughlin's first example of a *refundición* in 1772 may be a clue to approximately when this important change in presenting plays took place.

A front curtain made it possible to introduce scenery and thus replace the barren stage of the seventeenth century. Since many plays of the seventeenth century have numerous "imaginary" changes of scene within the act, this diversity presented a serious problem to the recaster. By extending the three-act play to five acts (French influence), it was possible

---

2 Coughlin, *Neo-classical refundiciones of Golden Age comedias 1772-1831*, unpublished dissertation, University of Michigan, 1965.

to overcome some of the difficulties that arose, but even so, some rather radical changes in the structure of the play were called for. In fact, it may be that the introduction of the front curtain was the principal reason for the appearance of the *refundiciones*.

Coughlin does not discuss any of the plays that have been considered in this "course," nor do we have at hand the *refundiciones* that he analyzes in detail. Therefore, in order to see what happens to a Golden Age play subject to a *refundición*, we must select another, say *La moza de cántaro* by Lope de Vega. With Lope, the first scene is in Doña María's house where she shows her utter disdain for her many suitors. Her father enters in a state of great agitation. He has been slapped by Diego, one of the suitors of María (Cf. *Las mocedades del Cid* by Guillén de Castro). He regrets that his son is away and cannot take vengeance. — The next scene is in prison (Diego is there) where Doña María enters (verisimilitude?), says she wants to marry Diego and thus put an end to the enmity between her family and him. As she pretends to embrace him, she stabs him to death. — The next scene seems to be in a street, and deals with the sub-plot. — Then the scene changes to a place called Adamus, where María, dressed as a peasant girl, takes up with an *indiano* and arranges to enter his service (verisimilitude!), and go with him to Madrid.

In the *refundición* by Cándido María Trigueros, all of the first act of Lope's play is omitted. The first act of Trigueros' play takes place in Doña María's house in Madrid, the second act in a street nearby; Act Three takes place in a "Campo ameno, y en él una fuente a lo largo;" Acts Three and Four are in Doña María's house. It is hard for Trigueros to keep strictly to the unity of place.

One trouble with the *refundición* is that we do not know the identity of Isabel (the María in Lope's play) until the very end of the play. Hence our interest in her is slight as compared with the original character, where the first scenes make it clear that she is a very remarkable woman. At the end of the *refundición* she identifies herself, tells about the affront to her father and of her killing the man who committed it. A considerable part of the *refundición* is otherwise almost a line by line rendering of the original.

To take another example, *El alcalde de Zalamea*, which we have studied in this "course." There were numerous *refundiciones* of this play. Perhaps as representative as any is the nineteenth century *refundición* by Abelardo López de Ayala. This author does not extend the play beyond the standard three acts, he sticks to three, the first and second acts take place in the home of Pedro Crespo, and the third in "Una Sala de las casas consistoriales de Zalamea."

The opening scene in the original depicting the rough and ready soldiers marching along the road, is omitted altogether. To one's surprise, Inés, the cousin of Isabel, says that the *consejales* will probably bribe the officers of the army to march on. She knows this, she says, because her father is one of the *consejales*. Obviously, it is one thing for Rebolledo to say this, as he does in Calderón's play, and quite another for it to come from the lips of Inés.

Some of the episodes in the *refundición* take place in strange places. For example, the episode in Act One where the Captain forces himself upon Isabel occurs, not up-stairs, but in the same room in which Pedro Crespo welcomes the Captain and later entertains Lope de Figueroa at dinner. In the second act (the same stage setting) the Captain expresses his infatuation for Isabel ("En un día") in the same house in which Lope de Figueroa is lodged. And in the third act it is in the Casa Consistorial that Isabel tells her sad story to her father.

Other *refundiciones* of *El Alcalde de Zalamea* are not any better. One perpetrated by a certain Magnolio Juárez follows along more or less the same lines as that by López de Ayala, but has nothing in it about bribing the officers. The third act takes place in the Sala baja en la Casa del Consejo. The printed version states that the play was put on at the Teatro Español on February 24, 1912.

A slight change occurs in the *refundición* by one José Brissa who has a "Telón corto" represent a street in Zalamea. The play begins by having the Captain announce that the army is not going on beyond Zalamea. The setting for Act Three is the same as that by López de Ayala.

When all is said and done, it appears that working out a *refundición* was not an easy task, and the results were far from satisfactory. We have no information about how much was paid for the *refundiciones,* but money must have been one of the incentives for taking the trouble to dream up an adaptation of a Siglo de Oro play and making use of modern scenery.

Coughlin was right in his conclusion that "all too frequently... the plays were divested of their vitality and color at the hands of the *refundidores.*"

Unhappily, *refundiciones* are the order of the day on the Spanish stage today. It is rare to see a Golden Age play presented in any form other than a *refundición.* [3] For one thing, we must say that the dramatists of the Golden Age are not getting what we commonly call a "fair shake."

Obviously, the public of today would not be prepared to accept a play with a bare stage and changes of scenery without visual evidence of

---

[3] Note: Jack H. Parker, "The Present State of *comedia* Performances," *Hispania,* XXXIX (1956), 408-411.

such happenings. It would be too great a departure from standard practice, and a dramatic company would hesitate a long time before producing such a play. And yet, it could be done.

After all, it is deplorable that the Golden plays are available only in printed form. There is a tremendous difference between reading a play in the quiet of one's home and taking part in the enthusiasm of an audience witnessing a live performance.

It is too much to hope, though, that we may see Golden Age plays on the stage as they were intended to be performed. The best we can do is to study them, as we are doing here, and try to imagine ourselves in Spain back in the seventeenth century.

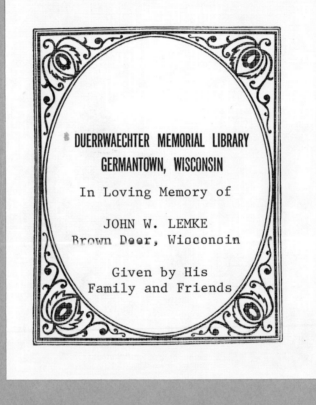

DOROTHY OF OZ

DOROTHY OF OZ
ROGER S. BAUM
ILLUSTRATED BY
ELIZABETH MILES

Books of Wonder
William Morrow and Co., Inc.
New York

Printed in the United States of America.
1 2 3 4 5 6 7 8 9 10
Library of Congress Cataloging-in-Publication Data
Baum, Roger S.
Dorothy of Oz.
Summary: With the aid of the Lion, Scarecrow, Tin
Man, and Tugg the talking boat, Dorothy battles the Jester,
who is using the dead Wicked Witch's magic wand to
turn the citizens of Oz into porcelain dolls.
[1. Fantasy]   I. Title.
PZ7.B327256Do   1989   [Fic]   89-6918
ISBN 0-688-07848-6

Dedicated to

Great-Grandfather
L. Frank Baum
The Guardian of the Gates
for all who are young at heart

My special thank you to my wife,
Charlene,
for her love, encouragement,
and her valuable time
and
Peter Glassman,
whose love of Oz is infectious
and whose advice is greatly appreciated.

List of Chapters

Dorothy
Returns to Oz

It was morning. Aunt Em and Uncle Henry were hard at work, trying to scrape a living from their land. A person could age quickly working under the hot Kansas sun. Uncle Henry's long beard was grayer now than when Dorothy had last come back from the Land of Oz.

Dorothy was making her bed. She straightened out the patchwork quilt Aunt Em had made for her, making sure its corners were straight and even. She could hear Toto's barking in the background. He had challenged the nearest barnyard chicken who happened along, running and barking and causing the little bird to flap its wings wildly. Chicken feathers flew in all different directions.

1

Dorothy Returns to Oz

The barking stopped for a short while, then started again as Toto found another chicken to tease. Dorothy looked out her window and gasped in astonishment. Only a stone's throw away was a bright and

Dorothy Returns to Oz

beautiful rainbow that filled the sky with brilliance. How beautiful it was against the morning grayness!

"Aunt Em!" Dorothy cried with excitement. "Aunt Em, look! Look at the rainbow!"

Aunt Em stopped her baking and looked. Sure enough, there it was, bigger and brighter than even Aunt Em, for all her years, had ever seen.

Dorothy burst out of the house and ran toward the bright colors as fast as her legs could take her. Toto was right behind her. She could hear Aunt Em calling after her from the porch, but her words were lost as they faded across the open prairie. Uncle

Dorothy Returns to Oz

Henry came out of the barn where he was milking cows and shouted to her, but Dorothy did not stop.

The farmhouse, Aunt Em, and Uncle Henry were soon out of sight. The rainbow seemed to move. As Dorothy ran, it remained just out of reach.

"Faster, Toto, faster," called Dorothy, urgency in her voice. She was drawn to the rainbow by something. Perhaps it was the rainbow's beauty, perhaps it was something more.

They finally stopped running, exhausted. The rainbow glimmered in front of them, seeming close enough to touch. Dorothy stared at it as she caught her breath. Toto just sat next to her, panting. He wasn't even barking, which was very unusual for him.

A very familiar voice whispered, "Hello, Dorothy, it's good to see you." Dorothy rubbed her eyes. There before her stood Glinda, the Good Witch of the South of Oz.

Dorothy could barely believe her eyes. Glinda's beauty was, in itself, mystical. Her long red hair flowed with the prairie wind. Her white gown changed colors as the rainbow's reflection danced upon the gown's strands of silk and lace.

Glinda's deep-blue eyes sparkled as she said, "Dorothy, you must return to Oz. The Tin Wood-

man, the Scarecrow, and the Lion need you. They are in grave trouble and only you can save them."

"But Glinda," Dorothy said, not wanting to believe what she had just heard, "the Wizard of Oz gave the Scarecrow his marvelous brains. He was once the ruler of the Emerald City. How could he be in trouble? He is too wise.

"The Tin Woodman has ruled over the Winkies in the country of the West since the Wicked Witch died. The Tin Woodman has a gentle heart. He is loving and giving to all creatures, for there is good in all of us. How could the Tin Woodman be in trouble with his kind heart?

"The once Cowardly Lion was given courage by the Great Wizard. He is now the King of Beasts. He can't be in trouble, can he?"

Glinda's beauty continued to reflect in an almost hypnotizing way. The rainbow's colors grew in their intensity. Glinda reached toward Dorothy. Her hand was up and her five fingers were spread. Dorothy placed her five fingers against Glinda's.

Their hands passed through one another and Glinda began to fade from sight. As she did, she said, "Dorothy, you must return to Oz and help." With that, Glinda disappeared, but the rainbow remained.

Dorothy Returns to Oz

Dorothy knew she must go back to Oz, but how? A cyclone like the one that took her there the first time was unlikely, and she had lost her silver shoes—which had the power to take you anyplace in the world—when they fell off over the desert on the way back from Oz.

Toto jumped up and started to bark again. He ran right into the rainbow. His little dark-brown body looked like a shadow among the red, yellow, and blue of the rainbow, and his eyes were wide as they reflected its colors. Dorothy watched in surprise. "Come here, Toto, come here," she called. Toto seemed very busy with something, but finally he ran out to Dorothy. In his mouth, he carried a pair of silver shoes.

Dorothy Returns to Oz

Toto was delighted at his newly found prize. He was fond of old shoes and slippers, sometimes taking Dorothy's or Aunt Em's and running away with them until he was caught and scolded. Now he ran just out of Dorothy's reach, the shoes still in his mouth.

"Toto, come here," Dorothy called again. This time Toto obeyed, dropping the shoes at Dorothy's feet. "Look," said Dorothy, "the silver shoes! Glinda the Good must have found them!"

Dorothy was putting them on when she found a note inside one shoe. The note said:

> Dear Dorothy,
>   The silver shoes will take you to Oz and back home again. The Impassable Desert has taken away much of their power, so they can be used only twice more.
>   Love, Princess Ozma and Glinda

Dorothy took Toto up carefully in her arms. She then clicked the heels of the silver shoes three times as she had been taught and said, "Take me to Oz!"

The rainbow became a blur. The prairie disappeared and they flew over the rainbow to Oz.

Candy County

They landed near a river, in a clearing surrounded on three sides by forest. Neither Dorothy nor Toto, in all their travels, had ever been here before. It was just a bit scary. They built a fire to warm and cheer themselves.

Dorothy always carried many things in her pockets. Today Dorothy was wearing her calico dress with the big red ribbon sash. Her pockets, one on each side, were stuffed with the things a young girl tended to carry. "Let's see what we have, Toto. We didn't have time to prepare for our trip and, unfortunately, I don't see any of those funny lunch-pail trees around for food. Tonight we'll just have to make do with whatever is in these pockets. Let's hope there is something to eat."

Dorothy reached into her pocket. Out came one

red crayon. She reached deeper and found a small mirror and a safety pin. The other pocket held a glass bottle and four of Aunt Em's home-baked oatmeal cookies. Dorothy gave Toto a cookie to eat and took one for herself.

Dorothy lay down on the grass and thought about her good friends. She had to find out where they were within Oz. She tried to think where they could be and what kind of trouble they might be in that Ozma, the fairy Princess of Oz, and Glinda, the Good Witch, could not get them out of. But she was very tired. Soon her thoughts drifted and both she and Toto fell asleep.

The next day they were up early. Dorothy was wondering in which direction they should walk when suddenly, out of the forest, a funny-looking bird appeared. At least Dorothy thought it was a bird. It had a large forehead and two big round eyes. Its neck looked like a rope that was attached to a small round body. Two birdlike claws protruded. Its whole body was covered with a sticky syrup, and it smelled like molasses.

"How do you do? I'm Wiser," he said.

"My name is Dorothy, and this is my dog, Toto."

"Nice to meet you," said Wiser.

Wiser looked a little bit like an owl, and owls were supposed to be wise. When Dorothy asked him,

Candy County

Wiser mentioned that he was indeed wise and became wiser each day.

Wiser had been up all night and was about to go to his nest to sleep all day, but before he did, he took a moment to ask Dorothy and Toto where they were going.

"That depends on where we are within the Land of Oz," Dorothy answered. "You see, we must find the Scarecrow, the Tin Woodman, and Lion. Glinda,

the Good Witch of the South, told us they are in grave trouble. I suppose we should first visit the one who is nearest to where we are now."

When Wiser heard this problem, he thought awhile. Finally he said, in a very wise voice, "You are in Gillikin Country. In order to find the direction to your nearest friend, it would be prudent to visit Candy County and ask the Giant Royal Marshmallow."

"Which way do we go to find Candy County and the Giant Royal Marshmallow?" asked Dorothy.

Wiser pointed a sticky, molasses-covered wing. "That direction. By the way," he added in his most wise-sounding voice, "all things are fun if you want them to be, and especially fun when you share your fun with another."

Wiser said good bye, then said suddenly, "Watch out for the molasses." Then off he flew, as well as he could with sticky wings, to wash and then sleep all day. Toto gave a couple of barks to say good-bye.

Hours passed. Finally, they climbed a hill that looked just like sugar and walked down it into the valley below. Dorothy and Toto looked around, and there, right in front of them, was a sign made out of candy. The sign pole was a peppermint stick,

C a n d y C o u n t y

and the sign itself was vanilla cream cake icing with black licorice letters, which read:

WELCOME TO CANDY COUNTY
HIS HIGHNESS
THE GIANT ROYAL MARSHMALLOW OF OZ

"Candy County," said Dorothy, looking around. "Wiser was right, Toto. There really is a Candy County." As Dorothy spoke, Toto was licking a big candy lollipop with delight.

Dorothy looked around and observed that lollipops were growing all over in a field of green cake crumbs. The lollipops were all different colors and flavors—purple for grape flavor, yellow for butterscotch, red

for cherry, green for lime. On and on and on the colors and flavors went. Dorothy reached down and picked a large cherry lollipop and joined Toto, who was already munching on his second.

In all their excitement, they had overlooked a white-chocolate sign with candy raisins, which read:

DO NOT PICK THE LOLLIPOPS

Toto had just finished his second lollipop and was studying his next one in delightful anticipation when a sticky-sounding voice bellowed from just behind them, "You, Dorothy, and you, Toto, have broken a law of Candy County. Therefore, you must see the Giant Royal Marshmallow, who will determine your punishment."

Toto was so startled that his ears went straight up. Dorothy and Toto turned around and, to their astonishment, there stood a large candy apple with large candy eyes and mouth and a yellow candy nose. He had two apple stick legs that seemed to reach right up to his apple head. The Candy Apple looked so funny that when Dorothy regained her composure, she almost laughed out loud.

"Who are you? And how do you know our names?" Dorothy asked in surprise.

C a n d y   C o u n t y

"I am the Royal Sheriff of Candy County," the Candy Apple said. "All people are known within the Kingdom of Candy County, for the Giant Royal Marshmallow knows all—well, almost all." The Candy Apple went on to explain that within the County, the Giant Royal Marshmallow was very powerful. Then he said they must be on their way to see the great ruler about breaking his law.

14

Candy County

"But," Dorothy pleaded, "we didn't know any better. The lollipops looked so good to eat and . . ."

The Candy Apple ignored Dorothy's plea, and so off they went. Presently the sheriff explained, in an almost apologetic way, the reason for protecting their land and candy so carefully.

"You see," the Candy Apple said, "everyone would like to come here and eat all our good candy and maybe even us, since all of us are made from things to eat. Our candy is made for the people of the Emerald City of Oz. I hope you both understand why we have to be so careful."

"I understand," said Dorothy.

Along the way to see the Giant Royal Marshmallow, Dorothy and Toto saw every possible type of candy you could imagine. They saw gumdrops, hard candy of all sizes, assorted chocolates in neat rows, and also chocolate drops hanging from candy trees.

Toto barked at a big white fluffy cloud overhead. Dorothy asked the Royal Sheriff what flavor the cloud was.

"Why," said the Sheriff with a broad grin, "that's cotton candy."

As little Toto walked in front of Dorothy and the Sheriff, he looked up again at the delicious-looking candy cloud. And then—*kerplop*—Toto

walked right into a puddle of gummy molasses. Dorothy laughed, and even the Sheriff smiled.

Toto now knew what Wiser meant when he said to watch out for the molasses. The thought didn't make him any happier.

Soon they could see the town up ahead. Right in its center was a great cherry-red castle where the Giant Royal Marshmallow lived.

As they walked through the town, they noticed that no one was smiling. How could all these people be so sad, Dorothy thought to herself, with all the wonderful colors and all these good things to eat around them? Something certainly must be wrong.

C a n d y C o u n t y

The people of Candy County were too busy working to notice the three as they walked slowly up to the castle's large forbidding gates. They all sadly went about their work. Some of the candy people were pouring candy syrup, including molasses, into kettles hung over stick fires.

Toto, having learned a good lesson about always watching where he was walking, was extra careful not to get any closer than he absolutely needed to this sticky stuff. He still hadn't quite finished the job of licking himself clean. One paw still looked awfully gooey.

Dorothy saw that some of the people were pouring liquid chocolate into molds to shape the word *Oz*, while others were decorating cakes with whipped cream and small candies. Each cake proudly had the word *Oz*, made of cinnamon, right on top.

Yet, with all this goodness around them, none of the people looked as if they were enjoying what they were doing.

Just then, they reached the castle's gates with the Candy Apple. Two candy royal guards with tall black licorice hats and red candy coats and black licorice pants appeared. Each was carrying a long gold maple-sugar sword. "Halt," said one royal guard.

"Halt," said the other royal guard. "Who ap-

proaches his Highness's royal castle?"

The Candy Apple answered, "What's wrong? I'm the Sheriff. Don't you know me?"

One guard apologized and explained that they were the new candy guards and that the other pair had been shipped to a candy store within the Emerald City.

"Yes," said the other, "shipped to a candy store within the Emerald City."

Dorothy asked the guards why one repeated so much of what the other said.

"Because," said one, "we are sold to candy stores in sets of two."

"Yes," said the other, "sets of two."

"Oh," said Dorothy, thinking how ridiculous the whole situation was.

"Who are you?" said first one guard and then the other. Dorothy politely introduced Toto and herself. The Candy Apple Sheriff explained to the guards that the two had been caught picking and eating candy lollipops.

The candy guards stepped back in horror, thinking Dorothy and Toto might be contemplating eating them, as well. Dorothy realized what their problem was and promised she and Toto would not take even one bite.

"In that case, you may pass," said one guard.

"Yes, you may pass," said the other.

They walked with the Candy Apple through the gates and into the main hall of the castle. Within the castle, grim-faced servants ran here and there on their special missions.

The Sheriff said, "You both must wait here."

Toto and Dorothy looked around them. The great hall with its glittering lights was magnificent. Candy always looked good to eat, Dorothy thought, but it was hard to believe it could be made to look so beautiful.

All at once, it became quiet. At the far end of the room, a large door made of chocolate bark opened. In walked his Highness, the Giant Royal Marshmallow, holding a strawberry sundae.

The Giant Royal Marshmallow bellowed angrily, "I've been told you two have been picking and eating our lollipops!"

"This is Dorothy and her dog, Toto, your Highness," broke in the Candy Apple timidly.

"I know who they are," bellowed the Royal Marshmallow. Around the ruler's neck hung a gold medal with the word *Oz*. It bounced up and down as he spoke.

His Highness started to say something else but,

to Dorothy's and even Toto's surprise, the Giant Marshmallow suddenly began to cry instead! Big tears of liquid sugar began rolling down his cheeks.

Dorothy felt sorry for his Highness and asked, "What's wrong, your Majesty?"

"It's my stomach," sobbed the Royal Marshmallow. "It hurts." Soon all the candy people within the hall were crying as well.

C a n d y   C o u n t y

Dorothy turned to the Candy Apple and Toto and said, "We have to help the Giant Royal Marshmallow. If we help him, we will also be helping all the people of Candy County. Isn't that right, Candy Apple?"

"Yes," answered the Royal Sheriff. "The people love his Highness."

"The Giant Royal Marshmallow isn't really so ill," Dorothy said. "It's just that he has a stomachache from eating lots and lots of candy. The people really do love their King and are worried about his health, but they don't know what to do. That's probably the reason no one is happy." Toto wagged his tail in agreement.

Dorothy asked his Highness whether she might try to help. He nodded as another big liquid-sugar tear rolled down his marshmallow cheek. "Your Highness," Dorothy suggested politely, "if you'll just eat marshmallows for a while and cut back on other sweets, you'll feel much better."

His Highness smiled. "Why, of course that's my problem. I feel better already." He put aside the strawberry sundae and promptly ordered a marshmallow sundae instead. "Since I'm made of marshmallow, then marshmallow would certainly agree with me, and I will feel better."

21

C a n d y   C o u n t y

The Candy Apple Sheriff then said, "The two of you are the first to take the time to help our King and our people."

Then the happy King said, "The lollipop-picking charges are dismissed, and you both are free to go. But first, may we help you in any way?"

"Oh, yes," said Dorothy. "Toto and I need to find the Tin Woodman, the Scarecrow, and the Lion, for we were told by Glinda, the Good Witch, that they are in grave trouble. Would you please give us directions?"

Noticing the silver shoes Dorothy wore, the Giant Royal Marshmallow said, "Your silver shoes have great power. Perhaps you could command them to take you to each of your friends."

"They did have great power, your Highness," said Dorothy, "but they were lost over the Impassable Desert. Glinda was able to recover them and give them back to me, but their power is almost gone. I may use them only one more time. Toto and I will need them to return to Kansas."

"Well," said the Royal Marshmallow, "at least we can help you get started with plenty of supplies."

At once two candy people appeared. Both were carrying baskets full of fruits and a whole assortment of candy and nuts. There were even several specially

made candy dog bones included for Toto. The baskets had a sling so Dorothy could carry them comfortably.

Then the King said, "You are very close to Gayelette's palace. Perhaps they will help you there." He instructed the Royal Sheriff to escort them to the borders of his kingdom and start them on their journey. The King's smile was very wide as they left the gates of the castle.

Then all the people of Candy County smiled, for this was the first time they had seen their good King smile in a long, long time, and it made everyone very happy. The people began to celebrate and insisted Dorothy and Toto stay a while longer as guests of honor. Dorothy was delighted and accepted. Toto just kept wagging his tail. It was the merriest feast to which anyone there had ever been.

Finally the hour grew late, and Dorothy was anxious to get started on their journey. The King and all his subjects cheered and waved good-bye as the Candy Apple headed them in the direction of Gayelette's palace.

Dorothy remembered that on her first trip to Oz the Winged Monkeys had told her the story of Gayelette and her prince, Quelala. Dorothy thought it would be fun to see a real prince and princess.

Candy County

Princess Gayelette and her prince were wise and strong. What better place to continue their journey! As it grew dark, Dorothy and Toto entered a small grove of trees for shelter. Dorothy opened one basket of candy and things. She gave Toto one of the special chocolate bones, and she ate a banana and some grapes. Soon the moon was shining down on the two as they slept. Dreams of meeting the handsome prince and the beautiful princess drifted through Dorothy's head.

The Jester

Meeting a court jester the next morning was the last thing Dorothy expected.

"Hello, my pretty princess," said the Jester as he came toward them on the road. He bowed low, taking off his hat as he did so.

The Jester wore purple and white, the colors of Gayelette's palace. He wore a five-pointed hat. At the end of each point, a tiny bell dangled. His purple shoes were too long for his feet, and at the end of each shoe, a single bell hung. He had a very long and sharp nose. His eyes were bright and a grin stretched from ear to ear.

"Hello," said Dorothy. The Jester was light-hearted and mischievous, as all court jesters were. Dorothy couldn't help but smile herself. Toto went

25

wild. He jumped up and down as the Jester's bells jingled.

"May I be of help or amusement for my little princess?" he asked. "I'm the Court Jester of Gayelette's palace."

Dorothy told the Jester that she was flattered to be thought of as a princess, but she did not truly think of herself as a real princess, although Glinda and Ozma did. She thought of herself as a little girl from Kansas. She then introduced Toto to the Jester.

"Oh, please be a real princess." The Jester's smile turned upside down. "I need a princess or prince or something so I may go back to work jesting."

Dorothy was confused. The Jester did a somersault, then explained. "Gayelette and her prince are gone and their palace is haunted. A haunted palace is no place for a jester, or anyone for that matter."

"Where did they go?" Dorothy asked.

"I will tell you a strange story," said the Jester as he did a cartwheel.

Dorothy invited the Jester to sit down and to enjoy a piece of their candy.

"It's odd," the Jester began. "One night, when the rain was falling and the wind was howling, Gayelette and Quelala were having a royal feast in the main hall of the palace. A large number of guests

were invited. All were dressed in costumes. I was there, doing what all jesters do best, and that is jesting.

"As I stepped into the hallway for a moment, I heard the tower bell toll midnight. The music stopped. I went back to the main hall, only to find Gayelette, Quelala, and the others had vanished. It was as if they were never really there. I looked and looked, hoping to find at least one person, but there was no one.

"I became tired and went to bed. The next morning, I woke up and thought it was all a bad dream. But, my dear Dorothy, it wasn't, because all the people were still gone.

"After three days, I heard voices, including the voice of Gayelette. When I called out to them, the voices stopped. I finally left the palace because there is no one left to jest." The Jester finished his mysterious story and started to juggle some red balls.

Dorothy thought about the Jester's story. Then she asked, "How far is it to Gayelette's haunted palace?"

"Just over the hill," said the Jester.

"Let's go," said Dorothy. "Maybe together we can find out where all the vanished people are."

Soon they were at the palace's gates. Not a soul

was around, just as the Jester had said. The palace looked attended, for it had not been very long since all its subjects had vanished, yet it was empty.

Toto ran up the wooden drawbridge that covered the moat, which completely circled the purple palace.

Once inside, the beauty of the tapestries and fine gold and silver ornaments overwhelmed Dorothy. The Jester skipped into the palace's main hall. It was eerie; not a person was there.

Toto found a large overstuffed chair and curled up in it while Dorothy looked at the long table in the center of the great hall, where all the people had been sitting and enjoying their sumptuous meal before they disappeared. As she looked, she found

something that chilled her to the bone. The wand of the Wicked Witch of the West was lying on the table. The old Witch had been destroyed when Dorothy spilled water on her and she melted, but the magic wand was hers, all right. Dorothy wondered how it had gotten there.

Dorothy searched the large table for bits of dama-fruit. People were tempted to eat the dama-fruit because of its heady perfume. She remembered how the dama-fruit made people and animals invisible. Finding none, Dorothy continued looking for clues to what had happened. The Jester also helped to search as he continued to jest, explaining to Dorothy that he must remain in practice. All good jesters practice because it takes practice to become good at something you really want to do. Meanwhile, Dorothy could find no one, and her disappointment grew.

Finally, her search led her to the royal bedchamber. The room was beautiful, fit for a princess and her prince. The bed was made of highly varnished wood with gold inlay. A silk cover was spread on top. Above the bed was a golden canopy.

The room was large. It also had a table and chairs made of gold. The chairs had purple velvet cushions. On the tabletop, Dorothy found a delicate china figure of a princess dressed for court.

Dorothy carefully lifted the doll off the table. "Please don't drop me," said the China Doll Princess. "If you do drop me, I will surely break into a million pieces."

Dorothy was so startled at the voice, she almost did drop the beautiful and delicate doll. She carefully placed the doll back in the center of the table and sat down on one of the velvet-cushioned chairs. She looked at the tiny doll and said, "You look very familiar to me. Haven't we met before?"

The Jester

"Don't you remember, Dorothy?" said the China Doll Princess. "We met in Dainty China Country."

"Yes, now I remember," said Dorothy. "How did you get here?"

"I was captured and brought here by the Jester. Be careful of him, Dorothy," pleaded the China Doll Princess. "He's cruel and will do something terrible after he becomes bored and is finished jesting and teasing you. Where is the Jester now?"

"He is helping me look for Gayelette and Quelala and their subjects, who have all disappeared," Dorothy said.

"He is teasing you," said the China Doll Princess. "The Jester made them disappear. He is dangerous and fears nothing. The Jester was a good person, but he found the Witch's wand and its evil overtook him. Now he is almost as bad as the Wicked Witch of the West. The Jester's power lies in the magic wand the old Witch used. Sometimes he becomes so carried away with his practical jokes he forgets and leaves the magic wand lying around. If you can get the wand, you will stop the Jester from his wicked deeds."

Dorothy was amazed and frightened at what the little China Doll Princess told her. Then she remembered Toto, all by himself, curled up on the stuffed

31

chair in the room with the Jester. "I must hurry and find Toto, my little dog!" Dorothy cried. "I left him alone in the great hall."

"Please, take me with you, Dorothy," the China Doll Princess called. "I'm so tired of being stuck here on this table." Dorothy carefully picked up the China Doll Princess, gently wrapped her in a piece of cloth, and put the doll in her dress pocket. Then she quickly turned and ran toward the great hall.

Laughter echoed through the deserted palace. Dorothy ran into a huge hall and saw the Jester turning a double somersault. "My good Dorothy," the Jester began.

"Where is Toto?" Dorothy interrupted in a voice touched with panic.

"Where is Toto? Why, I don't know, my good Dorothy. The last I saw him, he was curled up in that big stuffed chair. Why don't you look there?"

Dorothy ran to the chair. Toto was nowhere in sight. Then Dorothy looked down. On the chair's pillow sat a little dog made of china. Dorothy picked the dog up. It was Toto.

"My poor Toto," Dorothy cried. "What happened to you?" Toto could only manage a tiny bark.

Dorothy spun around and confronted the laughing Jester. "You did this, didn't you?" shouted Dorothy.

The Jester

The Jester was laughing so hard, he was forced to bend over.

Dorothy ran to the table where the magic wand had been lying, but it was gone. The Jester caught his breath. "Are you looking for something?" he asked sarcastically. "This, perhaps?" The Jester opened his jacket, and there, stuck through his belt, was the Witch's magic wand.

Dorothy was unable to contain herself. She ran toward the Jester. The Jester leaped over her, laughing, then turned to face her, his hands on his hips. He was very serious now.

"If you wish to see Toto as he was before," he said, "you must obey me. You must be my slave." Reluctantly, Dorothy agreed. She knew she could do nothing now. She had to bide her time and somehow get the wand.

"Do you want to see my superb porcelain collection?" the Jester offered.

Perhaps there were others in trouble besides Toto, Dorothy thought. She accepted the Jester's offer.

The Jester led Dorothy down a long and winding stairwell deep within the palace. As they walked, the Jester kept laughing and joking. His chatter echoed throughout the palace, giving his voice an almost ghostly ring.

At last, they stopped before a large metal door. The Jester giggled. Dorothy saw nothing funny about the whole situation. She held Toto firmly in her fist as the Jester took the Witch's wand and waved it, saying, "Open, metal door." The metal door opened, creaking sharply against its huge hinges.

Inside was a large room that was brightly lit by several chandeliers. A purple carpet lay on top of a stone floor. Around the walls were row upon row of shelves. Dorothy froze, for upon those shelves were hundreds of tiny porcelain figurines.

"How do you like my collection?" asked the Jester

gleefully. "They are collected from all over Oz. As a matter of fact, I was just starting on another collection trip when I stumbled on you and Toto. How lucky I am! I didn't have to travel far at all to find a most valuable addition to my collection. Come, Dorothy, take your time and look at the collection.

Perhaps you may see some familiar faces. Ha, ha, hee, hee, hee," the Jester laughed. He waved his wand, and a stuffed chair pulled up behind him. He sat down where he could keep an eye on Dorothy.

T h e   J e s t e r

"Over on the left side are my latest additions," the Jester said. Dorothy gasped in horror as she saw Princess Gayelette and Prince Quelala and their dinner guests from the great hall, all of them reduced to porcelain dolls.

"The Princess never suspected my beautiful china collection was right under her very own palace." The Jester laughed. "Gayelette is very powerful, so I had to be very, very careful." The Jester laughed raucously, shaking the china dolls upon their shelves.

Dorothy thought she heard a faint voice. She bent closer to Gayelette. "You must help us, Dorothy. Please help us," came the princess's plea. "We can talk, but we cannot move at all."

"I'll try," said Dorothy, whispering so the Jester could not hear her.

Dorothy walked down the rows and rows of tiny figures. They were from all over the Land of Oz. The captured people and creatures all seemed to know her and each pleaded with her to help them.

At the back of the room was a door. The Jester stood up and hopped over to stand in front of it. He said, "Would you care to see my special collection? I think you will find it most interesting. In fact, it is an ideal place to put Toto." He didn't wait for Dorothy to answer but immediately opened

the door, bowed low, and said, "Please enter, my good little Dorothy."

The room was much like the other room, only smaller. There weren't any shelves in this room, only a round, varnished wood table. At the center of the table was a box made of glass that reflected the light from a large chandelier directly above. On the floor of the glass box was placed a royal-purple velvet mat.

"Come closer, Dorothy," the Jester insisted. "And please hand me Toto." Dorothy had no choice. She carefully handed the tiny porcelain dog to the Jester.

"Don't you dare drop him," she said.

"Oh, I'll be very careful," said the Jester. "Toto is a most valuable part of my collection, as you will also be if you don't continue to obey me."

The Jester lifted the glass box and put Toto inside. "Dorothy," he said, "don't you think Toto looks comfortable next to these other three figures?"

Dorothy stepped closer. She could not believe her eyes.

"I believe these three are particularly close friends of yours. Let's see." The Jester pointed. "This is the Lion, this is the Scarecrow, and this is the Tin Woodman."

"Hello, Dorothy," said the Scarecrow. "I guess I'm not as wise as I thought, to have let the Jester trick me. I came to the palace to warn Princess Gayelette and her prince about the Jester and his magic wand, but instead I was caught by the Jester."

"Hello, Dorothy," said the Lion. "I'm sorry you have to see me like this. But it seems my courage overcame my wisdom. I came here to save our friend, the Scarecrow, and was also caught by the Jester. It seems courage, by itself, is not enough sometimes."

Then the Tin Woodman spoke. "Dorothy, Dorothy, we were hoping you would come to help us. I came here to save my friends, but it turned out to be a trap. It seems sometimes to take more than heart to get a job done. Now I see even Toto has been changed into a china figure." Toto barked once in frustration.

The Jester just smirked and chuckled. "Oh, be quiet," snapped Dorothy. The Jester was taken aback for a moment by Dorothy's boldness but soon regained his composure.

"Come," he said, "enough of this nonsense. I'm hungry for dinner."

The Jester lowered the glass box and left Dorothy's four friends staring up at her longingly from

inside their prison. Dorothy waved good-bye sadly.

The Jester led Dorothy out of his trophy rooms. The metal door clanked shut when the Jester waved the magic wand. They then climbed up the stairs to the palace's great main hall. Soon they were having dinner. No servants or cooks were needed. The magic wand did all the work.

It was dark outside and getting late. The palace was cold and silent. The Jester took one last bite of chocolate pie and got up from the table, yawning and stretching. He told Dorothy he was going to sleep and showed her to her bedroom. The Jester locked the door behind Dorothy. "I don't want any jesting from you," he cackled. "Jesting is a jester's profession." The Jester laughed at his remark, then said, "Good night."

Dorothy reached in her pocket and took out the China Doll Princess. "Thank you, Dorothy," said the doll. "It was getting stuffy in there."

Dorothy put the little Princess from Dainty China Country down carefully on the nightstand and looked around. There was no way to escape. The bedroom was high in the palace tower. The room was beautiful but it was a prison.

Dorothy climbed into bed and said good night to the little China Doll Princess next to her. She

thought and thought of ways to help her close friends and all the other people and creatures captured by the Jester. At last she had an idea.

Dorothy went to sleep with a slight smile on her face. Yes, she thought to herself, maybe there is a way to help my friends. The Jester's greed may very well be his undoing.

Tugg

The morning sun woke Dorothy. After she said good morning to the China Doll Princess, washed, and dressed, Dorothy walked to the window and looked at the land below. The countryside looked like spring in Kansas.

Her thoughts were interrupted by the sound of a key in the lock. "Don't forget me, Dorothy," the China Doll Princess said. Dorothy quickly wrapped her in the cloth and put her into her dress pocket just as the Jester entered to escort her to breakfast.

As they ate, Dorothy told the Jester her idea. He was pleased with what he heard. "What more could any collector of porcelain dolls want besides beautiful Glinda, the Good Witch of the South!" the gleeful Jester said.

41

"To bring Glinda back from the South of Oz will require the help of the Scarecrow, Tin Woodman, and Lion, as well as Toto," Dorothy told the Jester. "They must go with me."

The Jester wanted to refuse Dorothy's request, but the thought of adding such a prize piece as Glinda, the Good Witch of the South, to his porcelain collection was too much of a temptation. "The Scarecrow, Tin Woodman, and Lion may go with you," he decided, "but Toto will remain here as a hostage until you and your friends return."

The Jester waved his Witch's wand and immediately, Dorothy's three friends, full-sized and quite normal-looking, appeared before them—all but Toto.

The Jester, Dorothy thought to herself, was up to his not-so-good set of tricks.

The Scarecrow said, "You did it, Dorothy."

"Congratulations," said the Tin Woodman and Lion in unison.

"Not really," said Dorothy. "We have a great deal to do." Dorothy quickly explained to her friends what had to be accomplished. She could not tell them of her secret plan because the Jester was there, but they knew she was up to something. With a wink of an eye, they agreed.

Soon they made ready to leave. The Jester took Toto to Dorothy to remind her of her need to return to Gayelette's palace with her friends. Dorothy said good-bye to Toto, promising she would be back for him.

The five of them—Dorothy, the Scarecrow, the Tin Woodman, the Lion, and the China Doll Princess—who was safe deep within Dorothy's dress pocket—left the eerily quiet palace that had once sparkled with song and laughter. The only sound they heard as they departed was the high-pitched laughter of the Jester as it echoed throughout the palace halls.

Dorothy had more than enough food for herself on the journey. Many times in the past Dorothy had shared her food with the Lion, although the Lion generally preferred to hunt his food. The Tin Woodman and the Scarecrow never ate, nor did they need to sleep; neither did the China Doll Princess.

Dorothy took the Tin Woodman's jeweled oilcan and carefully oiled him so his joints would not rust. "Thank you, Dorothy," the Tin Man said. "It is nice for us to be with each other again, but it is sad that Toto and all the others are not free."

"Yes, it is sad," said the Scarecrow.

"What is our plan?" asked the Lion anxiously. Dorothy sat down on a large round purple rock, while the others stood by, listening.

"It is impossible to get the Witch's magic wand from the Jester," Dorothy explained. "Each time he carelessly put the wand down, I could not get to it before the Jester picked it up again. I knew/ he would do almost anything to add Glinda to his porcelain collection. It would have been just a matter of time before he traveled south in search of Glinda's castle to attempt to capture her by trickery."

"But, Dorothy," the Scarecrow advised, "Glinda, the Good Witch, is extremely powerful. Why do you believe the Jester could capture her?"

"Glinda is powerful, but the Jester is full of tricks. Don't forget, he has the Wicked Witch of the West's magic wand. He might be able to capture her. But since we were released by the Jester, we have an opportunity to warn her of the danger, as well as to ask her advice. Glinda knew the three of you were in trouble, but she didn't know where or how. Otherwise, I'm certain Glinda and Princess Ozma, the Fairy Ruler of Oz, would have attempted to save all of you themselves. Dorothy paused, then added, "We must save every captured citizen of Oz."

"Yes, all the citizens of Oz," came a voice from Dorothy's pocket.

"Oh!" cried Dorothy, reaching into her dress pocket, "I almost forgot. I've been most rude." Dorothy partially opened her hand to reveal the China Doll Princess. She reintroduced the tiny doll to her three friends. They had met once before in Dainty China Country.

"It's good to see all of you. I hope I will not be too much of a burden on our journey," said the China Doll Princess. "You remember how easily china dolls break."

Dorothy very carefully put the China Doll Princess safely back into her deep dress pocket. At that moment, Wiser flew down and landed on a nearby tree limb. He was cleaner without all the molasses sticking to him.

"Hello, Wiser," said Dorothy happily.

Wiser asked, "Where is that little dog, Toto?" Dorothy explained about the Jester and why they were on the way to see Glinda. Dorothy asked Wiser whether he knew the quickest way to Quadling Country, in the South of Oz, where Glinda lived.

Wiser thought a moment and said, "I would build a boat and travel down the Munchkin River, which flows south. The river is dangerous, but at least you

T u g g

would be going in the right direction. It will be less tiring for you and the Lion to travel the river than to go overland. But since the river is dangerous, be sure and build your boat from the Talk Trees that grow along the banks of the Munchkin River." Wiser pointed his wing in a southwesterly direction.

"Thank you," everyone said.

"No trouble at all," said Wiser. "By the way, Dorothy, did you watch out for the molasses?"

"Yes, thank you," said Dorothy, "but Toto forgot."

Wiser laughed and said, "I'm sure he will always watch where he is walking from now on." Then Wiser wished them good luck and said good-bye.

After walking for an hour in the direction Wiser had pointed, they arrived at a grove of trees along the Munchkin River's bank. The setting was serenely beautiful. The branches of the trees reached partway over the water, filtering the sun above. The river flowed quietly. It was a cool and pleasant spot.

The Tin Woodman sat down along the river's bank. He carefully made sure his feet were high above the current so they would not rust. Dorothy and the Lion washed and drank from the river's cool waters. The Scarecrow decided he wanted to sit close to the Munchkin River's inviting waters. He bor-

rowed Dorothy's red sash and tied one end to a nearby tree. Then the Scarecrow tied the other end of the sash around his waist for safety, because he was very light and didn't want to be washed away.

As the Scarecrow was about to take a seat next to the river, the tree to which Dorothy's sash was tied said, "Don't you think it would have been polite to ask permission before tying a sash to my trunk?"

The Scarecrow was so startled at hearing a talking tree that some of his straw flew everywhere. The surprised Tin Woodman fell forward into the river, getting his tin feet wet, while Dorothy and the Lion were so flabbergasted, they turned and bumped into each other, both falling completely into the river.

"Excuse . . . excuse me," said the Scarecrow, stammering and still very startled. "I just didn't think to ask for permission." Dorothy, the Tin Woodman, and Lion climbed back on the bank. Dorothy quickly dried the Tin Woodman's feet. Then she oiled his joints so he would not rust.

Dorothy introduced the Talk Trees to each of her friends. When she introduced the Tin Woodman, the whole grove of Talk Trees shook their branches. Leaves flew in all directions. "Perhaps," said the tree with the red sash tied to its trunk, "the Tin Woodman could stand back a little. You see,"

48

he explained, "all of us are afraid of woodsmen, whether they are made of tin or anything else." The rest of the trees were still shivering from fright. Their leaves floated down in masses.

"The Tin Woodman will not hurt you," said Dorothy. "The Wizard of Oz gave him a kind heart, so he wouldn't think of cutting down a Talk Tree."

"Are you sure, Dorothy?" asked the tree.

"Very sure," Dorothy quickly answered. All the trees in the grove finally stopped their shivering.

"By the way," said the Tin Woodman, "do you know Wiser?"

"Yes," answered the tree. "He sits on my tree limbs from time to time. Why do you ask?"

"Well," the Tin Woodman went on to explain, "Wiser suggested we build a boat and journey down the Munchkin River toward Glinda's palace. It is very important we talk with the Good Witch of the South."

"Wiser is a smart fellow," said the Talk Tree with the sash. "If you're going to build a boat, you will need wood." There was a moment of uncomfortable silence. Then the tree said, with a smile in his voice, "Perhaps you could make your boat using a limb from each of us. Soon you should have enough wood for a large boat that will talk."

"I've always wanted, at least in part, to be a boat," said another tree with delight. "We all have been watching the Munchkin River from this spot for many years. We've always wondered about the sights farther down. All we ever hear is bits and pieces about Oz from Wiser and our other friends."

"Let's take a vote," said the tree with the red sash. "All Talk Trees wishing to donate wood for a boat, please shake your limbs for yes. Those voting no, remain motionless. Now cast your vote."

All the trees shook so hard to vote yes that Dorothy and her friends were again covered with leaves.

"The ayes have it," said the tree.

Everyone's excitement grew as they went about the work of building a boat. The Tin Woodman

used his ax to cut the lumber. He cut a limb from one Talk Tree, then another. Very soon he had cut enough lumber to build a good-sized boat.

The Lion used his great strength to haul the lumber to the river's edge. While all this was going on, Dorothy and the little China Doll Princess, along with several of the Talk Trees, designed the boat. It would be very seaworthy. The Tin Woodman worked around the clock, as did the Scarecrow. The

51

China Doll Princess was placed near the riverbank and helped direct construction.

The boat had, of course, a timber frame and planking. Wooden pegs held it together. The Scarecrow gathered straw from nearby fields. The straw was soaked in pitch and then forced between the joints to make the hull watertight. With everyone working around the clock, the boat was soon finished.

The boat had three large staterooms and a wide deck. The ropes for the anchor and moorings were made of vines twisted together for strength. The anchor was made of bits of cloth sewn into a bag and filled with river sand. The Tin Woodman even carved a foghorn out of a hollow log and used a vine for a cord.

The boat looked like a tugboat. Dorothy had a special feeling that this boat would become well-known and loved by the citizens of Oz who lived near the banks of the Munchkin River. But something was wrong. The new boat should surely be able to talk, for it was made from the wood of the Talk Trees.

The Lion said, "I think we should paint a smile on our boat and name it Tugg. Perhaps Tugg will be able to talk with a mouth." All agreed.

Dorothy mixed some wild red berries with a little water. The mixture was just like paint. Then she

asked the Lion whether she could use the very end of his tail for a brush to paint the smile on Tugg. "Of course, you may use my tail," said the Lion. Dorothy carefully dipped the Lion's tail hairs into the red berry mixture and painted a large smile on Tugg's bow.

Then Dorothy took the glass bottle from her dress pocket and said, "For all of Oz, we name you 'Tugg.'" With that, Dorothy took the bottle and smashed it on Tugg's bow.

Everyone clapped and the tiny China Doll Princess shouted "hooray." The Talk Trees waved their limbs.

Then a very deep voice said, "I thought you would never get around to painting a mouth on me. It was difficult being unable to speak. By the way, this Munchkin River water is cold," complained Tugg.

They all looked at one another. It seemed that Tugg had a rough-and-tough personality. Perhaps that was good, Dorothy thought to herself, because on the river there could be some rough times ahead.

Dorothy thought how nice it was to have a part of the Talk Trees traveling the Munchkin River as they had always hoped and dreamed they might.

Tugg thanked everyone for making him into the fine boat that he was. He promised he would travel up the Munchkin River often to give all the Talk Trees a report on what he had seen and done.

"Now, if you don't mind," said Tugg in an annoyed manner, "there is a fish with very sharp teeth that keeps nibbling on my stern, so I would like to shove off as soon as possible."

"Of course," said Dorothy. Everyone crossed the gangplank and boarded the boat. The Lion pulled up the anchor, taking the vine rope gently in his mouth.

Tugg did not need an engine, just a propeller, since he was a living boat. Because he could talk as well as hear, all his captain needed to do was tell Tugg where to go and he would head in that direction.

Dorothy stood on the deck and gazed at the river. She said to Tugg, "We can now go downstream."

"Good," said Tugg in his gruff voice. "That is much easier for me than moving upstream."

Off they went. The Talk Trees waved their limbs good-bye. Tugg tooted his horn, and the crew waved back as they rounded the first bend in the Munchkin River.

The Maze

Dorothy removed the little China Doll Princess from her pocket and placed her carefully near the front windows. Then she tied her red sash around the China Doll Princess's waist and tied the other end to Tugg. Now the China Doll Princess would see all the sights along the river, and she could not fall and break.

"Thank you, Dorothy," said the little Princess. "This is the first time I've taken a boat ride. It's going to be fun."

Just then the water became very rough. "Hold on," said Tugg. They were caught in heavy rapids. The boat lurched and rocked. "Everyone inside," ordered Tugg. The Tin Woodman was already inside, afraid he would get wet and rust.

T h e M a z e

The Lion became a bit seasick with all the rocking.

The rapids went on and on. Every once in a while, Tugg would yell "Ouch" as a rock in the river scraped his sides.

Wave after wave splashed against the boat, but

Tugg was well constructed, and they made it safely through the rapids to where the water ran calm.

Eventually, they asked Tugg to dock himself next to the bank. Tugg steered to the right and pulled up next to the riverbank.

The Tin Woodman dropped anchor and said, "It will be dark soon. Why don't Dorothy and the Lion eat dinner while Scarecrow and I go on land and have a look around."

T h e   M a z e

"All right," said Dorothy, "but make sure you're back by dark. We're in a new and strange place."

"We will be careful," the Scarecrow assured her.

But darkness fell and the Scarecrow and Tin Woodman did not return. Dorothy and the Lion, as well as the China Doll Princess and even "rough and tough" Tugg, became more and more worried as the minutes passed. They could hear strange sounds coming from the land. Dorothy shivered at the noises. The China Doll Princess would have shivered, too, only she couldn't because she was unable to move.

The Lion looked about the bank with keen eyes, but it was too dark to see much of anything.

Dorothy asked Tugg to blow his foghorn. "Perhaps that will help them find their way home," she said. Tugg's foghorn blew loudly every few minutes, but the Scarecrow and Tin Woodman did not return.

"I will go and look for them," said the Lion bravely. "With all the courage that the Wizard of Oz gave me, I fear nothing."

But Dorothy suggested, "It might be wise to wait for light, in order to see better." The Lion quickly agreed.

Just then, more strange sounds were heard coming from land. The rocks and boulders near the water

seemed to move in the dark. Dorothy said, "Lion, do you see those boulders in the shadows? Are they moving or is it my imagination?"

The Lion looked again, and then the hair on his back stood straight up. "The boulders are moving!" he exclaimed.

Dorothy was very scared. She said, "We must wait until dawn to search for them. It is too dangerous at night." The Lion agreed.

It was a long night. Dorothy tried to sleep but could not. Neither could the Lion. The thought of their lost friends kept them awake.

When dawn approached, the strange noises stopped. "Look," said the China Doll Princess. "The rocks seem to be just as they were before."

"We'd better start looking for them right now," said Dorothy. "Who knows where they are and what kind of trouble they may be in."

Dorothy handed the Lion some fruit for nourishment and took some for herself. They said farewell to the China Doll Princess and Tugg and then they were on their way.

Soon they found a path that wound around one huge boulder after another. Dorothy remembered that Aunt Em had told her always to stay on a path or by the road while in the country, so as not to get lost.

They walked at a fast pace for a long time. The Lion would send out a loud roar every so often in hopes the Scarecrow and Tin Woodman would hear him.

The Lion spotted something in the middle of the path. It was straw from the Scarecrow. Dorothy took off her apron and placed the Scarecrow's straw in it. This way she could easily carry the straw without losing any. As they walked, they found more straw. Dorothy kept picking it up and saving it.

"It appears," said the Lion, "that the Scarecrow is marking a trail for us to follow."

The Scarecrow's straw suddenly left the main path and made a right turn onto a smaller path. Dorothy's load of straw continued to grow as she collected it along the way. Finally, the Lion said, "Why don't you tie the bundle of straw on my back?"

"Thank you," said Dorothy. She tied the straw on her friend's back, using her apron ties to secure it. "The Scarecrow cannot have much straw left," she said.

As the two rounded another turn, they came upon a sign. The sign read:

SINCE YOU HAVE COME THIS FAR,
PLEASE CONTINUE STRAIGHT AHEAD.

T h e   M a z e

"What a strange sign," said Dorothy.

Dorothy and the Lion traveled straight ahead. Soon they came upon another sign, which read:

> SINCE YOU HAVE GONE STRAIGHT AHEAD,
> PERHAPS YOU WOULD LIKE TO TURN AND
> GO STRAIGHT BACK.

"What a strange sign," said the Lion.

"Yes, you might say that," said a voice. Both the Lion and Dorothy turned to find a kind-looking man with a broad smile. He carried several oversized keys and large clocks with big red second hands. The man was dressed quite formally in a white starched shirt. His pants were black, as was his coat. His shoes were well polished.

"Pardon me. I'm the official gamekeeper here. It is my job to see that you obey the rules and finish the game on time."

"My name is Dorothy, and this is my friend, the Lion. Do you know where the Scarecrow and Tin Woodman are?"

"They are playing the game. Let's see," the Gamekeeper continued, looking at one of his large clocks. "My, how time flies! They began the game nineteen and one-half hours ago. That gives them

just another four and one-half hours to finish the game, or they lose."

"Lose what?" asked Dorothy.

"The game, of course," answered the Game-keeper.

"Nothing here seems to make sense," said the Lion.

"I hope not," said the Gamekeeper with a smug laugh. "You see, you both are about to play the

T h e   M a z e

Game of the Maze. You both have twenty-four hours to find your way out of it, just as the Tin Woodman and Scarecrow have, or you all will vanish forever." He laughed again. "By the way, I let the boulders roll around at night just to confuse things. It's all part of the game."

"What happens if we solve the maze and get out?" asked Dorothy.

"If you solved the maze, then I, the Gamekeeper, would vanish and so would the maze. You would not vanish but would be free to go. However, as you can guess, of the many who have tried, no one has ever solved the maze. Otherwise, I would not be here any longer." The Gamekeeper laughed. Then he said officially, "It is time to start the game."

"But what if we don't want to play the game?" said the Lion.

"Then you automatically lose by forfeit. Anyway," said the Gamekeeper, "I'm sure you want to find your two friends before you all lose."

He chuckled and added, "All you need to do is stay on the paths and find the way out. Remember, you have twenty-four hours to finish." Then the Gamekeeper wound up another of his large clocks and said, "Please step up to the starting line." He pointed to a broad line across the path.

The Maze

The Lion and Dorothy had little choice but to do as he asked.

The Gamekeeper's voice took on an even more official-sounding tone as he said, "Get on your mark. Get set. Go!" The large clock started, and so did Dorothy and the Lion.

The Gamekeeper called out after them, "By the way, the Tin Woodman and the Scarecrow now have only four and a quarter hours left to win the game, or they will vanish forever. Good luck," he added with a sneer.

As they walked, one path broke into another path

and these paths split into others. It was very, very confusing. The boulders beside the path began to look just like one another. The Lion roared again and again, hoping the Scarecrow and Tin Woodman would hear him.

The Lion reminded Dorothy that the large rocks moved at night and would confuse them even more.

"We'll never find our way out!" the Lion cried.

"Yes we will," said Dorothy. "We have to. Toto and all the others are counting on us!"

As they passed another huge boulder, they found more of the Scarecrow's straw on the path. Dorothy placed it with the rest of the straw on the Lion's back. Then, she glanced up and yelled, "There they are!"

Dorothy and the Lion ran to the Scarecrow and the Tin Woodman. They all embraced, except for the Scarecrow. He was nothing more than his blue Munchkin suit and his support sticks. All his straw was gone except for the straw in his head, and he hung limply on the Tin Woodman's back. "We've been trying to solve the mystery of the maze for hours," said the Scarecrow in a weak voice. "I used my straw to mark the path for you to follow. It's a good thing you found us when you did. I just ran out of straw."

T h e   M a z e

Dorothy helped the Scarecrow off the Tin Woodman's back and carefully stuffed his straw back into
him. "There," said Dorothy when she finished, "you
look as good as new."

"Thank you," said the Scarecrow. "I feel much
better." The Scarecrow patted and shaped the straw
here and there to his liking.

"I'm afraid we're running out of time to solve
the maze," said the Tin Woodman. "Our twenty-
four hours are almost up."

Just then the Gamekeeper appeared on top of a
nearby boulder. "I'm afraid you are correct." He
chuckled. "Both you and the Scarecrow are running
out of time to solve the maze before you both vanish

forever. Don't feel bad, though," he added sarcastically. "No one has ever solved the maze. By the rules of the game, I'm required to give you a warning when you're down to your last hour. When you hear the bell, you will have one hour remaining to solve the maze. Also, when you have one minute left, the bell will ring each second."

The Lion roared very loudly to show his anger, and the Gamekeeper fell backward off the rock, his clocks tumbling every which way. "Now see what you have done!" said the Gamekeeper as he attempted to brush off his soiled clothes. "I will have to clean my suit to look proper for the end of the game." The Gamekeeper stood up, dusting off his formal black pants. Then he gathered up his clocks and looked closely at one of them. A sly grin crossed his face. "Good luck, Scarecrow, and to you, Tin Woodman," he said. "You now have only one hour to solve the maze." He took out a silver bell with writing on its side. The inscription read:

IN HONOR OF THE
WICKED WITCH OF
THE WEST

He rang the silver bell loudly and then suddenly vanished in the middle of another ominous chuckle.

The Maze

"One hour! We have to solve the maze in just one hour!" said the Tin Woodman.

The Scarecrow looked up at the sky where the sun was beginning to set in the west.

"Wait," said the Scarecrow, using his wonderful brain. "Remember when we left Tugg and went ashore, the sun was setting behind us. That means we need to go west. That will bring us to Tugg and the China Doll Princess."

"Yes, you are right," said the Lion excitedly. "We must follow any path that travels west—the direction of the setting sun."

"Let's hurry," said Dorothy. Off the group ran, following path after path, all leading west.

Finally, they reached a spot where the boulders blocked their way. "The rocks must have moved," the Tin Woodman said. Just then, they heard a foghorn tooting very near.

"That's Tugg!" Dorothy shouted. "He's still trying to guide us back to him. It sounds as if he is right on the other side of this big boulder."

"We must get to the other side before the time runs out," said the Tin Woodman. "But how can we get around it?"

Then everyone froze. In the distance, they could hear the Gamekeeper's official silver bell ominously counting off the last sixty seconds.

The Maze

"What do we do? What do we do?" repeated the Tin Woodman.

"Lion," cried the Scarecrow in an excited voice. "Can you jump over the boulder, get the rope we use to moor Tugg, and bring it back? Then maybe he can pull us over the rocks."

"I'll try," roared the Lion. He took a few quick steps backward and ran toward the huge rock. Up, up he bounded, over the boulder. Just as quickly, he jumped back again, but this time he carried Tugg's rope with him. In the background, the Gamekeeper's bell sounded off the last few seconds.

"Hurry! Everyone grab hold of the rope," said the Lion. Dorothy, the Tin Woodman, and the Scarecrow held Tugg's rope tightly. The Lion, with all his might and courage, jumped high up to the boulder's top and roared a signal to Tugg. The rope started to move, slowly at first, then faster and faster as it pulled all three up and over.

They landed on the other side of the boulder with a crash, but they were out of the maze. The Lion jumped from the top of the boulder just before the last second rang from the Gamekeeper's silver bell.

There was a rush of air, and the water of the Munchkin River became very rough. Dorothy's hair flew straight up. The Scarecrow, who was so light,

held tightly to Tugg's rope but was still blown at least six feet off the ground, while the Lion's tail was going around and around in circles. The Tin Woodman was heavy. He just stood and stared in the direction where the maze used to be.

The maze, with its paths, boulders, and Gamekeeper, was gone. In its place was a beautiful flat land of purple flowers, silver trees, and a small village of little people going about their business. The people noticed Dorothy and her friends. One small man, who looked exactly like the Gamekeeper, came forward, bowed low, and said, "Permit me to introduce myself. I'm the Schoolmaster. Thank you for giving us back our town of Purplefield. The Wicked Witch of the West left a spell on our town long ago. Now, thanks to each of you, the spell is broken and we are free again to fish the Munchkin River and farm our land."

Just then, the school bell rang and they all looked up at it. It was a silver bell with a school clock just beneath it. The bell and the clock were exactly like the ones the Gamekeeper had used, but this time the silver bell had another inscription on it, reading:

IN HONOR OF THE
TOWN OF PURPLEFIELD
AND ITS CHILDREN

T h e M a z e

It was signed and dated:

THE WIZARD OF OZ
MAY 15, 1856

The Schoolmaster invited them to be his guests for the night, but Dorothy and the others politely declined, explaining that they must be on their way to see Glinda, the Good Witch of the South.

Boarding Tugg, they waved good-bye to the people of Purplefield. "Thank you, Tugg," said Dorothy, "for pulling us out of the maze."

"No problem at all," said Tugg as he floated slowly away from shore.

"It is nice to know we all helped each other," said the Tin Woodman.

Later that night, after washing and eating, they told the full adventure of the maze to the little China Doll Princess and Tugg.

The Munchkin River was very calm that night as they traveled south all safe and sound.

Dragons

The next morning, after breakfast, Dorothy carefully oiled the Tin Woodman's joints. The Scarecrow laughed as he noticed that the hair at the end of the Lion's tail was beginning to return to its natural color. They all laughed as the Lion, in a moment of shyness, hid the end of his tail beneath his body. Tugg said, "Thank you for allowing Dorothy to use your tail hairs for a paintbrush."

As Tugg and his crew continued on down the Munchkin River, the China Doll Princess saw a sign along the bank of the river and asked the Lion what it said. "It says, LAKE ORIZON AHEAD. MUNCHKIN RIVER—USE SOUTH FORK. That means we have to go to the right to stay with the Munchkin River and continue south."

Dorothy said, "We must be in Munchkin Country."

"We will see the Yellow Brick Road if we watch carefully," said the Lion.

"That is a long way from here," said the Tin Woodman. "We are now entering the long south stretch of the river. I've heard some of it is still uncharted."

The China Doll Princess, who was watching the river ahead of them, called out, "There is a large hill straight ahead."

"The river must flow around the hill," said the Lion.

"The river is gaining speed," said the China Doll Princess.

"Wheee," said Tugg as he raced along, "this is fun!"

"Be careful, Tugg," said Dorothy.

"Don't worry, Dorothy," said Tugg as he raced along.

"Back inside, everyone," warned the Scarecrow as Tugg's speed increased.

"Look," said the China Doll Princess. "The Munchkin River doesn't go around the hill. It flows inside of it."

"Can we stop?" said the Scarecrow to Tugg.

"No, it's too late to stop. The current is too strong. I'll just have to ride this one out," said Tugg. With that, the torrent plunged Tugg and his crew into the complete darkness of the tunnel.

"Can anyone see anything?" asked Dorothy.

"No," everyone answered.

"Do we have a light?" asked the Scarecrow. He hoped a candle would not be needed, because scarecrows in particular are not fond of fire, for obvious reasons.

"No, we didn't bring a light of any kind. We didn't plan on this happening," said Dorothy.

Around and around Tugg turned in the darkness. He had instinctively stopped his propeller when he entered the cave, and he didn't dare try to start it again for fear of running into something he couldn't see.

On they floated, caught in the Munchkin River's strong current. It was so dark they couldn't see their hands in front of their faces.

All at once, circular lights appeared in front of them. The lights were scattered in pairs. Some pairs of lights were small, others large. Every once in a while, the lights would blink.

"Some light is better than no light," the Lion remarked.

"I'm not so sure," said the Tin Woodman.

D r a g o n s

"What is that?" said a much deeper and fearsome voice that echoed about them.

"Oh no!" exclaimed another, tinier voice.

"Quiet!" demanded yet another voice.

"Who are you, and why has our sleep been interrupted?" asked the deep-sounding voice.

"We're very sorry," said Dorothy timidly. "Our boat got caught in the raging waters of the Munchkin River, and before we knew it, we were carried down here."

The large round lights were blinking more rapidly than before. "Who are you?" asked Dorothy.

"Dragons," shouted the one with a deep voice. "Dragons who are trying to sleep. As you may know, we live under the earth because everyone is frightened of us. We only go above ground to search for

food. We'd love to live above ground, but no one wants us for neighbors."

"I'm hungry," said a baby dragon.

"If I have told you once," said the baby dragon's mother, "I've told you a hundred times, you are not to eat between meals, even if it is one hundred years between meals."

"But," said the baby dragon, "they look especially good to eat, and anyway, the last meal got away."

Just at that moment, another dragon at the rear of the cave woke up and yawned deeply. Fire shot out of his mouth and singed the largest dragon's tail, causing him to roar loudly in pain.

The largest dragon was very upset, having been awakened from his sleep by Tugg and his crew and now, to top it all off, having his tail burned. "Enough is enough," he said. "This time we will make an exception. We *will* eat between meals."

"No, please!" Dorothy cried as she shivered.

"Wait," interrupted the Scarecrow. "What if we were to help you find a nice safe place on the surface of Oz where you could live with room to roam and throw fire like dragons are supposed to?"

The baby dragon ignored the Scarecrow's offer. He snorted some fire and said, "I'm still hungry. I could eat all of them myself."

Dorothy believed him. The baby dragon was not

very little, except when compared to the full-grown dragons. The baby dragon was as big as two elephants standing one on top of the other.

Before anything could be done, he grabbed the Tin Woodman with his huge forked tongue and lifted him right off Tugg's deck and into his open jaws. The baby dragon blew a flame from his mouth. Then his eyes grew wide and giant tears rolled down his long dragon's snout. He jumped up and down with his eyes open wide for a moment. Then he took a deep breath and roared so loudly it even startled the much older and larger dragons. When the baby dragon roared again, a red-hot flame popped out of his mouth, along with a red-hot Tin Woodman. His tin glowed in the semidarkness of the cave.

"Ugh!" said the little dragon, jumping up and down again. "I've never ever tasted anything so awful in all of my six hundred and thirty-eight years. I thought the rhinoceros was terrible-tasting with his tough skin, but this man made of tin tastes worse than ten rhinoceroses."

"Perhaps you would like to eat me next," challenged the Scarecrow.

"You're the first creature that has ever offered to be eaten," noted the baby dragon. He paused, then said, "I'll just take a sample bite."

"Certainly," said the Scarecrow. He unbuttoned

his blue Munchkin shirt. Then he grabbed a handful of straw, laid it on the floor of the cave, and said to the baby dragon, "Please help yourself."

The baby dragon used his large tongue to lick up the Scarecrow's straw in one swoop. "Ugh!" said the baby dragon again. Making a sour face, he said, "You taste just like straw!"

"I am made of straw," said the Scarecrow.

"Ugh," said the baby dragon. "Maybe horses and cows and other animals like straw, but not dragons."

Dorothy decided she would take a big chance and try to fool the little dragon, since he didn't find either the Tin Woodman or the Scarecrow tasty.

D r a g o n s

Dorothy took a deep breath and said, "Why don't you try to eat me and the Lion?" The Lion's eyes went wide at Dorothy's offer, but then he realized it was only a trick to fool the baby dragon into thinking that they were not any good to eat, either.

By this time, the baby dragon had had enough unpleasant food and exclaimed, "You cannot fool me. I know you two aren't any better-tasting than the others." Dorothy and the Lion smiled knowingly at each other.

"Enough is enough," bellowed the big dragon in frustration. "What is your plan for a nice place for us to live on the surface of Oz?"

"I will tell you in a moment," said the Scarecrow, "but first, we must cool down the Tin Woodman."

Dorothy wet one of Tugg's ropes in the water so it would not burn and tied one end around the Tin Woodman's waist, being careful not to touch him. She handed the other end to the Lion, who took it gently in his mouth. Then the very, very hot Tin Woodman jumped into the river. The water boiled around him.

Soon the Tin Woodman was cool to the touch. The Lion pulled up the rope, and the Tin Woodman was safely back on board. Dorothy wiped the Tin Woodman dry and then added fresh oil to his joints.

"How do you feel?" asked Tugg in his gruff voice.

"Great," said the Tin Woodman. "All that heat sealed some of my seams. In fact, I feel better than ever."

"As I was saying," interrupted the big dragon, who was obviously getting impatient, "what is your plan for a new home for us?"

The Scarecrow said, "We know of a palace that would be just right for you to live near. However, you must trust us and let us go. Tugg will return later to guide you, but first we must visit Glinda on a very important mission."

The big dragon snorted. A small flame flickered in his huge mouth as he said, "We're certainly not getting much sleep while all of you are here, and you aren't very tasty, so it will be all right for you to leave here. I hope," the big dragon added, "that you will be back soon. We really do need a better place to live than a cave."

With that, Tugg gave two toots from his foghorn. Dorothy held the little China Doll Princess in her hands, and they all said good-bye to the dragons, who were almost asleep again.

Down the Munchkin River they floated. Complete darkness soon overtook them once more.

The Secret
of the
Yellow Brick Road

They floated in total darkness for hours. At one
point, Tugg let out a loud "Ouch!" and complained
that his keel was scraping the rough sand on the
river's bottom.

"Perhaps I can swim behind you for a while," said
the Lion. "Without my weight on board, you'll be
able to float higher in the water and not scrape the
bottom."

"But you could lose us in the dark," said the
China Doll Princess.

"We will put this rope to good use again," said
the Tin Woodman. The Woodman untied Tugg's
rope from himself and then tied it around the Lion's
body.

The Yellow Brick Road

The Lion jumped from Tugg's deck into the Munchkin River with a very loud splash. "That feels better," said Tugg, much relieved. "Thank you," he said to the Lion, but there was no answer.

The Scarecrow, Dorothy, and the Tin Woodman all rushed to the back of the boat. It was still dark. Nothing could be seen or heard.

Dorothy called out twice. Still there was no answer from the Lion. The only sound was the rushing of the Munchkin River. Worried, Dorothy yelled again, "Are you all right?"

"Of course I'm all right," said the Lion.

"Then why didn't you answer the other times when I called to you?" asked Dorothy.

"Because," answered the Lion, laughing, "I was just swimming underwater and couldn't hear you."

"Oh," said Dorothy and the others, laughing in relief.

"Oh!" exclaimed the little China Doll Princess from her vantage point. "Look at that!"

"Look at what?" asked the Scarecrow. "It is too dark in here to see anything."

"There is a speck of light up ahead," said the China Doll Princess. They all turned and, sure enough, they could see light ahead. As they watched, the speck of light grew larger and larger.

The Yellow Brick Road

Tugg said, "We are about to come out of the cave."

"You had better get back on board," said the Scarecrow to the Lion. The Lion clawed his way back onto the boat.

"Be careful," said Tugg. "Those claws hurt."

"Sorry," said the Lion.

Suddenly, Tugg and his crew were drenched in sunlight. Behind them were the large hills and the cave where they had just been. On either side of the river were groves of trees and meadows filled with wild flowers of every imaginable color and kind.

"How beautiful," exclaimed the China Doll Princess.

"Gorgeous," agreed the Tin Woodman.

"The Munchkin River is calm here. Let's have lunch and stop awhile," said the Lion. Tugg moved toward the bank and found a nice quiet spot to stop. The Tin Woodman dropped anchor. Soon they were all relaxing while Dorothy and the Lion enjoyed a lunch from her supplies.

After lunch, they set out again. They were eager to reach Glinda's castle and had no time to waste. They traveled all that day past the beautiful meadows, watching fat honeybees buzzing gently as they flitted from flower to flower gathering nectar.

The Yellow Brick Road

The shadows lengthened. Dorothy and the Lion ate dinner as Tugg carried them farther down the river.

Tugg and the China Doll Princess, who was his volunteer lookout, decided it would be all right to travel the river at night.

The next morning, it was raining hard. The wind howled. Tugg rocked back and forth as wave after wave broke against his hull. No one dared to venture out on Tugg's deck. They all stayed inside their cabins because it would be easy to fall overboard. Tugg complained he had to work hard to maintain a steady course.

The Munchkin River twisted around one bend, then another. The banks of the river gave way to high, menacing canyon walls. The river was swollen from the storm, and its raging torrent moved Tugg very rapidly. Although it was dangerous to travel so fast, they were making good progress.

The next morning, several large rocks, loosened by the rain, broke free from the steep canyon walls and tumbled down to the river, nearly hitting Tugg. One small rock did hit him. "Ouch!" said Tugg. "I didn't realize being a boat could be so hazardous."

The rain continued all that day. By the time night came again, they had traveled a long way down the

The Yellow Brick Road

Munchkin River. The crew noticed
the canyon walls were lower than
they had been before. Soon they
were only as high as Tugg's
windows, and finally, they were
no higher than Tugg's deck.

   The rain let up enough for
the travelers to see a good place
to dock. Tugg yelled, "Whoopee,"
and headed for safety. The
Tin Woodman tossed out
the anchor.

The Yellow Brick Road

The worst of the storm passed soon after they docked, and the Munchkin River returned to normal. It was still cloudy, but there was just enough sunlight for a distant rainbow to arch across the land. The rainbow reminded Dorothy and the others how important it was to reach Glinda's castle as soon as possible. Dorothy thought of the cold evil of the Wicked Witch's magic wand. The Jester could do many evil things with the wand. There was no telling what he might do next if he tired of capturing the citizens of Oz for his porcelain collection.

From the river, they could see tiny blue cottages scattered throughout the landscape. Each cottage was round, with a large domed roof. Dorothy felt a happy glow warm her from head to toe, for she knew they were in the land of the Munchkins.

Dorothy remembered how she had first met the Munchkins after she had been blown to Oz by the Kansas cyclone, and how they, as well as the Good Witch of the North, had thought she was a noble sorceress for having accidentally killed the Wicked Witch of the East. She had died when Dorothy's house landed on top of her. The Good Witch of the North gave Dorothy the Wicked Witch's silver shoes and kissed her on the forehead, for the Good Witch knew the kiss would protect her on her journey

to the Emerald City. It was near here that Dorothy had started her travels upon the Yellow Brick Road.

"The Yellow Brick Road must be around here," said the Scarecrow, interrupting Dorothy's thoughts.

"Yes," Dorothy agreed, growing more excited by the minute.

"It must be farther down the Munchkin River," said the Tin Woodman. "The river travels right through it."

Dorothy asked the Lion whether he was hungry. "I think I will catch some fresh breakfast, perhaps chicken and eggs," said the Lion as he bounded from Tugg's deck onto the river's bank.

After an hour went by, the Tin Woodman gazed upward at the sky. The wind was beginning to blow. "Look," said the Tin Woodman. "It's starting to storm again."

"Something is not right," said the Scarecrow.

"Something is very wrong," agreed Tugg. "In all of the years the Talk Trees have lived along the bank of this river, I cannot recall it ever having rained this much."

"The sky was starting to clear, and now it's cloudy, and it's beginning to rain again," said the China Doll Princess.

"Batten down my hatches," said Tugg with a

disappointed sigh. "I was enjoying having my hatches open for a while."

"Look!" said the Scarecrow. "The Lion is returning with someone."

Dorothy was breathless with excitement. "It's Boq," she cried. "My old friend, Boq!" Dorothy grinned from ear to ear as the Lion and Boq jumped on board. Dorothy and Boq hugged each other and tears of joy rolled down their faces. Mixed with their tears were raindrops from the new storm. "Let's all go inside," said Dorothy. "We're getting wet out here."

Dorothy introduced Boq to her friends. She told them how Boq and the other Munchkins had invited her to supper and to pass the night with them before she continued her journey along the Yellow Brick Road on her first visit to Oz.

The Tin Woodman offered Boq a cup of fresh hot broth. Even though the Tin Woodman was not made of flesh and blood and did not eat or sleep, or feel hot or cold, he had a loving and giving heart and anticipated the needs of others. Boq accepted the Tin Woodman's polite offer and thanked him.

"I'm very happy to see you, Dorothy, and to meet your friends." Boq paused a moment, then asked, "Where is Toto?"

The Yellow Brick Road

"Toto is being held prisoner by Princess Gayelette's Jester at her palace in Gillikin Country in the North of Oz," Dorothy explained sadly. "The Jester has the magic wand of the Wicked Witch of the West."

When Boq heard this, he was visibly shaken. "But," said the China Doll Princess, "we are on our way to Glinda's castle to warn her of the Jester and seek her help to free Toto and the others."

"I'm sure the good and powerful sorceress can help," said Boq. "I only hope someone will help us."

"What do you mean?" asked the Tin Woodman.

Before Boq could answer the Tin Woodman's question, a loud clap of thunder rolled overhead. Tugg said, "It's getting kind of rough out here. I'm afraid we're in for another big storm."

"That's the problem," said Boq. "It hasn't stopped raining for several months. The storms come one after another. It is too wet to plant our crops. In fact, many areas of Munchkin Country are flooded. Most of us are very low on food."

"I couldn't even find breakfast this morning," the Lion said.

Boq took another sip of broth, savoring its warmth and nourishment. "My friends," he said, "I have

some more sad news."

"What is it, Boq?" asked the Tin Woodman. He wondered how things could get any worse for the Munchkins.

"It is the Yellow Brick Road," said Boq. Tears filled his eyes. "The Yellow Brick Road is no longer yellow, and all the rainwater has it in terrible disrepair."

"Oh, no!" cried Dorothy.

"The secret of the Yellow Brick Road is known by only a few citizens of Oz. I am one of those few," said Boq. "The Good Witch of the North, at the request of the great and powerful Wizard of Oz, mixed the first brick laid for the Yellow Brick Road with magical ingredients. All the rest of the bricks

90

The Yellow Brick Road

were made from the same magical recipe. The bricks were laid side by side until they reached the gates of the Emerald City. The road connected the people of Oz as friends, just as the great Wizard wished. The Yellow Brick Road's magical ingredients are quite simple in their nature. The Good Witch used sunshine, mixed with the same kind of love that makes the Emerald City green.

"The Wizard of Oz, as we all know," said Boq, "was more than just a humbug wizard. He gave great love and understanding to all the peoples of Oz. The Emerald City, of course, is green. It is beautiful because the people who built it loved the city and the Wizard who designed it. And the green-tinted glasses the Wizard had the people wear only added to its beauty."

Boq paused as Tugg rocked from side to side when an especially large wave rolled under him. The storm was getting worse.

"But," the Tin Woodman noted, "we don't need yellow-tinted glasses to see that the Yellow Brick Road is yellow."

"No," said the Scarecrow, thinking very hard. "Instead of tinted glasses, the Yellow Brick Road uses sunshine and love for its color."

Boq spoke. "That's right. When the sun shines,

The Yellow Brick Road

the road is yellow, and even when it rains once in awhile, it remains yellow. But with so many storms coming in, one after another, there isn't enough sunshine for the magical bricks to remain yellow."

"Well," Dorothy observed, "at least the Munchkins are full of love, which is half of the secret ingredients.

"Yes," agreed Boq. "At least no one can take that away from us. If we add sunshine, the bricks will again become yellow."

"I notice," the Scarecrow said, bracing his body against the side as another large wave hit Tugg, "the storms seem to come from the east."

"That's correct," confirmed Boq. "Each storm comes from where Dorothy's Kansas house set down."

"The storms must be the work of the Wicked Witch of the East," said the Scarecrow. "She hated the sun and she hated love. She must have really hated the Yellow Brick Road."

"But the Wicked Witch is dead," said the Lion. "She died when Dorothy's house fell on top of her."

"Yes, I believe she is dead," said the Scarecrow. "But isn't it possible that she cast a wicked spell in her dying moments?"

"Yes," answered Boq, "that could be the reason

for all the storms that block out the sunshine. The Wicked Witch couldn't stop love, but she could block out the sunshine with storm clouds."

"Every spell has a key to break it," said the Scarecrow, using the brain that the Wizard had given him. His brain was working as hard as it had ever worked. As a matter of fact, because he was thinking so hard, the pins and sticks and straw his brain was made of were sticking out from his head in all directions. "All we have to do is find the key, and then we can end the Wicked Witch's spell," added the Scarecrow.

"It looks like another break in the storm," called Tugg, relieved.

"The breaks between the storms do not last long," said Boq.

"Let's hurry," said Dorothy, "and go to where my house landed on the Witch. Perhaps we'll find the key to breaking her spell there."

"Quickly," said Boq, "follow me, before the next storm begins."

They said good-bye to Tugg and the China Doll Princess. Tugg's rope was tied to a nearby tree and his hatches were fully secured. Dorothy made sure the fragile China Doll Princess was tied safely to Tugg, in readiness for the next storm. Then the rest

of them followed Boq down a Munchkin road toward the east.

Soon they saw Dorothy's house, just as it had landed. It hadn't aged at all, for in the Land of Oz nothing ages. Dorothy swallowed with difficulty as all the warm memories came flooding back to her.

The farmhouse door was ajar. Dorothy and her friends walked inside. The house looked the same inside, too. The rusty cooking stove, the cupboards, the table, the chairs, and the beds were all there, except they were scattered all around, just as the Kansas cyclone had left them. There was the trapdoor to the cellar, through which Toto was almost lost to the whirling winds when the farmhouse was high up in the sky.

Boq interrupted Dorothy's thoughts. "Look out the window. Another storm is coming. I'm glad that we are inside your farmhouse."

"Yes," agreed a tiny voice from beneath the stove. Startled, Dorothy looked down and saw her old friend, the Queen of the Field Mice.

"It's good to see all of you again," said the Queen. Everyone bowed as low as they could before her Highness. The Lion bowed especially low. He would never forget how she and her subjects had saved him by pulling him from the poppy field where he had been overcome by the heady perfume.

The Yellow Brick Road

The Queen also made a special bow before the Tin Woodman. The Queen was forever grateful to the Tin Woodman for saving her and some of her subjects from the fierce Wildcat.

"Dreadful, just dreadful with all of these storms," said the Queen. "The Yellow Brick Road is no longer yellow, and the water from the storms has caused us to leave our burrows for the higher ground of your farmhouse. Dorothy, I hope you don't mind us staying here until things get better," said her Highness.

"Of course not," said Dorothy. She noticed hundreds of tiny eyes looking gratefully at her from all kinds of hiding places.

"Your Majesty," said the Scarecrow, "we believe the storms are caused by the Wicked Witch of the

The Yellow Brick Road

East, who placed a curse upon this land and the Yellow Brick Road in her dying moments." The Queen of the Field Mice agreed with their conclusion.

"My friends, we have heard the dead Witch's spirit laughing at night," said the Queen.

"That only confirms our suspicions," said the Scarecrow.

Just then, a bolt of lightning flashed against the deep, dark, storm-ridden sky, followed by a clap of thunder. The sound of thunder echoed all around them. The group huddled close together for protection.

Suddenly, the old Wicked Witch's spirit laughed and chuckled. The Lion's hair stood straight up on his back. The Scarecrow looked up and down. Boq left the group and moved around Dorothy's farmhouse, searching for the laughter's source. The Tin Woodman had his ax at the ready, but the Wicked Witch was nowhere to be seen. Only her eerie laughter could be heard.

Then, everyone froze. "Go home to Kansas, Dorothy. Go home, go home," came the low, cracked voice of the Wicked Witch. "Go home before it's too late."

Dorothy turned quickly to Boq and the Queen

of the Field Mice. "Hurry," Dorothy said. "Show me the shortest route to the start of the Yellow Brick Road."

"No!" shouted the Witch's spirit as a bolt of lightning just missed the farmhouse.

"Hurry, hurry!" shouted Dorothy. "We must leave at once." The Lion told the Queen of the Field Mice to jump on his back. Dorothy quickly re-oiled the Tin Woodman to protect him against the rain. The Queen ordered her subjects to remain in Dorothy's farmhouse.

Boq led the way to the start of the Yellow Brick Road.

"Run, run!" yelled Dorothy as another bolt of lightning landed at their feet.

"No! Stop!" screamed the spirit of the Witch. But they didn't stop. They ran as fast as they could after Boq. The Scarecrow fell in a puddle of water as he was running, and the Wicked Witch's laughter could be heard in the distance.

"This way," shouted Boq as the rain poured down on them. Over a hill the six of them raced. None of them looked back for fear of what they might see.

When the Yellow Brick Road was yellow, it was easy to pick out its bright color from the other roads,

The Yellow Brick Road

but now they all looked the same. With the sun hidden behind the storm clouds, all the roads were a dull and depressing gray.

The Queen of the Field Mice exclaimed, "It's the one with a spike tree growing from its start."

"But there was never a spike tree there before," said Boq.

"It is the Wicked Witch's spike tree," the Queen replied. "It guards the beginning of the Yellow Brick Road."

"Look," said the Lion, "the road's first brick—the one that the Wizard requested be made with love and sunshine—has been loosened."

"We must place it back where it belongs," said the Scarecrow.

"But the spike tree won't allow it," said her Highness. "It stabs any creature who comes too close to it."

"There must be a way to destroy it and replace the Wizard's brick," said the Scarecrow.

Just then, two flashes of lightning burned holes in the ground right next to them and another clap of thunder rolled across the dark sky. The rain poured down in a solid sheet.

"I know what to do," said the Scarecrow. "The Tin Woodman cannot be hurt by the tree's spikes.

The Yellow Brick Road

If he can get close enough, he can chop it down."

The Tin Woodman strode toward the tree with his ax raised. The sharp spikes of the tree glistened with rain as they moved to meet the Tin Woodman's challenge. The Tin Woodman's ax plunged down, cutting off several of the spikes. The tree moaned and slashed at him. Its swordlike spikes stabbed at his tin body, but they did little harm.

The Yellow Brick Road

The Tin Woodman started to raise his ax ever so slowly to strike the spike tree again. Then he stopped, frozen, with the ax raised high over his head.

"Oh, no!" cried Dorothy. "He's rusted and cannot move."

The sky echoed with the Wicked Witch's laughter and turned a deeper, more menacing gray. "The Witch's spell is going to flood everything! We must hurry," said the Scarecrow.

The Scarecrow hurried over to the Queen of the Field Mice, who was sitting on the Lion's back. He whispered something quickly to her and she nodded in agreement. Then the Scarecrow did something unexpected. He ran to the spike tree, yelling loudly while he ran. The spike tree turned its long swords in the Scarecrow's direction.

"Spike me if you can," challenged the Scarecrow. The tree poked with one spike, then another, but because the Scarecrow was made of straw, the spikes couldn't hurt him at all. In fact, they tickled. The Scarecrow only laughed. This made the spike tree all the more angry. It slashed and slashed at the Scarecrow. The Scarecrow laughed some more, but his Munchkin shirt was becoming a ragged mess. Straw was going in every direction.

The Yellow Brick Road

While the spike tree's attention was diverted by the Scarecrow, the Queen of the Field Mice ran toward the dangerous tree from the other side. She scampered between the immobile Tin Woodman's legs and under the sharp spikes of the tree.

By then the spike tree realized what had happened, but it was too late. Underneath, its spikes were harmless, for to use them there would surely mean it would cut itself.

The spirit of the Wicked Witch of the East screamed over the wind. "No! You will not move the special brick!" But the tiny Queen of the Field Mice was not deterred by the Witch's voice. The little Queen pushed hard against the loose brick that the Wizard of Oz had designed for the Yellow Brick Road.

The Yellow Brick Road

As the Queen pushed the brick closer, it glowed a brighter and brighter yellow. Her Majesty pushed and pushed the brick. Her tiny feet slipped against the wet ground. Finally, the special brick was almost in its proper place.

The Wicked Witch's spirit and her spell pounded the air with thunder and lightning. The lightning struck the ground all around the Queen, but with all of her remaining effort, she pushed the yellow glowing brick one more time. It slid into place. The magical brick's yellow glow spread from one brick in the road to the next. Soon the brick road was the beautiful glowing yellow that the Good Witch and the Wizard of Oz had mixed from love and sunshine. It gleamed in all its splendor.

The rain stopped suddenly and the sunshine splashed everything with its bright warmth. The spike tree withered and vanished, along with the Wicked Witch's spell, when the sun touched it.

Dorothy, the Lion, and Boq ran toward their friends. Dorothy took the Tin Woodman's oilcan, oiled his rusted joints, and gave him a big hug.

Boq removed the Scarecrow's ripped and tattered blue shirt and replaced it with his own. He then picked up the straw that was scattered around and put him back together. The Scarecrow said,

The Yellow Brick Road

"Thank you."

"No," said Boq, "thank you, for helping us."

The Lion gave the Queen of the Field Mice a big lick with his tongue and nearly knocked her over! Then he lay down so her Majesty could climb up on his back again.

The sun was shining again as the group headed back to Tugg and the China Doll Princess. When they reached him, he gave the longest and loudest welcome ever with his foghorn, to show his excitement. A tear rolled down the tiny cheek of the China Doll Princess. She was very grateful to see her friends back safe and sound.

Boq and the Queen of the Field Mice spoke quietly with each other. They left Tugg and his crew, but quickly returned, bringing with them all the Munchkins and all the field mice in the land. The Munchkins were all dressed in their finest Munchkin blue. The field mice wore tiny colored ribbons around their necks. It was an impressive sight.

They all brought what food they had, and that night everyone danced and ate and shared in the celebration. Now the Munchkins could plant their crops and the field mice could go safely back to their burrows.

Dorothy could not help remembering the first

The Yellow Brick Road

celebration she'd had with the Munchkins when her farmhouse landed on the Wicked Witch of the East. Then Dorothy's thoughts turned to Toto. It was time to leave. Toto and the rest must be saved from the Jester.

The tiny Queen of the Field Mice and Boq hugged each of them in love and gratitude. The crew boarded Tugg and waved good-bye to the rest of the field mice and the Munchkins as Tugg pulled away from shore and started down the Munchkin River. A tear

rolled down Dorothy's cheek. "You know, my dear friends," said Dorothy, "the Yellow Brick Road is now golden yellow again in the land of the Munchkins, whose favorite color is blue. When you mix those colors together you have green, the emerald green of Emerald City."

"What a beautiful thought," said the Tin Woodman.

Tugg rounded a bend in the Munchkin River and the waving Munchkins and field mice disappeared from sight.

The
China Doll Princess
Goes Home

Tugg seemed extra energetic. As he rounded each bend in the Munchkin River, he sounded his horn. The hours passed as they watched the countryside roll by. They saw beautiful flowers on the hillsides. The flowers were covered with small dots of dew in the morning, creating a silver shimmer across the land. Later, the midday sun awoke the flowers to their full beauty. Their colors glowed with many hues until sunset. Then they became a sea of orange as the sun dipped lower, finally giving way to the dark blue of night.

From time to time, they would see strange-looking houses grouped together into villages along the river. On the river itself were tiny boats with little creatures

aboard. The creatures would watch Tugg and his crew travel by, but they made no effort to talk to them. Dorothy and the others wondered about these tiny beings and their boats, but there was no time to stop and inquire. Perhaps someday they would have time to introduce themselves to these beings and the others who lived along the Munchkin River. Now, however, they must continue their journey to Glinda's castle and seek her help to save Toto and all the others from the evil magic of the Jester.

One morning, the China Doll Princess grew very excited. "Tugg, please slow down," said the China Doll Princess. "We are very close to where I live. If we travel south from here, we will cross Dainty China Country. Then we will be only a short distance from Glinda's castle."

Tugg floated toward a spot along the river's bank that looked like a safe place to dock. He was very quiet, not at all his old self. "What is wrong, Tugg?" Dorothy asked him.

"Oh, nothing," replied Tugg. He tooted his horn, but it was so quiet it almost sounded like a squeak.

"Something is definitely wrong," whispered the Scarecrow.

The Lion realized what Tugg's problem was.

The China Doll Princess

"Tugg won't be able to go with us to Dainty China Country or to Glinda's castle because he cannot travel on land."

All of the crew stood still, and it became uncomfortably quiet.

Tugg soon broke the silence. "All of you must travel on to save Toto and the rest of the Jester's captives," he said. "In the meantime, I will travel back up the Munchkin River and tell the Talk Trees what we've seen and done along the river."

"Good," said Dorothy. "We promise we'll see you again as soon as it is possible. We will have to return to Gayelette's palace and the Jester, but I'm sure we'll travel north by whatever means Glinda suggests. It would not be fair or safe for you to remain docked here."

"It might be wise for all of us to meet by the Talk Trees," said the Scarecrow. "We will ask Wiser to let you know exactly when we will all meet."

"Good idea," said the Tin Woodman. Tugg felt much better.

Dorothy and the Lion packed some food for their journey on land. The Tin Woodman re-oiled some of his joints. He also used some oil to seal Tugg's wooden fixtures. Tugg was very grateful for this extra protection from the weather. Finally, they were all

The China Doll Princess

ready for the journey to Glinda's castle. Everyone said good-bye to Tugg and thanked him for delivering them safely. They all hoped it would not be long until they were back together again.

Dorothy carefully put the fragile China Doll Princess into her dress pocket, and off they went along the path to Dainty China Country.

Tugg would toot his horn every few moments, even when they were out of sight, just to let them know he was still there. But as Tugg's crew walked farther and farther away from the Munchkin River, the sound from Tugg's foghorn grew faint, until finally it could not be heard at all.

After a while, the sun began to set and long shadows appeared. The Lion said he would run to the top of a nearby hill to scout the land and look for shelter before night came.

It wasn't long before the Lion returned. "My friends," said the Lion, "there is a cave at the base of a hill that will provide us with shelter."

When they reached the cave, the Lion led them in. As they moved deeper into the cave, a tiny, tiny voice said, "May I light the way?" The Lion was so startled, he jumped in the air, but it was only a firefly.

"I should say, may we light the way?" At least

The China Doll Princess

twelve more fireflies appeared with their tails aglow.

"That's very kind of you," said Dorothy. The fireflies gathered together in the shape of a globe and flew deeper into the cave, followed by the Lion and the others.

The cave was very large. The Scarecrow suggested that they settle down close to the cave's entrance. The Firefly said, "My friends and I will stay here with you all night and keep the cave lit."

"You're very kind," said the Tin Woodman.

Dorothy carefully removed the China Doll Princess from her pocket. "Thank you, Dorothy," she said.

The Scarecrow lay down on the cave's floor. "Please put the Princess on my arm, where she will be safe," he said. "My straw is soft and will protect her from harm."

"Good idea," said Dorothy. Dorothy put the China Doll Princess carefully down upon the Scarecrow's soft straw. Dorothy then took out food and shared some with the Lion.

The Tin Woodman placed himself between his friends and the cave's entrance to guard against intruders.

Finally, after discussing the trip ahead and asking the fireflies how much farther it was to Dainty China

The China Doll Princess

Country, the Lion and Dorothy went to sleep. The fireflies dimmed their lights, while the others kept very quiet.

When midnight came, a warm wind rushed through the cave. Frightened, the fireflies turned off their lights completely and hid between two large rocks. Their light was replaced by a bright glow. Both Dorothy and the Lion woke up. The Scarecrow held the China Doll Princess carefully in his hand. The Tin Woodman and the Lion huddled together with them.

The China Doll Princess

The glow became even brighter, and Ozma and Glinda appeared in its center. Glinda said, "Our dear friends, it is good to see all of you again. We just heard about the Jester and the danger Toto and many of our citizens are in. We will explain further when you reach my castle. To help speed your way, the Sawhorse will meet you at the gates to Dainty China Country at noon the day after tomorrow. The Sawhorse will pull a wagon in which all of you can ride. Please don't be late." Ozma and Glinda waved good-bye and vanished. The warm wind stopped

The China Doll Princess

blowing and the fireflies came out again to light the cave.

Dorothy was happy to see Ozma and Glinda, but she sensed the urgency in Glinda's voice. "We must leave early tomorrow morning and reach Dainty China Country as soon as possible," she said. Her friends nodded in agreement, and Dorothy and the Lion went back to a restless sleep.

The next morning, the group left the cave early. Dorothy put the China Doll Princess in her pocket, bracing her upright with a piece of cloth so her head appeared over the edge. Although this was not as safe for the China Doll Princess as staying completely covered, it did allow her to see and help guide all of them to Dainty China Country.

That morning, the sky was a particularly deep blue. Two butterflies played around the Scarecrow's head, causing him to joke, "At least butterflies are not scared of me, even though crows sometimes are."

Along the way, the China Doll Princess would call out directions to them from time to time. Finally, she said, "Make a right here. My home is just over this next hill." Her voice trembled with excitement.

They all walked faster and were soon over the hill. Dainty China Country was below them. As everyone knew, when the China Doll Princess entered

The China Doll Princess

Dainty China Country, she would be able to move, just as Dorothy could. In fact, all the china dolls could move about. However, should any of them leave the Country's borders, they would become as rigid as ordinary china dolls.

Dainty China Country was surrounded by a wall made from white china. Beyond the wall, the Country was just as Dorothy, the Scarecrow, Tin Woodman, and Lion remembered. There were small china houses and china barns, china barnyard animals penned in with china fences. There were dolls dressed as princesses. Each one had a doll prince. There were doll shepherds tending their china flocks and china doll milkmaids. All of them were color-fully dressed.

From the hill, they could see the china church that the Lion had accidentally broken with his tail on his last visit. The church had been marvelously repaired by the skilled

114

The China Doll Princess

china menders who were themselves made from porcelain. A few cracks were still visible, giving the church a beautiful antique appearance. The Lion was especially pleased to see it standing again.

Off to one side was a forest. This great forest was the one the Lion ruled as King of Beasts.

Down the hill they walked until they reached the white china wall surrounding the Dainty China Country.

"Follow the wall to the right and look carefully for a crack in it," instructed the Princess.

It was only a short walk before they reached the crack. Although it was at least three feet wide, it was considered just a crack, because the wall completely encircled all of Dainty China Country.

Dorothy entered the crack in the wall's otherwise smooth white surface. She removed the China Doll Princess from her pocket and carefully held her with both hands. The Tin Woodman, Scarecrow, and Lion followed her through. The Lion had a tight squeeze but managed.

The crack in the wall opened into a beautiful courtyard. Around the courtyard were miniature china pine trees and in its center was a water fountain, also made of china. Placed around the fountain were four oversized porcelain love seats. Their sides were

The China Doll Princess

decorated with china inlays. The trees, fountain, and love seats were so beautiful, it was hard to imagine anything could be so stunning.

The little China Doll Princess asked Dorothy to place her down carefully on the smooth white china surface of Dainty China Country. Dorothy slowly lowered the China Doll Princess to the surface. The group carefully gathered around her, watching. The Lion made sure his tail didn't break anything.

At first, the China Doll Princess didn't move. Very slowly, however, one of her fingers moved, and then her hand. Then her arms moved. Finally, she was able to take her first step in months. Tears

The China Doll Princess

of pure joy rolled down her tiny cheeks.

The China Doll Princess looked up at them and said, "Thank you for bringing me with you on your journey. Each of you has given me your love. I will never, never forget any of you. Please let me know if there is anything my people or I can do to help save Toto and the others who are captured by the Jester. I know how it feels not to be able to move on your own."

She walked to the nearby water fountain and love seats. "While you are waiting for the Sawhorse to take you to Glinda's, please sit here. These love seats are especially for our visitors," she said. "They will make you feel relaxed and comfortable. Also, while you sit in the seats, food and drink will appear magically before any who wish it. I know both Dorothy and the Lion must be hungry.

"When visitors come to Dainty China Country, they are always requested to sit in these love seats," the China Doll Princess explained. "They are not only magical but they help keep Dainty China Country's visitors in one place so they cannot accidentally break the fragile china around them. The love seats were a special gift from Glinda the Good."

It wasn't long before Dorothy and the Lion were rested. Of course, the Scarecrow and Tin Woodman

The China Doll Princess

did not need food or rest, but they sat in the magic love seats because they knew it would be safer.

While they sat in the love seats, many of the people of Dainty China Country stopped by to visit and to thank their guests for the safe return of their China Doll Princess.

Time went quickly, and before they knew it, it was morning again. Soon the little Princess came by. She looked especially beautiful because she was so

The China Doll Princess

happy to be home. The little Princess said, "The Sawhorse will be here in a few minutes to take you to Glinda's castle. Before he arrives, I want to thank each of you again for my safe return. I've talked with many of our citizens and they all want you to know that if there is anything we can do to save Toto and all those captured by the Jester, we will be happy to help."

Dorothy, the Lion, Scarecrow, and Tin Woodman all thanked the China Doll Princess for her offer, as well as for her help aboard Tugg. Dorothy curtsied before the little Princess, and the Lion, Tin Woodman, and Scarecrow all bowed low.

A porcelain guard dressed in a red uniform, black parade hat, black boots and belt, and carrying a toy rifle, strode over to the group from the open crack in the wall and announced, "The Sawhorse has just arrived." It was time to leave Dainty China Country.

The Plan

The Sawhorse, with Dorothy, the Lion, Scarecrow, and Tin Woodman on board his Red Wagon, moved like the wind. He was not only swift, he was powerful. He pulled the almost fully loaded wagon with ease. It took only moments before they reached the hill of the Hammer-Heads. The Hammer-Heads, as Dorothy and her friends knew, did not allow anyone to cross over their hill. To prevent everyone from crossing their territory, they hid behind the rocks on the hillside and used their flat heads and thick necks to strike intruders. Normally, it would be impossible to cross over their hill, but the Sawhorse was not to be delayed by the Hammer-Heads.

The Sawhorse increased his speed threefold. The

The Plan

Red Wagon became a blur. The Hammer-Heads tried to strike the Sawhorse and the Red Wagon, but as fast as the Hammer-Heads were, they were still too slow for the Sawhorse. Over the hill they zigzagged, around the large rocks that shielded the Hammer-Heads, until they safely reached the other side.

They followed the road south toward the castle of Glinda the Good. The Sawhorse reached the castle quickly. One of the three young girls who attended the castle gates said, "Welcome, Dorothy." The three bowed to Dorothy and her companions, who descended from the wagon.

The Plan

"Please follow us," said another of the gate girls. "Glinda and Ozma are anxiously awaiting your arrival."

They said good-bye to the Sawhorse and followed the young girls directly into the reception hall of the castle. Dorothy had little time to stop and talk with the many friends she saw along the way.

When they reached the reception hall, Ozma and Glinda were there to greet them. The four bowed to Ozma, the Fairy Ruler of Oz, and Glinda, the Good Sorceress. Then Dorothy and Ozma embraced. Though the circumstances were dire, the two young girls could not help but be happy at seeing each other again. Glinda kissed Dorothy on her forehead as Ozma hugged each of her other dear friends.

Glinda led them from the reception hall to a beautiful room with thousands of jewels decorating the walls. In the center of the beautiful room was a ruby table with many chairs around it.

"Come, my dear friends," said Glinda, "please sit here around the ruby table while we discuss the Jester and his witch's magic. We have no time to waste."

Glinda and Ozma asked Dorothy many questions concerning the Jester and the Wicked Witch's wand. They listened carefully to her story, obviously con-

T h e   P l a n

cerned about the dangerous plight of Toto and the other prisoners.

Finally, Ozma said, "The Wicked Witch of the West's wand is indeed powerful and obviously as

wicked as she was. And the Jester is breaking the laws of Oz by using witchcraft without my permission.''

"Your Majesty,'' Dorothy said, ''the China Doll Princess thought the Jester was really a good person, but the wand's evil overtook him.''

"I have little doubt that Princess Gayelette's Jester is basically good,'' answered Ozma. ''But he is doing evil and he must be stopped.''

"From what you have told us,'' commented Glinda, ''the Jester may be even more dangerous because he is so unpredictable.''

"True,'' agreed the Scarecrow.

"The Great Book of Records, which records all the events in Oz, told me that the Scarecrow, Tin Woodman, Lion, and others were in trouble,'' Glinda said. ''However, the Great Book also warned that the Jester's magic could not be fought with other magic. Any use of magic would only worsen the captives' predicament. It was then, Dorothy, that we decided to ask you to return to Oz and help. We knew that your love for the Scarecrow, Lion, and Tin Woodman would help you find them faster than anyone else could. And, as you have no magic of your own, you would not endanger them more.''

"I am glad you asked me to help,'' said Dorothy.

The Plan

"But I don't understand why the use of magic would increase the danger."

"I am sure," Glinda explained, "that you have all wondered at one time or another why neither I nor the Good Witch of the North was ever able to free the Munchkins and Winkies from the evil of the Wicked Witches. The reason is that the Wicked Witch of the East's silver shoes and the Wicked Witch of the West's wand both have the magical ability to become more powerful and evil when they come close to other magic."

"But then neither of you can go near the Jester," said the Scarecrow.

"That is true," replied Ozma, "but we will give you all the help we can."

"How can we ever defeat the Jester without magic?" asked Dorothy.

"You forget, my dear," answered Ozma, "that you destroyed both Wicked Witches without magic. It was nature, not magic, which dropped your house on the Wicked Witch of the East, and you used water, not enchantments, to melt the Wicked Witch of the West."

"You see, there is more than just magic and wizardry involved," added Glinda. "All four of you have the same quality Dorothy used to destroy the

The Plan

Wicked Witch of the West—the gift of winning hearts and love."

"There is no time to lose," said Ozma. "Glinda and I have a plan to recover the Witch's wand from the Jester and change Toto and the captured people from porcelain dolls back into themselves. But it is not without risk."

"I will put all the heart I have into saving Toto and the others," said the Tin Woodman.

"I will use all the courage I have," said the Lion.

"I will use all the brains I possess," said the Scarecrow.

Dorothy took only a second to answer. "I miss Toto, and I want to help all the Jester's captured people." Dorothy looked at each of her friends around the ruby table and said, "It's nice to know we all can count on each other."

"You will need all the brains, heart, and courage you four possess," said Ozma. "Now, here is our plan."

The plan to stop the Jester and save Toto and the others was discussed in great detail. After a long while, the plan was finalized.

Looking at Dorothy, the Tin Woodman, Lion, and Scarecrow, Ozma said, "We are indeed proud of the four of you already."

T h e   P l a n

"It doesn't always take magic or wizardry to solve a problem," added Glinda. "Just working together, as you have in the past, is usually all that is necessary."

When they left the ruby table, Dorothy was shown to her room, where she could wash and change into clean clothes. The Scarecrow's room had plenty of fresh straw to replace his old straw. The Tin Woodman, in his own room, was given the finest oil to replenish his oilcan, and he was polished to shine brighter than ever. The Lion's room had an extra-large bath, and he was provided with a brush so he could groom himself.

The next morning, the four of them were up early, ready to leave Glinda's castle. They met with Ozma and Glinda one last time to say good-bye and wish each other well.

It would be the swift and sure Sawhorse with his Red Wagon who would carry Dorothy and her friends back to Gayelette's palace. But there would be one important stop along the way.

Excited
and Anxious

The Sawhorse had his instructions. He traveled so fast that the Scarecrow had to crouch low in the Red Wagon so he would not be blown away.

Back over the hill of the Hammer-Heads they rode. This time, very few Hammer-Heads tried to stop the Sawhorse, because they knew by now it would be impossible.

It was not long before the Sawhorse stopped at the entrance to Dainty China Country. The four travelers got out of the wagon and walked through the crack in the white porcelain wall.

In the courtyard, a china doll soldier greeted them.

"Please request that our friend, the little Princess, come to meet with us," said Dorothy. "It is very important that we talk to her."

Excited and Anxious

"Of course," answered the china doll soldier. "I will ask her to meet with you at once. In the meantime, please sit in our love seats."

"Thank you," said the Scarecrow.

They all sat down. The china soldier left the courtyard and soon returned with the China Doll Princess.

"It is good to see all of you," the China Doll Princess greeted them, "but why are you back here so soon? It must be important."

"Yes," agreed Dorothy. "It is important."

The China Doll Princess listened carefully as Dorothy explained the plan they had devised with Ozma and Glinda to save Toto and the others from the Jester. Then she got up and requested the presence of those who mended the china dolls of Dainty China Country when they accidentally broke. Soon twenty-five china dolls, all wearing the dress of china menders, entered the courtyard.

Dorothy said, "All of you are among the finest china craftsmen in the world, and we need your help." Dorothy explained about the Jester and how he had captured Toto and the many other citizens of Oz and turned them into china dolls who could not move, only talk.

"We need your skills to make a life-size china

doll of Glinda and to make dolls that look exactly like the Lion, Scarecrow, and Tin Woodman," Dorothy said at last. "They must be well made and look lifelike, but the Lion, Tin Woodman, and Scarecrow will need to be inside to give each doll a voice. We hope this will fool the Jester into thinking they are the real thing."

After Dorothy explained the plight of Toto and the others, the China Doll Princess asked the mend-

ers whether they could make the dolls just as Dorothy requested. At first, the china doll menders were silent. Then they grew excited. It would be a challenge, but they agreed it could be done. They thought it would not be too difficult to make doll replicas of the Lion, Scarecrow, and Tin Woodman because a mold of each could be made with their help. However, making a doll likeness of Glinda would be quite a challenge. It was fortunate that Glinda had visited Dainty China Country from time to time. Many of the china doll menders remembered exactly what she looked like. They were artisans and had an eye for doing just this sort of work from memory.

The Tin Woodman asked how long it would take to complete the life-size dolls. One of the china doll menders said, "If we work day and night, it will take at least five days."

The China Doll Princess then said, "Please stay here in our courtyard and use the magic love seats to provide your food and rest. We will begin work immediately on the life-size dolls."

For the next five days, the menders of china would no longer be only menders; they would be creators, too. First the Lion was called to the workshops and made to stand very still as a plaster mold was made

Excited and Anxious

of him. Then it was the Tin Woodman's turn, and finally, the Scarecrow's.

Because the Scarecrow was made of soft straw and a few sticks, he had to be wrapped up completely in wax paper. Then plaster was poured over him to make his mold. The Scarecrow didn't seem to mind as long as they didn't cover his head. The Scarecrow laughed and said, "You know, with this plaster poured around me, I've never felt cozier."

Drawings were made of Glinda. The menders were excited at the prospect of reproducing in porcelain the Great and Good Witch of the South. The doll would truly be a work of art.

The five days went by quickly. For the china

menders, it was a time of hard work, the kind of hard work that is rewarded, not only for its artistic value but, more important, for its purpose. Never in the history of Dainty China Country had the citizens been able to do something to help so many others.

Finally the China Doll Princess entered the court-

yard, accompanied by the twenty-five china menders. They announced their work was finished. Everyone followed the group back to the workshops, and there before them stood the most beautiful and exquisite porcelain dolls anyone had ever seen. The life-size dolls sparkled as the workshop lights reflected from one to the next and back again.

The Lion's golden fur glistened. He had deep-set, courageous-appearing eyes. The Scarecrow was so detailed that small sticks of straw seemed to protrude from beneath his blue jacket and his pant legs. They could see by the set of his head that he was in deep thought. The Tin Woodman doll was shiny and gleamed as if his tin had been freshly polished. His ax looked so real, one would have thought it could cut wood.

As Dorothy, the Lion, Tin Woodman, and Scarecrow moved around to the other side of the workshop, they froze in complete awe. There before them was Glinda, the beautiful Sorceress of Oz. Her red hair seemed alive and she was wearing a beautiful royal-red gown that flowed just like her hair. She held a wand raised above her head, and her deep blue eyes looked straight ahead. The doll was a masterpiece, and it reflected the love the china doll menders had for their work.

Excited and Anxious

Dorothy, the Lion, Scarecrow, Tin Woodman, the China Doll Princess, and all the menders were smiling as they looked at the magnificent china dolls. Dorothy said, "All of you should be proud of your craftsmanship. If our plan to free Toto and the rest of the captured citizens of Oz from the Jester works, it will be in a large part because of your contribution."

"Thank you," said the China Doll Princess. "We are truly grateful. All of us hope you will be able to accomplish your mission, and we consider it an honor that you called upon us to help."

There was still much work to be done. The four lifelike dolls had to be crated so that they would not be broken on their trip to Gayelette's palace. Then the four dolls were carried, one at a time, on the Lion's back and loaded on the Sawhorse's Red Wagon. As the Lion carried each doll, the Tin Woodman, Scarecrow, and Dorothy held the crates steady so they would not fall.

When all four china dolls were loaded, Dorothy, the Tin Woodman, Lion, and Scarecrow returned to the courtyard. To their amazement, they found that the courtyard was filled with the many citizens of Dainty China Country, who had come to bid them a fond farewell. All of them kept their distance from Dorothy and her friends because each was fragile

and did not want to be accidentally broken. Standing in the front were the twenty-five menders and the China Doll Princess. The China Doll Princess stepped forward and carefully handed Dorothy, the Lion, Tin Woodman, and the Scarecrow a key to Dainty China Country, symbolizing their friendship and everlasting welcome.

The four bowed low and thanked the china dolls. Then they walked back through the opening and climbed aboard the Red Wagon. Within seconds, the Sawhorse and his Red Wagon, loaded with its precious cargo, were out of sight, headed back to Gayelette's palace and the Jester in the North of Oz.

The Spell Is Broken

Once again, the Sawhorse traveled as fast as the wind, but he tried to move as smoothly as possible so as not to damage the valuable porcelain dolls that looked so much like the Lion, Tin Woodman, Scarecrow, and Glinda. Dorothy and her friends tried to help balance the crates to keep them from bumping about in the fast-moving Red Wagon.

As they journeyed back to the North of Oz, Dorothy began to worry about Toto and the others held captive by the wicked Jester. "We have been gone such a long time," she said. "I hope that the Jester hasn't done something terrible to Toto and the others. And I hope our plan will bring an end to the evil of the Wicked Witch's magic wand."

Although the Sawhorse sped north as fast as he

The Spell Is Broken

could, it still seemed like a long time before they came close to Gayelette's palace. Dorothy and the Lion began to grow tired, though they had rested for a long time in Dainty China Country. The two slept fitfully as the Red Wagon flew through the night, heading ever closer to Gayelette's palace.

Just before sunrise, Dorothy asked the Sawhorse how close he was to the palace. "We are almost there," the Sawhorse told them.

"Please stop, then," said Dorothy. "We must finish our preparations before the Jester sees us."

As the sun rose over the hills of Oz, spreading a cheery glow across the meadows, the Lion, with his great strength, lifted the crates containing the Tin Woodman and the Scarecrow dolls very carefully out of the wagon and set them on the ground. He left the crate with his own life-size china doll in the Red Wagon, along with the one of Glinda.

Dorothy and the others climbed out of the wagon and stood next to the two crates. "Now we all understand what we have to do, don't we?" asked Dorothy. Her three friends all nodded. The Lion twitched his tail just a bit nervously and the Scarecrow patted down the straw inside his blue shirt.

Each of the dolls created by the china menders

The Spell Is Broken

of Dainty China Country was hollow. The Lion,
Tin Woodman, and Scarecrow could each fit inside
his own doll. This way, the porcelain figurines would
be able to speak, just as all the miniature china dolls
in the Jester's collection could.

"Tin Woodman, can you pry open one side of
these crates with your ax?" Dorothy asked him.

"Certainly," said the Tin Woodman. In just a

The Spell Is Broken

few moments, he had loosened each crate just enough so that he and the Scarecrow could crawl inside their dolls. The china dolls were a tight fit, and it took some effort and some pushing from Dorothy and the Lion to get them safely inside.

The Scarecrow laughed. "Why this is just as cozy as when they wrapped me in sheets and made a plaster cast of me in Dainty China Country. It's a good thing that the china menders placed almost-clear china in these dolls' eyes so we can see what's going on."

The Tin Woodman agreed and added, "Don't lose my oilcan, Dorothy. I think I may be a bit stiff by the time I climb back out of here."

Once the Tin Woodman and Scarecrow were safely inside their porcelain dolls, the Lion helped Dorothy wedge the open sides of the crates back in place. Then, very carefully, he lifted the two crates back onto the Red Wagon. Dorothy helped to steady them. The Tin Woodman's crate was heavier now, but the Scarecrow's was hardly different, as his straw body was so light.

All this time, the Sawhorse had been standing quietly, waiting to finish his journey to Gayelette's palace. Suddenly he said, "Someone's coming." Dorothy and the Lion looked up to see Wiser stepping

The Spell Is Broken

carefully out of the morning shadows.

"Hello, Dorothy," Wiser said. "Did you find Glinda in the South of Oz?"

"Yes, we did," Dorothy said. "But things did not turn out quite as we thought."

"I can see that," Wiser said, staring at the interesting-looking crates in the wagon. "Can I help you?"

"Yes, thank you," said Dorothy. "I would appreciate your help with the Lion and this crate."

Dorothy was glad to see Wiser, as she had not been sure how she would get the Lion into his life-size doll and seal the crate again by herself. Dorothy and Wiser helped the Lion squeeze into his look-alike doll. She explained to Wiser the plan they had worked out with Ozma and Glinda for fooling the Jester.

"It will take great courage to make your plan work," Wiser said. "And it will require more than magic to overcome the evil in the Wicked Witch's wand."

When the Lion was safely inside his doll, they put the side of the crate back on. Dorothy noticed that the tip of the Lion's tail, which had grown to its natural color, was peeking out of the hole in the bottom of his doll. Quickly, she reached between the slats of the crate and tucked it in.

The Spell Is Broken

"Well, good luck to you," said Wiser. "I hope your plan works."

"Thank you for your help. You came along at just the right time. Now I need to ask you for one more favor, if you don't mind," said Dorothy.

"Not at all," replied Wiser.

"We had to leave Tugg, the boat we made from the Talk Trees, who carried us to the South of Oz. He could not travel overland with us to Dainty China Country and Glinda's castle. We promised to send him word of our progress. Could you please locate him and tell him that we are just about to arrive at the palace and face the Jester?

The Tin Woodman spoke up from inside his porcelain doll, his voice slightly muffled. "Tugg is a good friend to all of us. I hope we can see him again soon. He has much heart."

"And he had the brains to help us out of difficult situations," added the Scarecrow.

"He always showed great courage, too," the Lion said. "We are lucky to have such a friend."

Wiser promised to find Tugg and give him their message. Wiser then said good-bye and flew off into the early morning sun.

Finally, Dorothy and her three friends were ready to return to Gayelette's palace and meet the Jester.

The Spell Is Broken

Dorothy told the Sawhorse to please hurry. She was eager to see whether the plan would work. She was also a little afraid, but she was hopeful, too.

Moments later, the Sawhorse pulled up in front of the gates of Gayelette's palace. The drawbridge was down across the moat, as if the Jester was waiting for their return. Dorothy turned to her friends hidden inside their china dolls and whispered, "Remember, I will do everything I can to keep you safe and to get the Wicked Witch of the West's wand away from the Jester."

With that, the Sawhorse clattered across the drawbridge and stopped at the very gates of the palace.

The Spell Is Broken

Dorothy stepped down from the Red Wagon and knocked politely at the gate. As she did so, it swung open and the Jester greeted her with a double somersault.

"I knew you would come back as long as I kept Toto here with me. I knew you would return. Hee, hee, hee, ha, ha," he laughed. "Now I shall have all the very best pieces in my porcelain collection." He did a cartwheel through the entrance.

"I have brought you something," said Dorothy. She pointed to the crates in the Wagon behind her.

"Goodie, goodie!" said the Jester. "But first you must come with me to get the Wicked Witch's wand. I don't dare leave it lying around with you here." He chortled.

Dorothy followed him through the empty hall of the palace. The beautiful gold and silver ornaments seemed dull in the stillness, and the once-bright purple of Gayelette's palace seemed to have grown deeper and darker under the Jester's wicked rule. She followed him into the great hall, where Toto had curled up in the overstuffed chair and then been turned into a china figure.

To her surprise, all the walls were lined with shelves filled with the fragile porcelain figures of the people and animals of Oz. There were Princess

The Spell Is Broken

Gayelette and Prince Quelala. There stood all her courtiers, dressed in their finery. In the middle of the room was the varnished round wood table with the glass box on top. Under the glass was Toto.

"You see," said the Jester, "now that I have captured Gayelette and Quelala, I don't need to hide my collection anymore. I moved them here to the great hall so I could see them all the time, and so they could see me." He began to juggle the three red balls that he carried in his pocket. "The glass case on the table is all ready for the Lion, Tin Woodman, Scarecrow, and Glinda. Where are they?" he asked, suddenly suspicious. The Jester dropped one of the balls and reached for the Witch's wand, which was lying just out of Dorothy's reach on the great hall table. "Where are they?" he asked again.

"Come with me. I have a surprise for you," said Dorothy. She led him back outside to the courtyard where the Sawhorse waited. There she showed the Jester the four crates in the Red Wagon. Using the magic wand, he lifted the crates and set them on the cobblestones of the palace yard.

"What are these large crates for?" asked the Jester. "Where are the Lion, Scarecrow, Tin Woodman, and Glinda?"

"Open the crates, Jester," said Dorothy, taking

The Spell Is Broken

a very deep breath. With a wave of the powerful wand, the Jester had the china dolls out of their crates in an instant. A smile spread across his face and he tossed the wand in the air, spinning it over his head. "What fine large china pieces these are! Where did you get them?" He chuckled as he danced around the four figures.

Dorothy knew how important her words would be. She must convince him that these were really her four friends turned to china.

"We traveled to the South of Oz to try and bring Glinda back here for your china doll collection," Dorothy began, "but we could not trick Glinda into coming back with us. It was her idea that she and the Lion, Scarecrow, and Tin Woodman should be exchanged for the many citizens of Oz held captive here." Dorothy did not like to lie outright, but this was nearly the truth. And it was all part of their plan to save Toto and the others.

"Glinda turned herself and your three friends into china so that I would set all the others free?" The Jester was confused. "Why would she do that, and why would they let her?"

Dorothy thought fast. "As a Good Witch of Oz, her first concern must be for the citizens of this land. Her own interest and those of a few seem small in

comparison." Dorothy wasn't sure the Jester would believe this. He was a selfish person who might not understand what friends would do for one another. Then she remembered that the China Doll Princess and Ozma thought the Jester was basically good, and her hopes rose.

The Jester stopped dancing around and stood thinking for a minute. He even stopped laughing. "You're not jesting me, are you? Jesting is a jester's job, remember?"

"I'm not jesting you," Dorothy said quietly. She turned away from him with tears in her eyes. She was so worried about Toto and her friends. What if their plan failed?

Suddenly, in the hush of the courtyard, a wind began to stir. In the wind, a high-pitched voice could be heard. "No! Stop! It must be a trick," shrieked the voice. It reminded Dorothy of the voice of the Wicked Witch of the East when she took the yellow out of the Yellow Brick Road. This must be the spirit voice of the Wicked Witch of the West. Dorothy could only hope the Jester wouldn't listen to her.

"Turn her to porcelain, quickly! It must be a trick," howled the spirit voice.

The Jester was startled. "Maybe this is a trick, Dorothy. How do I know these porcelain figures are

real?'' he asked. Without waiting for an answer, he spun around and went to the statue of the Lion, once cowardly, now so filled with courage. He looked closely at the beautiful statue.

Suddenly, the Lion's voice came out of the china doll. "I am the Lion, King of Beasts," he said.

The Jester jumped back. "It's real! Oh, what a fine piece for my collection! Hee, hee, hee, ha, ha, ha," he laughed, flipping backward. He ran over to the Scarecrow.

"And I am the Scarecrow, made of straw but blessed with a brain given to me by the Wizard," he said from within the doll. The Jester jumped high in the air, spinning the wand again.

Finally, the Tin Woodman spoke up. "My caring heart makes me eager to see Gayelette and her subjects set free from your spell."

The Jester was delighted. He danced over to the beautiful Glinda statue, its red gown glimmering in the morning sun. Her hair shone, too, with all the colors of the rainbow. Quickly, before the Jester could ask the figurine to speak, Dorothy spoke up, "You may keep these four if you free all the others."

"Beware, Jester, beware of a trick," came the spirit voice of the Wicked Witch. The Jester laughed at her.

The Spell Is Broken

"I do want these four life-size dolls," he said, "but Dorothy, I could take them and keep all the others, too. I have the Wicked Witch's wand. Did you forget?" He waved it at her threateningly. "I could turn you to china right now."

Dorothy held her breath. The Wicked Witch's evil laugh echoed from the walls.

"Oh, well," said the Jester suddenly. "I'm bored with these little statues anyway. You can have Toto and the others in trade for your four life-size porcelain dolls."

As he said this, he cartwheeled toward the palace gate. His foot brushed against the china Lion. All at once, the Lion's tail fell out of the hole in the china figure and landed right on the Jester's feet.

The Jester's eyes got very small and his face became red. He turned to Dorothy, who stood there horrified that their plan had failed. "You did try to trick me, didn't you? Tell your friends to climb out of their fancy hiding places!" he shouted. The Witch began to laugh again, high and shrill.

The Lion, Tin Woodman, and Scarecrow slowly crawled out into the courtyard and stood next to Dorothy. Dorothy was trying to think fast, but all she could do was wish Glinda and Ozma could help with their powerful magic. How could she save her

The Spell Is Broken

friends on her own? The Jester was furious. Slowly, he raised the magic wand over his head, looking every bit as mean as the old Wicked Witch ever did. "You will pay for this," he said. "You will all remain with me forever as pieces of my collection. And I will go find Glinda myself!" He started to wave the wand, preparing to turn Dorothy and her friends into motionless porcelain.

Suddenly Dorothy remembered what Glinda and Ozma and even Wiser had said—that it would take more than magic to defeat the Jester and the wicked wand. She remembered what Glinda and Ozma had said about love overcoming evil. And she, too, became

The Spell Is Broken

angry, angry that the Jester could be so mean to so many people.

Dorothy reached into her deep dress pocket, pulling out something and holding it in her hand. "You should be ashamed of yourself!" she yelled. "Jesters are meant to make people happy, to make them laugh and have fun. They're not supposed to bring sadness. You've changed because of that wicked wand! Look at yourself. Look at what you've become!" She uncurled her fingers from around the small mirror and held it up in front of the Jester.

In the bright light, he could clearly see the expression of rage and wickedness on his face. He knew that he had turned from a laughing jester into an evil one. The Jester stopped, the hand holding the

The Spell Is Broken

wand frozen over his head. He suddenly remembered when he used to make others laugh. Now he was the only one who ever laughed. He remembered how much Gayelette and Quelala had liked hearing his stories and jokes and how kind they had been to him. He thought of the love and friendship that bound Dorothy and her friends together. As he stared into the mirror, feeling very confused, his face began to soften. "You're right, Dorothy. I have changed," the Jester said with tears in his eyes.

The Witch's spirit voice shrieked, "No! Don't be foolish! Turn her into china! Turn her into anything!"

But the Jester shook his head. Slowly, he handed the wand to Dorothy. "I'm sorry," he mumbled. "I've made many people unhappy. I'm not a very good jester, I guess."

Dorothy quickly took the wand from the Jester. Lifting it above her head with both hands, she brought it down hard over her knee, snapping it in half. From the wand's broken ends came a cloud of nasty black smoke. It drifted up into the sky. As the horrid smoke rose, the spirit of the Wicked Witch of the West let out a long shriek that finally faded away to nothing in the still air of the courtyard.

There was commotion inside the main hall of

The Spell Is Broken

the palace. The spell was broken, and all the china figures were turning back into the people and creatures they had once been. The Lion, Scarecrow, and Tin Woodman threw their arms around Dorothy and gave her a huge hug, shouting, "You did it! You rescued Toto and the others from the Wicked Witch's spell!"

Right into Dorothy's arms jumped a wiggling, barking Toto, trying to lick her face and her hands all at once. Dorothy laughed, glad to get her faithful little dog back.

Dorothy and her friends could hear the sound of

The Spell Is Broken

laughter as Princess Gayelette and Prince Quelala and all their subjects began to run through the palace.

With all this going on, Dorothy forgot about the Jester and the broken wand until the Lion asked her, "What are you planning to do with the Wicked Witch's wand? It may still be very dangerous."

"I don't know," she said. "What do you think, Scarecrow?"

The Scarecrow scratched his head, then said, "I think we should give it to Glinda and Ozma. They will know how to prevent this sort of thing from happening again."

"That's a good idea," added the Tin Woodman. "Until you can give it to them, let's lock it in the glass case in the hall. It will remind everyone how courage and love defeated the wicked wand's power."

Dorothy carefully picked up the pieces of the broken wand and entered the hall. The others watched as she placed them on the purple mat under the glass.

The room was now filled with happy people. Princess Gayelette and Prince Quelala welcomed Dorothy and her friends and invited them to stay for a celebration dinner. Toto just kept barking and running around in circles, as if he was trying to make up for when he couldn't run at all.

The Spell Is Broken

Everyone had forgotten about the Jester. He stood quietly in the corner, nearly lost among all the bright and shiny ornaments and laughing courtiers. It was Dorothy who remembered him. She went to Gayelette and Quelala and said, "Do you think the Jester could stay and jest for you again? I think he would be glad for the chance to prove to you all that he is sorry. I think he would like to make you laugh again."

Gayelette smiled and said, "Of course. Come here, Jester. You are an important person. You alone of all of us have had to overcome evil in yourself. That makes you special, because you chose love over evil, with the help of your friends."

The Jester, for once, was speechless, but he did the highest jump and the fanciest double backflip he had ever done in his life.

While everyone was singing and dancing and eating and laughing, a warm, bright light suddenly appeared in the great hall. Slowly, Glinda and Ozma stepped out of the light. Beside them was the Wizard of Oz. All the people in Gayelette's palace quickly began to bow and curtsy to the good and powerful figures before them. Little Toto sat quietly.

Ozma came right up to Dorothy. She shimmered with many lights and colors, brighter than all the beautiful things in the palace. "We are all very proud

155

The Spell Is Broken

of you, Dorothy," she said. Glinda and the Wizard nodded in agreement. "Glinda's Great Book of Records told us that you had defeated the Wicked Witch's magic. You used your own wisdom and caring,

The Spell Is Broken

not magic and trickery, to save your friends. Within your heart was the belief you could save Toto, the Jester, and the captured subjects. Within your heart, you believed in yourself and your friends.''

Glinda promised to take the Wicked Witch's broken wand and put it where it could never cause trouble and sadness again. Then the Wizard, Ozma, and Glinda joined in the celebration, adding a special glow to the gathering. The beautiful life-size porcelain figurines were taken into the hall, where they would serve to remind all the people of the friendship of the citizens of Dainty China Country, and of the love, courage, wisdom, and heart of Dorothy, the Lion, Scarecrow, and Tin Woodman.

Suddenly, from the direction of the Munchkin River came the insistent sound of a foghorn. Dorothy and her three friends jumped up and ran out of the palace, across the drawbridge, and through the meadows toward the sound. There at the edge of the Munchkin River, hazy in the gathering twilight, was Tugg. All along the riverbank behind him, pairs of lights flickered in the dusk.

From Tugg's deck, Wiser shouted, "Hello, everybody. It is good to see all of you safe and sound."

Wiser explained that he had found Tugg at the Talk Trees. Tugg had told him of their promise to

the dragons and thought perhaps the dragons might help if Dorothy was in trouble. So Wiser had flown down the river to get the dragons from their cave beneath the hill. It was their eyes that glowed so brightly along the river behind him.

"Well," said Tugg in his deep voice, "it looks as if you've got everything taken care of. I remembered the promise to the dragons of finding them a home near a palace, and since I felt certain the evil Jester would be defeated, I went ahead and invited them to come with me." Tugg added softly, "It's really good to see you all again."

The whole party from the palace had followed Dorothy to the river's edge, and there were many introductions and explanations to be made, including the marvel of a talking boat. Wiser stepped past the others to Toto and checked his fur for molasses. "I heard you got a little sticky," he said.

Princess Gayelette and Prince Quelala were delighted to give the dragons a home in the palace moat.

The largest dragon bowed formally to the Princess and Prince and said, "Thank you for your warm welcome. Rest assured no one from your principality will ever be harmed as long as we live near your palace." All the other dragons nodded agreement,

The Spell Is Broken

letting out little puffs of flame
and smoke. The baby
dragon blinked his eyes and
said, "I'm sleepy. Can't
I just go back to sleep?"

Dorothy knew that it was
time for her to go home.
She knew Uncle Henry
and Aunt Em would be wor-
ried about her. All her
friends were safe and well
and would always be here
for her to visit. Just the
same, she would miss
them very much.

The Spell Is Broken

Dorothy said good-bye to the Princess and Prince and all their subjects. Then she turned to Ozma, Glinda, and the Wizard. Ozma said, "Remember, Dorothy, though you may live in Kansas, you are a princess in Oz. You are always welcome here. Your friends here will never forget you and the things you have done for them." Glinda smiled and the Wizard patted Dorothy on the head to say good-bye.

The Spell Is Broken

Next Dorothy spoke to Tugg and Wiser. She was very sorry to leave her newest friends. Dorothy patted the side of the talking boat, then turned to say goodbye to the others. She hugged the Lion, Scarecrow, and Tin Woodman tightly. They had known each other so long and so well that words were not really necessary. Only the Lion said, "Until we meet again."

Finally, Dorothy turned to Ozma once more. Their fingers touched and their eyes met in love and understanding.

With tears in her eyes, Dorothy picked up little Toto. She glanced down at the silver shoes, which had the strength and magic for only one more trip. She smiled at all her friends and waved. Then she clicked her heels three times and said, "Take me to Aunt Em and Uncle Henry!"

Home

There was a rush of air and quick blur of lights. Dorothy felt solid ground under her feet. She was standing on the grasslands of Kansas, just after sunset. Dorothy looked down and saw that her feet were bare. The silver shoes had vanished.

Dorothy set Toto on the ground and said, "Let's go home, Toto. I'm sure Aunt Em and Uncle Henry are worried about us." Toto barked once and set off at a run. Dorothy walked slowly behind him. When she saw the lights of the farmhouse ahead of her, she grabbed Toto and started to run. "Auntie Em, Auntie Em! Uncle Henry! I'm back!" she called.

Aunt Em threw open the front door. Uncle Henry was standing just behind her. In a moment, Dorothy and Toto were enveloped by the warm light of the

farmhouse and the even warmer hugs of Aunt Em and Uncle Henry. They were home safe at last.

"Look at that!" Aunt Em said suddenly. Dorothy looked outside. She couldn't believe her eyes.

There in the twilight sky was a beautiful rainbow. Dorothy had never seen a rainbow after sunset before. She knew it must be Ozma, Glinda, and the Wizard's way of saying good-bye to them. The rainbow shimmered over the prairie with all the bright and true colors of Oz.

Afterword

When L. Frank Baum wrote *The Wonderful Wizard of Oz* in 1900, the last thing he was thinking about was writing a series of stories about Dorothy and the Land of Oz. But when the book became the best-selling children's book of the year and was turned into a hit Broadway musical a few years later, the appeal of a sequel became overwhelming.

Still, Baum only planned one sequel, not a series, when he wrote *The Marvelous Land of Oz* in 1904. The children who read it, however, had other ideas. They wrote to Baum asking for more stories about Dorothy and her friends, and so Baum complied. In his contract for the third Oz book, *Ozma of Oz*, Baum agreed to write several more stories about Oz for later publication.

Baum tried to end his series for good in his sixth Oz book, *The Emerald City of Oz*, by making Oz invisible and intangible to all who did not live there. But like A. Conan Doyle, who failed in his attempts to end the career of Sherlock Holmes, Baum could not end the adventures in Oz. Despite his desire to continue a new series of fantasies for children, his readers kept sending him letters demanding more about Dorothy and Oz. So in 1913, Baum returned to Oz and wrote a new Oz book every year until he died.

Baum's last Oz book, *Glinda of Oz*, was issued in 1920, after his death. So popular had the tradition of a yearly Oz book become that

A f t e r w o r d

Baum's publishers firmly believed that Oz books written by someone other than Baum would also do well. With the permission of Baum's widow, they hired a young woman from Philadelphia named Ruth Plumly Thompson to continue the Oz series. Thompson wrote a new Oz book every year from 1921 to 1939, for a total of nineteen novels about Oz—five more than Baum himself had written. Although Thompson's books may have lacked some of the originality and distinctive American flavor that made Baum's first Oz books so special, by the time children had read all fourteen of Baum's Oz books and "graduated" into Thompson's, they were ready to overlook any minor differences for the joy of sharing a new adventure with their well-loved friends from Oz.

When Thompson chose to retire as "Royal Historian of Oz" in 1939, the publishers asked John R. Neill, who had illustrated all but the first Oz book, to try his hand at writing an Oz story. Clearly, Neill's strengths as an artist were far greater than his skills as an author, but still, the three Oz books he wrote before his death in 1943 delighted the legions of readers who always wanted more Oz.

After World War II, sporadic attempts at publishing new Oz books were made by Baum's publishers—and others as well—but none met with the popular success of Baum's and earlier successors' works. In fact, during the 1950s and 1960s, Oz began to lose favor with librarians and teachers as "series" books began to be seen as lacking in literary merit and fantasy began to be frowned upon for children.

In the late 1970s, however, fantasy for children began a strong comeback. With a growing recognition of the importance of developing imagination in children and the essential role that children's books play in this development, works of juvenile fantasy began once more to be considered an important part of children's literature. As part of this movement, the cornerstone position of *The Wonderful Wizard of Oz* and its sequels in American children's literature was reestablished.

Since then, the popularity of Oz has continued to grow—although to the millions of people who grew up on these stories, their popularity never waned. The number of literary figures who have written about their love of Oz reads like a who's who of modern American literature: James Thurber, Ray Bradbury, Paul Gallico, Martin Gardner, and Gore Vidal are just some of these writers.

A f t e r w o r d

Certainly a major role in perpetuating America's (and the world's) love of Oz was played by the 1939 Metro-Goldwyn-Mayer film *The Wizard of Oz*. Capturing both the humor and tenderness of Baum's first novel, it led millions of children (and adults) to the works of Baum and his successors.

It is therefore fitting that the first true Oz book written by a direct descendant of L. Frank Baum be published in this year, the fiftieth anniversary of the MGM film. Roger S. Baum, a great-grandson of L. Frank Baum, has not copied his great-grandfather but, like the most successful of his many successors, has let the elder Baum's spirit infuse his work.

Dorothy's plucky spirit and tender heart are evident throughout the story, as are the qualities of loyalty, compassion, and courage that endeared her companions to us. And, as in most of the elder Baum's tales, it is not great sorcery that saves the day but steadfast determination mixed with ingenuity and a dose of good old-fashioned American humbug.

In illustrating this new tale of Oz, Elizabeth Miles has allowed the tone and spirit of John R. Neill's work to influence her, while giving to her pictures a distinctive new vision all her own. And, like the Oz books of L. Frank Baum, this tale is filled with numerous illustrations to capture the excitement and humor of the story and add to the enjoyment of young readers who, like Lewis Carroll's Alice, cannot see "the use of a book without pictures."

By creating a story of Oz that is both new and exciting and, at the same time, familiar and welcoming, Roger Baum has paid elegant homage to his great-grandfather while helping to satisfy the endless desire for more stories about Oz that L. Frank Baum first began nearly ninety years ago.

—PETER GLASSMAN